Fragments: The Prophecy

Fragments, Volume 2

Cole Stephens

Published by Chris Cole, 2023.

This is a work of fiction. Similarities to real people, places, or events are entirely coincidental.

FRAGMENTS: THE PROPHECY

First edition. November 18, 2023.

ISBN: 979-8201969073

Written by Cole Stephens.

Also by Cole Stephens

Fragments
Fragments: The Revelation
Fragments: The Prophecy

Watch for more at https://www.chriscolebooks.com.

Table of Contents

Fragments: The Prophecy 1
Chapter 1: Trippin' 2
Chapter 2: Advantage, Us (Knock on Wood) 19
Chapter 3: I Totally Know What I'm Doing 37
Chapter 4: Just a Slight Kidnapping 55
Chapter 5: The Eye of the Shitstorm 76
Chapter 6: Till Death Do You Part 94
Chapter 7: Shaken, Stirred, and Screwed 112
Chapter 8: Shit Gets Really Real 134
Chapter 9: Am I in an RPG or Something? 153
Chapter 10: Sharkbait – Ooh Ha Ha! 173
Chapter 11: *Mockingly* That's Classified 190
Chapter 12: Governments... They Know Shit 207
Chapter 13: Parental Choices and Their Effects 229
Chapter 14: Two Worlds Collide 246
Chapter 15: A Totally Normal, Everyday Conversation 262
Chapter 16: Wormhole? Blackhole? Hellhole. 280
Chapter 17: I Make a Choice 294
Chapter 18: Fragments of Truth 310

To those who understand that the fight between good and evil is filled with many gray areas.

To Trent, who lights my fire.

And to Russell and Anthony. Who knows - maybe you'll like this when you're older?

Cover by MIblArt.

Fragments: The Prophecy

By Cole Stephens

Chapter 1: Trippin'

I sat on the couch, remote in one hand, a bag of popcorn engulfing the other. The screen was frozen with the image of Jordan, my boyfriend, being chased by our enemy, Sebastian Benedetti.

My companion came back from the bathroom and plopped down. "You know, my people have developed not only a self-cleaning toilet, but an orifice-cleaning toilet."

I stared at their main pair of eyes, frowning in amusement. "You're telling me you don't even have to wipe yourself clean?"

They shook their head, their upper eyes looking at the screen while their lower eyes stared at me. "It is not a convenience, but a necessity, to have clean excreta areas."

I blew a raspberry, turning back to the screen. "Speaking dealing with some shit, we have to watch Jordan go through all this alone."

"He is not alone. He has you. And his friends."

"I've heard things about leadership, though. It's lonely when you're the accountable one." I unpaused the movie, and the scene began to play out, Jordan running through the warehouse and Benedetti using his powers to send diamond spikes at him.

"I wish I knew how to do that."

"We can teach you, when the rest of us arrive."

I tilted my head to the side, pausing the movie again. "The rest of us?"

They nodded, and that was when I started noticing more about them. Their sideways, lipless mouth, the inside like an upside-down human mouth. Their eyes, the pupils looking like black hourglasses surrounded by pools of silver.

"Yes, my people know of your existence," they said. "And when the time comes to meet them, you must make a choice. And once that choice is made, you cannot back away from the challenges. If you choose one way, Jordan will live with the consequences. If you choose another, the burden will rest on your shoulders. You will not know what you choose until the moment arrives."

I scoffed. "So, like all decisions then. I can't know what's coming until it comes. I mean, you can't even give me a hint? You're the one that keeps visiting me when I'm unconscious."

"I cannot help you until you release me."

Blackness began to fill my vision. The TV screen was getting wider, ready to completely envelop me.

"Who are you?"

"I am the Praetorian."

"Who's the Praetorian? What is that?"

"Find The Praetorian. Find Cemparius. I will help you. But you must free me. Free me."

I shouted over the noise the darkness was making. "Where am I going?"

"I can only see sand. Sand... and human constructs."

I tried to get more information, but suddenly I was sucked into the screen, into the warehouse itself. Jordan jumped and turned around.

"Oh. There you are." He walked over and embraced me, kissing my forehead. "I haven't been able to find anyone else. Help me."

"Benedetti's here."

"Then we better hurry. We have to get the submarine loaded onto the truck before he finds us."

We began to jog until we reached the end of the hall. There were only two ways to go—left or right. The left hallway went into darkness. I could see some spiderwebs dangling and couldn't make out much after that. The right side stayed in the light, and I could see people laughing at the end.

"Jordan, we should split up. We'll find them faster that way. You go ask those people and I'll take this way."

Jordan frowned at me. "We should stick together."

"We both have so much to do. This will help us."

He sighed. "You're right. I'll go ask them."

He gave me a soft kiss, then turned and jogged away, into the light. I turned and, grabbing my cell phone, activated the flashlight and ventured into the darkness.

I didn't want to be here. But I knew something in the darkness was important. I continued walking, only then realizing how loud my footsteps were. I stopped walking, and, a few seconds after that, the echo of my footsteps stopped.

Or someone else stopped.

I wasn't one of those dumb horror movie people. I took off my shoes and, taking a deep breath, began running faster into the darkness.

You know, like one of those dumb horror movie people.

I tripped, falling hard and crying out. My cell phone skittered out of my reach, the flashlight the only way to find it. I quickly stood, grabbed the phone, and turned to see what I had tripped on.

Grace. Her body was on the ground, billowing purple robes flared out. Her eyes were open, but unseeing. Blood was pooled around her.

"Look what you did," a voice hissed, and I turned and continued running. Suddenly, bodies began to swoop down at me from the ceiling, suspended by ropes around their necks. Isaac. Jack. Bree. Kieran. Patti.

Just as I thought I dodged the last one, another barreled into me, and I fell again. I stared directly into Blair's dead eyes, the hole in his head oozing bright red blood.

I stood and turned to run, completely forgetting my phone, only I ran into someone, who grabbed my shoulders and squeezed tightly.

"Is this how you help people?" Vic whispered, pointing to the tattered remains of his ear. "You're a monster."

"No," I said, struggling to get away. "No, I didn't want any of this!"

I squirmed free and turned to run again, only the lights suddenly came on, brighter than anything I'd seen.

But I was in a large room, facing the wall, and gut-wrenching sight.

They were lined up in front of me, hanging and bound like the others. I couldn't say anything. I couldn't stop staring at their decaying bodies.

Zeke. Will. Lex. David. Ari.

Where was Jordan?

"You're searching in the wrong place." I knew who was speaking, but I couldn't see him. I whipped around, looking for him, but I didn't see anything.

It was the two of us left. I had to get the Omnia Fragment.

"Look up." Benedetti's voice rang out again, and I lifted my eyes to the ceiling, and ice promptly flooded my veins.

There he was. Body bloodied and beaten, face swollen and bruised. Eyes closed. Suspended by his neck as well.

"You did this to him." He finally stepped into view. Benedetti was wearing a white suit, with a matching bright red shirt and tie. He grinned, but not in his normal aggressive way. "If you had all cooperated with me, none of this would have happened. And you made the decision that ultimately got him killed."

"You forced me," I said, glaring at him through tears. "We had no choice but to fight you."

"There's always a choice."

He leaped at me, wrapping his hands around my neck before I could react. I couldn't breathe. I kicked at him, but he didn't let me go.

"Jake!"

Can't breathe. Dying.

"*Jake*!"

I reached out but someone grabbed my arms. How—?

coffee and caffeine when you were raised to not partake in any of those things. The LDS church frowns on it."

I frowned at her, taking a sip of my wine. "You were raised in the LDS church? But you're from New York."

She laughed and wiggled her fingers at me. "We're everywhere."

I laughed. "Do you still go to church and maintain those beliefs, even after learning about, um, world history?"

She raised an eyebrow. "Church beliefs and Keeper beliefs aren't exclusive. The church was founded by someone who found ancient writings—if you believe that story—and the Keepers were founded after they found the fragments and had the visions—if you believe *that* story."

"But we've all seen the same visions," Zeke said. "No one else saw the visions what's-his-name did."

"Joseph Smith. And who's to say we actually have seen the visions? I haven't seen the vision you've seen, or that Jake's seen."

"No, but they all circulate around the same theme." Will's face looked rather malicious. "Joseph Smith was a con artist, babe."

Lex rolled her eyes. "Believe what you want. I don't call the founder of your belief system names."

"Because my belief system is entirely based on RuPaul. Long live the queen."

Lex shook her head, frustrated. "You never take anything seriously."

"Only the things that are serious. Organized cults claiming to follow a spiritual leader are something I actually take very seriously, thank you."

"Jake goes to church, too." Ari gestured at me, much to my chagrin. "Is he in a cult?"

"All churches are cults in some way or another. Organized praying—corporate worship—is always concerning to me. So, yeah."

I let out a noise of protest. "I wasn't raised in church, so I don't have strong beliefs. I don't think my church is the *right* church, but I go there because I like the people. Besides, they have every Keeper take an oath at the beginning of a Crossing, don't they? Making people swear to live life according to what the Keepers want is a little culty."

"The Keepers actually eliminated any kind of ceremony that was based around spirituality." Jordan cleared his throat after taking a sip of his whiskey on the rocks. "When they used to do the Crossing, there was this whole chant and prayer in the name of Jesus Christ, because that's pretty much who started this whole thing. But the Keepers Council in 1871 did away with it."

I nodded. "Yeah, that would have been terrifying and off-putting to have people chanting around me while I tripped out on a vision."

"Speaking of the Keepers, we should make it a goal to rebuild them. They're all scattered right now, but we can find a new place to call home once all this is finished."

I shrugged. "Sure. I mean, I know Kevin was actually a Disciple, and Vic. Maybe we can ask Spencer about others and make sure they don't get the invite."

"Oh, they'll get an invite," Jordan said with a frown. "They'll serve as a lesson to the rest of the Disciples. Once we have the power of the Primarch, we tell them in no uncertain terms that anyone who was against us before we had the Omnia Fragment is our enemy, and we treat them exactly the way they treated us. We kill them."

"What?" I raised my eyebrows at his cold statement. "The Disciples don't want us dead. They want us for our power. Even Benedetti didn't want us dead. He just wants to control us."

"Seriously? Benedetti wanted us to cooperate because it was beneficial to him. In Sanctuary he didn't even have enough control over his people to stop them from trying to kill us. In his eyes, if he doesn't have the power, then no one should."

"I mean, that does make sense, but I don't think it's true." I was genuinely surprised by his stance. "Benedetti values the power of the fragments above everything, even if it's driven him to extreme measures. And he's amassed a following of the same people who are even more extreme than him. He wants the power for power's sake. But if he doesn't get it, I don't think he'd order us killed. I think his followers want to kill us no matter what, as they want him to be the one with the power."

"We've seen what extremists can do in this country." Ari finished their mixed drink. "I agree with Jordan. Once we get the power, Benedetti may back down, but his followers won't. We need to show them we're willing to fight exactly like them to protect the fragments."

I shook my head. "Stooping to their level isn't the answer. I won't participate in a planned slaughter of people."

"Even if they'd be willing to do the same to you?" Ari regarded me like I was the stupidest person on the planet. "That's super naive."

"More murder isn't the answer. I don't want revenge."

"You'd feel differently if the people who were murdered were your family."

I gazed at Jordan. He had spoken lightly, but his words seemed to carry a heavy weight. "The people almost *were* my family. You were there. My dad almost died. That doesn't mean I'm going to go out and be like Benedetti."

"The world would be a better place if he wasn't alive," Jordan said, his voice rising. "People like him are all the same. They want power and will get it any way they can. I'm telling you, his death will bring us peace."

"His death would only enrage the Disciples to come after us and kill us all, Jordan." I matched his tone and volume. "All you're doing is letting your fear and anger control you. If you start killing Disciples, you're just like him."

Ari gasped. "Jake—"

"You think I'm like him for wanting to keep the people I love safe?" Jordan's eyes were wide, and I could feel actual heat radiating from him. "I have done nothing but try to keep everyone safe and keep the fragments out of Benedetti's hands!"

"You've been recruiting us since your parents died because you want revenge." My fists were balled up in rage. "Your entire life has been consumed by grief, and it almost got all of us killed. You're the reason all this happened!"

I had crossed the line. The pub, who already had people looking around for the source of the raised voices, became still as Jordan stood and slammed his fists on the table, sparks flying out of them.

"This happened because I wasn't *murdered* along with my family! You're blaming this on me? *Fuck you*!"

And he stormed out as our server came over, holding several plates of food and looking completely done with other people's drama.

"Who had the bacon cheeseburger?"

I sighed and held up my hand. Our server quickly distributed the plates, except for Jordan's.

"Quesadilla?"

Throw it away, I thought angrily. Instead, I said, "If you put it in a box, I'll make sure it gets to him. Thank you, and we're sorry about the noise."

She walked away and I stared at the door, wondering if Jordan was waiting outside. The others all gaped at me.

"I can't believe you blamed this whole thing on Jordan," Ari said quietly. "That was... so wrong."

"Is it?" I shot back. "If Jordan hadn't recruited any of us, our families would be whole and intact. Ari, your mom would be alive, and so would Logan."

Ari stood as well. "Or we'd all be dead because Benedetti would have the power. You don't know my life, Jake. So, fuck you."

They snatched up their own burger and left as well.

I blinked back tears. "My parents wouldn't be in hiding right now. We all would have a home."

"I wouldn't." Zeke shrugged as if making a simple statement. "Jordan saved me from prison and the streets. I'd be dead if it weren't for him."

I didn't know what to say to that. "I'm sorry. But I still don't think seeking out people and killing them is the answer."

"No. But blaming Jordan for making choices in the circumstances he's in is shitty, West." David raised his eyebrows. "The Disciples murdered my sister right as I was being recruited. And I don't blame Jordan for their choices. You shouldn't, either."

"I... you're right. I can't believe Jordan is willing to kill even after all this is over."

"We're all dealing with a lot of loss right now, Jakey." Will's face was a rare mixture of serious and compassionate. "We can't keep making decisions like we have the luxury of being on the moral high ground."

I wet my lips. "If we don't have morals, how are we different from Benedetti?"

And no one had an answer to my question as we ate in silence.

Chapter 3: I Totally Know What I'm Doing

After we finished eating, we all went back to the hotel, me carrying Jordan's quesadilla in a biodegradable container. I messaged him to ask where he was so we could talk, and he gave a short reply saying he was taking a walk with Ari to cool off. He said he'd find me in our room later.

Will and Zeke went off to explore the hotel, and David and Lex went to bed. I sat in our room, looking out the window and wondering where Jordan was, and what would happen when he got back to the room.

The door opened and Zeke came in, looking pale and out of breath. My heart stopped.

"Jordan? Is he okay?"

"It's Will." He pointed behind him, then ran his hands through his hair. "He... he asked me to marry him."

My mouth fell open in shock. "What?"

"He fucking *proposed* to me. On the roof! He had a ring and everything."

My heart leapt at the news, but Zeke didn't seem to be taking this well.

"Did he... do something wrong?"

"No. I mean, yes! I mean..." Zeke began pacing. "He had this whole other thing planned, but Sanctuary was destroyed. So, he took me to the roof, and he told me he loved me, and that he didn't want to waste any more time because we may not have any more time to waste, and he got down on one knee and asked, and I told him I needed to think and left. I bet I hurt his feelings. What if I do say yes, but he takes it back? What if he doesn't forgive me? What if—"

"Hold on." I held out my hands. "What was your first thought when he got down on one knee? What was your first feeling?"

"I was... excited. And scared. Like, about the same amount. I guess... Ugh, I need a soda." He turned and walked out the door. Right before it closed, he came back. "Uh, you coming?"

"Oh, sure. I didn't know I was invited."

"Duh." His response very much made me wonder if Will channeled all the sass Zeke repressed.

We walked down the hall together, looking for the nearest vending machine.

"See, we've talked about marriage, and I do want to, but we've got a lot going on right now. And it's dangerous stuff, so, like, what if—"

"What if he's proposing because he thinks we're all going to die, and he won't have to follow through?"

He looked at me, nodding slowly as we rounded the corner to a little hallway with the ice machine. There had once been a vending machine here, judging by the black marks on the floor in a big square. "Where are the fucking vending machines?"

"Let's try the front desk." We turned and walked back to the elevator. "As for your worries? He said he'd been planning all this before our lives blew up. It doesn't sound like he's proposing because he thinks we're going to die. He's proposing because he wants to live."

He clicked his tongue, pressing the button to go down. The elevator door opened at once.

"I don't even know if I believe in marriage." We stepped in and he pressed the button for the lobby. "Growing up, gay people had barely been allowed to marry, so I naturally wanted to. But now that I can have it, I look at it and think... why?"

"Marriage means something different to everyone, doesn't it?"

The doors opened and we stepped into the lobby, finding the snack shop easily. "Three dollars for a soda? You must be out of your damn mind."

"Candy bars are two bucks," I suggested.

He pulled a crumpled five dollar bill out of his pocket. "Well, this is all I've got, so it's all we're getting."

We presented the front desk agent with the cash and our items. She wished us a good night, and we made our way back to the elevator.

"You know, Will and I can be committed to each other without going through an expensive ceremony where people buy us stuff we don't need. Plus, I know my dad wouldn't go. *And*! If marriage is so great, why do so many people get divorced?"

We stepped back into the elevator as he opened the soda and took a long drink.

"I... am probably not the best person to ask for advice about relationships, especially adult ones," I admitted. "This is the first relationship I've been in since high school."

He stared at me in shock as the doors opened to our floor. We stepped out and walked down the hall to our room.

"Really? But you're... well..." He was a little bashful for a moment. "You're cute."

I laughed. "I'm also highly emotionally damaged, as Spencer alluded to."

"Yeah, what was all that about?" We got to the door and looked at each other expectantly. "Um, you have the key, right?"

"No. I thought you did."

We both sighed, then sank down on the floor. I opened my candy bar and broke off a piece to give to him. He passed me the soda in return, and I took a drink.

"My brother sexually assaulted my sister when she was twelve." I blurted it out, trying to get through the initial trauma as quickly as possible. "He was eighteen. I was nine, and... she told me about the whole thing. We didn't tell anyone because we thought it was something we'd both done wrong. He gaslighted us. Then, this girl came forward and accused him of rape. She was sixteen, and he was twenty-three, barely finishing college. My parents supported him until Kate finally told them what he'd done to her. He admitted to it, and to the rape after that, so they kicked him out and cut off any financial support they were giving him as well. He spent four years in prison before he got out. While he was in prison, he basically blamed our parents for him being the way he was, and they cut off contact for good."

Zeke slowly mulled all this over in his head while he chewed. He finally swallowed and cleared his throat. "That's a lot for someone to go through. I'm sorry for your sister. And now I think it's even more nice of you to want to save him if he were in trouble."

I shrugged. "He doesn't deserve to pay for my choices."

"Even though you're paying for his?"

I laughed darkly. "I just... I want to be a better person to others than he was to me and my sister. Anyway, I think that's enough about me. Back to your stuff."

Zeke rolled his eyes and shook his head. "I still don't know what to do."

"I mean, other people may get divorced or have unhappy marriages, but that doesn't mean you have to. That was one of the big arguments I remember, is that people for marriage equality kept saying that gay people's marriages were nobody's business. You decide what your marriage or relationship means, not the law, or the Bible, or anyone else. Sure, you'll get some legal benefits, but you decide what changes on top of that. You have friends you really love you and would be there for you—I'd totally be there—but you and Will need to decide together on what you want."

He took another drink of soda. "So, you're saying I should talk about my relationship with the person I have a relationship with?"

I nodded. "It sounds like he loves you, so I don't think he would take it back or say no after you walked away. Tell him why. Besides, with how dramatic he can be, he should forgive you for *one* instance of drama."

He smiled and nudged me. "You know, for only knowing you about a month, I think we could be good friends."

"Same." I frowned as a thought occurred to me. "You know, I should be able to unlock the door with my powers."

We stood and I held my hand to the doorknob, feeling the metal in my hand and trying to connect to the parts I couldn't see. Concentrating carefully, I pulled away and held my hands to the door, and gently pushed. The door opened, and I poked at Zeke excitedly.

"I can't believe that actually worked." We stepped inside to find Will sitting on the end of the bed. He glanced up as we both stopped.

"You were in here the whole time?"

Will nodded.

"Right." I grabbed the soda from Zeke. "I'll wait outside."

"Here." Zeke walked over to the little table and grabbed the keycard, handing it to me.

I waved at Will, who pursed his lips and widened his eyes as I closed the door behind me. "'Kay, thanks. Bye!" I decided I didn't want to sit in the hallway, so I went back down to the lobby, where I snagged a seat, waiting for Jordan and Ari to come back.

I didn't have to wait long. I used some of my cash to buy another soda, and as I was talking to the front desk agent, Ari and Jordan walked in. I met his gaze and he muttered something to Ari, who looked over at me as well. Then, he walked toward me while Ari went to the elevator.

"Hey."

"Hi." He put his hands in his pockets, looking at the floor.

"So, I have a lot to be sorry for, and I am."

He swallowed. "Yeah, I should also say I'm sorry."

"Will and Zeke are talking in our room, and David and Lex are already asleep."

"Let's talk here." He gestured to a table in the corner. We went and sat down, neither of us speaking for several long moments. "You're right," he finally said. "It is my fault everyone's in this mess."

"No, I'm not. And no, it's not. Benedetti killed your parents and your brother. The choices you've made since then all stem from that one decision. You can't—you shouldn't—be blamed for having to make choices because of what he did. I mean, I also feel awful for challenging you like that. You're our leader—"

"No, I'm not."

I frowned. "I mean, we didn't vote on it, but you—"

"I don't want to be the leader," he burst out, then took a steadying breath. "I may have helped some people out by making them a Keeper, but everyone else would have been more than fine without me. I lied about recruiting them. I lied about where they came from. I lied for so long because I was... I *am* obsessed with getting justice for my family. If I keep leading, everyone's probably going to die."

I stared for a second. Two lines of thought went through my head. I could be supportive and explain that I really felt for him, or I could give him tough love and get him out of his low-self-esteem mindset. I decided on a mix.

"Hon, I wish you had a choice. But you don't. None of us do. You're the most experienced out of all of us, and you know the most about the Omnia Fragment. It has to be you." I paused to see how my words were affecting him. His expression was unreadable. "Yes, you recruited us and changed our lives. But one of us is the Primarch. And we need to figure out who that is before Benedetti does. I know it's not ideal, but it's the best we can do. I... I want you to know you can lean on me in private, and I'll support you. But you have to lead us."

He blew out a big breath, then patted my leg. "I'm sorry I yelled."

"I'm sorry I was such a shit."

He smiled. "You know, for being a leader, I can see one huge flaw in our plan."

"What's that?"

"We don't know enough about NEMO. Is it open to the public? What kind of security do they have? Where's the sub? Who pilots it? How do we get it from NEMO to Saipan? There's so many hurdles."

"It's a good thing we can jump, then." I reached over and stroked his face, gently petting his beard with my thumb. "Why don't you want to be the leader?"

"I really don't like the burden of leadership. Grace would tell me about the pressure she felt to keep everyone safe, and I didn't want that in my life. But, like you said, I don't have a choice right now. So, I'll do my best."

I nodded, standing and grabbing his hand. "Let's get back to the room."

As we walked back to the elevator, he nudged me. "Why don't *you* want to be in charge?"

I laughed, starting to tick off reasons on my fingers. "Are you kidding? I'm the newest to the group, newest to the powers, I'm most unfamiliar with everyone so they don't trust me for shit, and... well, I've never done any leading before."

"Doesn't mean you wouldn't be good at it."

"It doesn't mean I *would* be, either."

The doors closed as we made our way up to our room.

"You know, this is my first time in San Francisco."

"I only came here when I recruited Zeke."

"Yeah, I heard about that. Is he a good kisser?"

He turned to me and smiled, wrapping his arms around me. "Not that it's a competition, but I like kissing you much better."

We shared a long kiss, only breaking apart when the doors opened.

"I wish we could have peace, you know?" he whispered.

I nodded. "The problem is that we have to fight for it right now. But once we have it, I hope we'll never let it go."

"I hope so, too. I don't want to have to fight forever."

We made our way back to the room and opened the door. The lights were low, and Will and Zeke were snuggled up in bed.

I made my way to my bag, realizing I didn't have any pajamas. I turned to Jordan, shocked to see him stripping down to his underwear.

"What are you doing?"

He stared, wide-eyed. "I'm going to bed."

"But... you're naked."

"I have underwear on." He laughed, running his thumbs along the inside of the waistband and snapping the elastic. "Besides, it's not like I'm going to put any moves on you while we're sharing a room with these two."

"Thanks for that," Will hissed into his pillow. "Now stop being a little bitch and get into bed with your boyfriend, Jake."

I sighed, climbing into bed fully clothed. Jordan turned out the light, and I was surprised to find how tired I was. His hand found mine under the sheets, and he intertwined his fingers with mine.

"Goodnight," he whispered.

"Night."

And with that, I closed my eyes and fell into a fitful sleep.

When I awoke, I only remembered the odd part of my dream where a giant crab told me I was cute and tried to kiss me, but I refused because my boyfriend, some actor I'd seen in a movie years ago, would be angry.

So, probably not a vitally important vision.

After breakfast in the restaurant downstairs, we met together in our hotel room to discuss plans.

"Okay." Jordan rubbed his hands together. "We need to get into NEMO. How do we do that?"

He looked around for any ideas. Nobody volunteered any information. I had an idea, but I didn't want to be the first one to say anything. Finally, the silence was long enough that I couldn't stand it.

"We kidnap the director of NEMO and make them do whatever we want."

Will considered me, impressed but shocked. Lex immediately shook her head and Ari grinned, completely onboard.

"Um, I think that might be a last resort, but it still might be necessary." Jordan spoke slowly, and I'm sure he was avoiding trying to hurt my feelings. I nodded, feeling like maybe I'd started way too far in the extreme.

"I investigated NEMO on the way here." David held his phone up, showing the NEMO website. "They'll sometimes do tour groups. Maybe we could schedule a tour?"

Jordan nodded. "That's a good way in. But once we're in, we need a way to convince them to let us have the sub and its pilot."

"I don't think there's any way we can casually convince the pilot to come with us." Lex was massaging her temples.

Jordan glanced at me. "Well, we may have to resort to kidnapping after all. I have an idea."

Over the next few hours, we went over the plan to get into NEMO, get the sub and a pilot, and get transportation for the sub to the airport in San Francisco, where we would also have transport waiting to take us to Saipan.

We all had our parts to play. Mine was going to take a shit ton of confident lying.

"You can do this." Jordan squeezed my shoulder. "You kept a cool head under stress when it came to Benedetti. I believe in you."

"We believe in you." Zeke gave two thumbs up, his new engagement ring sticking out on his fingers.

"Um, what is that?" Ari asked, pointing right to it.

"Oh. We forgot to say anything—"

"*We* didn't forget shit." Will had his standard look of raised eyebrows and pursed lips. "*You* forgot."

"Yes, okay, I'm sorry, I forgot to tell everyone that we got engaged last night."

Ari and Lex both squealed, grabbing at Zeke's hand to see the ring, and David clapped them both on the shoulders, grinning.

"The ruby is Will." Zeke pointed to each stone inlaid in the simple silver band as he explained the meaning. "It's July's birthstone. Then a diamond for Fortis and a black diamond for Ionis. Then my birthstone, an opal."

"Ooh, that reminds me of your birthday!" Ari grabbed at Zeke excitedly, but he shook his head and gestured to me.

"Sh. We've got work to do. Starting with making the phone call."

"Yes." Jordan nodded, though he was grinning as well. "Let's get started."

I took a deep breath, and, with everyone watching, I dialed the number.

"Naval Exploration, Mapping, and Oceanography Center. This is Melanie, how may I help you?"

"Yes, this is Marley Wagner calling from Mark Buchanan's office here at Vostell." I was doing my best to keep the shake out of my voice. "We understand it's short notice, but he was hoping to schedule a visit tomorrow with our director of Aquatic Initiatives."

"Oh, tomorrow?" Melanie sounded surprised, and I heard a few clicking noises. "Let's see here... Yeah, I don't think I can schedule a group on that short notice. I'm so sorry. The earliest I can do is Wednesday next week."

"Oh, no!" I tried to sound disappointed, though I knew to expect a no. At least, at first. "It's—well, this is a bit embarrassing. I'm the new executive assistant to the CEO, and Mr. Buchanan had asked me to schedule this last week, but it completely slipped my radar. I know my emergency isn't your emergency, but I've got such a great opportunity here, and they're all counting on me. Is there any way...?"

Assistants are probably the most powerful people in the world. Forget about all the people with the money—the people who assist those people can approve or deny access to them and more.

"Well, let me see what I can do." I heard her typing on the computer. "Let's see here... it looks like Renee actually has an opening tomorrow at nine o'clock, and I bet she would be willing to lead the tour herself, as Vostell is one of our most important partners. How many should I expect, so I can make sure you all get some swag?"

"Melanie, you're a lifesaver!" I meant it in the literal sense. "There will be the four of us on the tour. Mr. Buchanan wanted to meet with the director, but his schedule was too full for this trip."

"I know how it is to have a busy boss." Melanie laughed and I heard her finish typing. "Well, it looks like we've got you all set, Marley. See you tomorrow at nine o'clock."

"Thank you so much, and I look forward to meeting you in person."

I hung up, and Jordan grabbed me and spun me around in a hug.

"You did so good! I love you!"

He let me down, and I kissed him. It was the first time he'd said those words to me, and I knew as soon as he said it, I wanted to say it back.

"I love you, too," I whispered as we broke apart. We stared at each other for a moment, me feeling more confident than ever before.

"Um, other people exist on the planet. In this exact moment. At this precise location."

I rolled my eyes. "Maybe that should change, Will."

"While I would love nothing more than to leave and let you two bask in the glorious splendiferousness of your lovikins... we've got things to do, Jumanji Jake."

Jordan sighed and slowly increased the space between us. "He's right."

"Annoyingly right."

"Aggravatingly right."

"Literally couldn't be more irritatingly right."

Will clicked his tongue. "Are you done yet? 'Cause this bitch needs to get her shopping on."

Jordan frowned at him. "Shopping for what?"

Will laughed. "You don't expect us to fake-represent Vostell as business professionals wearing jeans and t-shirts, do you?"

A few minutes later, we drove the seven blocks from the hotel to the nearest stores.

San Francisco buildings all seemed huge in comparison to King buildings. We drove by what I thought was a twenty-story apartment building, but after I counted the balconies, it was only thirteen. Still, double the size of anything we had in King.

"Do they call it the Bay Area because so many windows are bay windows?" I asked Zeke as he drove. He laughed and rolled his eyes.

I was also surprised to see so many people walking around, especially on a slightly overcast Tuesday morning. Even in downtown King you didn't see so many people out and about in the morning.

Finally, we arrived at our destination, a large cluster of clothing stores.

"Let's meet back here in half an hour." Jordan tried to meet everyone's eyes to confirm, but we deferred to Lex.

"Two hours, back in this spot. Byeeee."

"Lex, you aren't dressing up as a Vostell employee, so why—"

"I'm not spending the rest of this trip in sweats, Jordan. Don't worry, I'll get some fun t-shirts for everyone!" She waved and bounded away, David jogging to catch up.

"This guy's probably going to need some help." Will shook Zeke by the shoulders. "He loves to do this unique-top-with-dress-pants look that's supposed to look professional but never does."

"Excuse me, I rock that look."

"Of course, dear." Will steered Zeke toward another store.

"Okay." Ari stared at Jordan and me. "So, I know I never got to see any of the money, but Vostell pays well. We need to invest in our attire."

As we shopped, I asked Jordan about Zeke. "He totally avoided the question about his birthday earlier."

"It's tomorrow." Jordan quickly added, "But he doesn't like to celebrate it at all, so please don't do anything."

"Hmm." I crossed my arms as we sifted through suit jackets, Ari browsing the ties a few rows over. "Well, he got engaged, so maybe we can have a celebration tonight for that instead?"

He shrugged. "I mean, we should have some fun while we can."

"Because we're all going to die tomorrow?"

He closed his eyes and shook his head. "Yes. That's exactly what I meant."

I got on my phone and ordered balloons and a cake to be delivered to the hotel around six o'clock, giving us plenty of time to get back from shopping. They didn't have any engagement cakes, but they did have a happy birthday cake. I decided if Zeke had a strong reaction, I would tell him the half-truth that they didn't have engagement cakes but leave out the fact that they had plenty of blank cakes to choose from.

"And, done. There. Now we can have some semblance of normalcy, at least for a night."

Ari tossed a couple ties to me. "You do realize everything was pretty much normal before you came along, right? I mean, not to say it's your fault, but I'm saying things seem like they haven't been normal for only the time you've been there. Before that, it was chill."

I shrugged, drawn to the bright green tie. "Yeah, that's probably true. Which means I could use a break. So, party tonight. Our room."

Jordan grabbed a black suit for himself. "I guess we should give the man what he wants."

Two hours later, we were back at the cars with bags of new clothes. It was funny how everyone chose a color associated with their powers, except for Will, who chose all black with a pink tie.

"Jake decided we're having a party in our room tonight," Jordan told everyone.

"I love parties!" Will clapped his hands. "Drinks for everyone!"

"This will not be an excuse to get plastered," Jordan reminded him.

"I do my best lying when I'm hungover, though," Will complained.

David, Will, and Lex went to get drinks and food, leaving the rest of us to decorate the hotel room once the decorations arrived.

We were a few hours into the party, the cake having gone over fine, when Zeke, who'd had more than a bit to drink, sidled up to me.

"I haven't ceberelated—celebrilated my birthday since I was twelve."

"Why?"

"Because my mom was killed on my twelfth birthday." Seeing my shocked look, he clicked his tongue a little. "Shh. 'S okay. You didn't know. But this is a fun night. Right now, I feel happy and relaxed."

He smiled, kissed me on the cheek, and made his way back to the group that had formed to play Truth or Dare.

"You can't dare everyone to streak," David was saying.

"Like anyone wants to see you naked." Will blew David a kiss. "Besides, I have the best dares *ever*."

Ari gave a wicked smile. "Bet."

"I dare you to act like a chicken for the next thirty seconds."

Everyone stared at Ari, wide-eyed, until they made an odd noise with their throat.

"Buk-buk... bu-gawk!" They put their elbows out and jerked their head back and forth, acting like they were pecking. Everyone roared with laughter.

The game soon turned into showing off cool tricks with powers. Zeke pretended to be a snake charmer while Will floated in the air. David kept holding his hand out to shake, only to shock people with increasing voltage. Zeke got Lex's braids to almost stand on end, and Ari kept making sure everyone's drinks had ice shaped like butts.

As I observed the smiling faces of my friends, I couldn't help but think of something my grandma had told me before she died. "Enjoy each day, because tomorrow's never guaranteed."

When I tried to fall asleep much later that night—technically the next morning—I wondered why she suddenly popped into my head. As I lay in bed, my brain kept repeating an answer I really didn't want to hear.

Maybe it's because you'll be seeing her soon, Jake.

Chapter 4: Just a Slight Kidnapping

"Hi! How may I help you?"

"Hi!" I hoped my confident smile disguised my writing insides. "My name is Marley Wagner. I'm here with Gordon Hailey, the director of Aquatic Initiatives from Vostell."

"Ah, yes." The woman at the desk stood and extended her hand. I shook it, hoping my palms weren't too sweaty. "I'm Melanie. We spoke on the phone yesterday?"

"Yes! It's nice to meet you in person." I turned to Will and Ari. "This is Gil James, and KC Smith, the assistant director and one of our technicians who worked on the contract between NEMO and Vostell."

"It's nice to meet you all." She shook everyone's hands. "Ms. Lloyd is waiting."

We walked through the facility, looking around at what we'd first seen online. The front part of the building was a large, angled glass structure, housing their offices and research labs. Then there was a roadway between that building and the warehouses and docks, which would be our final destination.

"You know, Vostell has been the topic of conversation here for the last few days." Melanie led us down a hallway lined with paintings of ocean life. "I was surprised to get your call, especially with the news breaking this morning."

The question was out of my mouth before I thought better. "What news?"

"Oh." She looked around as if afraid the walls might be listening. "I thought you would all have to stay back in Idaho, what with the majority of your staff not showing up to work. Plus, the news said something about Mr. Buchanan, um, being investigated."

Jordan and I exchanged a panicked look. Luckily, Will was right there.

"Oh, you know how it is, Melanie. We can't talk about an open investigation or personnel issues, but work still has to be done."

"Ah." She nodded, but I wasn't entirely sure she was convinced. "Just through here."

We had reached a beautifully decorated office that had clearly been designed by someone obsessed with winter, as all the glass was frosted. Orange, red, and yellow walls all invited us inside. Plants and water-themed decorations hung on walls and sat on two desks that were separated by a large pane of glass.

Across the room were two—you guessed it—frosted glass doors. A sign on the left side had the name "Lindsay Cooper, CFO," on it, and a sign by the other door was labeled, "Renee Lloyd, Director."

"Wait here for a moment." Melanie walked over to the director's door, knocking lightly before opening. My stomach gave a thrilling leap. There was no turning back.

Melanie said something to someone inside, and then held the door open for the NEMO director.

A middle-aged woman stepped out of the office. She was a little shorter than me and wore a crisp black business suit with a shiny purple button-up shirt underneath. For some reason, I couldn't take my eyes off the pointy purple collar.

Her silky black hair, parted in an almost too-straight part, fell down to below her shoulders. Her black square-framed glasses also seemed severe, but the look was tempered by her kind, smiling eyes.

"You must be Gordon." She stepped forward, shaking Jordan's hand. "I'm Renee. It's nice to meet you."

"The pleasure is all ours." Jordan's smile would have won anyone over. "This is Gil James, my assistant director, and KC Smith, our head lab technician. And Marley Wagner, executive assistant to our CEO."

"Oh, is Mark not joining us today?" She raised her eyebrows at me expectantly.

"Unfortunately, he had a last-minute change of plans and was unable to attend."

"That is unfortunate." Renee clicked her tongue sympathetically. "We've all heard about Vostell's troubles."

"Yes, it's been a difficult few days to say the least." I hoped she would accept that and move on.

She did. "Well, make sure to give Mark my best when you see him next. You know, I've always loved his passion for exploring the unknown. Which is exactly what we do here, as I'm sure you're aware. Is this your first time at our facility?" We all nodded. "Perfect, then I'll give you the full tour. Here, these packets have some of our basic information."

She handed out some clear binders and went on.

We walked around the building with her as she went through the many wonderful things NEMO was doing to advance our knowledge of the oceans, the creatures that lived in the deepest depths, and the many mysteries we still had yet to uncover.

Overall, I would have enjoyed it tons more if I wasn't so focused on getting to the sub and kidnapping its pilot.

Eventually, we stopped in a dark room with a large sandbox, where we got to see how their instruments measured the depth of the ocean floor.

Jordan's phone dinged, and he quickly checked it while Renee explained the intricacies of ocean floor mapping. He focused on me and nodded, and as she took a breath, I seized the moment to ask a question.

"Ms. Lloyd?"

"Please, call me Renee."

I smiled. "Part of your ocean mapping work is what the *SeaSearch* program was developed for, correct?"

"Yes. That actually takes us to the next stop on the tour." She led the way out of the dark room and out of the main building, into the bright sunlight. She strode across the road and into a plain brick warehouse.

We walked inside and saw the prize: *The Ancora*. It was about twelve feet tall, and twice as long. The front was a large, round bubble, and I could see three seats crammed in next to each other. The rest of the submarine was sleek, in a silvery chrome color.

The propellers on the back of the submarine seemed tiny for such a big piece of machinery, but it also looked like there were propellers on the bottom. There was a large, three-point claw tucked under the front.

Renee came to a halt as we walked in, and I understood why. The large double doors were open, and the submarine had been loaded onto a flatbed. Just like we'd planned.

"Does anyone else think it looks like a giant metal sperm?" Will whispered.

"Why... Robert? Is there a reason *The Ancora* is on a flatbed?"

A man with curly black hair stepped out from behind the front of the semi, holding his hands up. Lex followed him, pointing the gun we had 'borrowed' from Spencer.

"Do whatever they tell you, Renee!" The man was shaking and crying, which made me feel horrible.

Zeke was adjusting straps on the bed of the truck, as was David, making sure the sub was secure.

"Ms. Lloyd, we don't mean any harm." Lex then spoke to Jordan. "This is the pilot, Robert Friedley."

I was surprised by Renee's reaction. She didn't freak out and didn't raise her arms.

"So. This really is how Mark and Vostell do business."

Jordan's eyes widened, alarmed. "What do you mean?"

She raised an eyebrow. "Oh please. I know people who work for Vostell. They said he murdered some of his employees and went on the run. The FBI and CIA are investigating. I'm surprised Mark thought I was special enough to send cronies to kill me in person."

Jordan swallowed. "We don't actually work for Vostell, but he does send cronies. A lot."

She scoffed. "Oh? Then how do you know so much about Vostell's work with the *SeaSearch* program?"

"The people he murdered were our friends... our family." I glanced at Ari, who scowled back. "We're here to stop him from taking some of his assets to escape justice."

"So you're stealing our sub to stop him from... stealing it."

"It's necessary, we promise." Jordan peered earnestly into Renee's eyes. "His real name is Sebastian Benedetti, and he is willing to kill you to get what he wants. We're here to make sure you and the submarine are safe."

"If you wanted to save us so badly, why the gun? Why the lies? Why not call the police?" She folded her arms over her chest.

"If we called the police, he would have known we were planning on taking the sub and would have killed you to get to it before us."

"Where's your proof?" She glared at him. "I'm supposed to believe the people who are willing to shoot my pilot?"

"We're not going to shoot him at all." Jordan's frown was sincerely troubled. "We need him to pilot the sub to our destination."

She tilted her head to the side. "You're not taking Robert."

And, before I knew what was happening, she had kicked Jordan in the face and knocked Will into Ari, sending them both falling to the ground. She advanced on me, but I shot vines out of my fingertips, wrapping them around her, pinning her arms to her sides.

"What the fuck?" She struggled and fell over, Jordan barely catching her before she hit the ground. His face was red from where she had kicked him.

"Oh my God, who are you people?" Robert's eyes were wide in horror as I detached the vines from my fingers and helped Jordan stand Renee up, who was also looking like she'd seen a ghost.

"We're the Keepers of the Fragments." Will crossed his arms over his chest, looking like he was posing for a movie poster. "We're here to save the fucking day."

Rolling her eyes, Lex escorted Robert over to Renee, where they both sat, and we told them everything. The quick version.

"And now Benedetti wants the Omnia Fragment to be the most powerful man in the world. If he gets the fragments, he could create armies of superpowered people. It would be..."

"A disaster and a half." Ari finished Jordan's thought.

Renee shook her head. "And I'm supposed to take your word and these vines as proof?"

Will shrugged. "Like you said, it's all over the news. I mean, if you wanted, you could wait until your murder makes the news next. You'd have your proof, but you'd be all dead and stuff."

She arched her eyebrow at him.

"Aaaand you definitely have kids because that's a total mom look." Will stepped back and deferred to Jordan.

"Look, we've had plenty of opportunity to hurt you, but we haven't. We've tried to tell you why we're here, and that we want to keep your pilot safe. Doesn't that say anything?"

She thought for a moment. "I'm coming with you."

"You're actually *not*," Ari began, but Jordan raised his hand.

"Why?"

"I've invested twenty years of my life into this submarine, this company, and the people here." Her jaw was set. "Not to mention the significant financial investment. But... my priority is Robert." She turned to him, hardness melting quickly into compassion. "You won't be alone in this. We'll get you back to your family."

Jordan studied her face carefully. "We'll treat you well, but if you try and get us captured, or try to alert the authorities... we'll have to make you a prisoner. And we'll need your phones."

David, Lex, and Zeke had already taken Robert's phone, so I snagged Renee's. I put it in my pocket, and she shook her head. "You're all so young. This is going to stay with you for the rest of your lives. You can't undo kidnapping, and theft, and whatever else you've done to get here."

"We know." I gave her a stern look. "We're not doing this because we want to. We're doing this because we have to. Let's get you and Robert in the truck."

"I'd like a private word with him first," Renee said, but Jordan shook his head.

"We need to hear what you have to say."

She strode over to Robert and gave him a hug. "We'll get through this together."

"You don't have to do this." He squeezed her back.

"I really do."

She let go of him, unbuttoned her suit jacket, and strode over to David, gesturing to his tie downs. "You have those in the wrong spot. Go for the central weight points. I don't want my sub getting destroyed because of your incompetence." She turned to Jordan. "You. Come help me with this."

Jordan and I shared a look, and he followed her over to the semi.

"I can't believe we got her to cooperate with us." I glanced at Lex, who was still holding onto the empty gun. "Should we seriously bring her along?"

"We want her safe, right? Would it be better for Benedetti to think she helped us and leave her here?"

Ten minutes later, Robert and Renee declared the sub was steady and ready for transport. Zeke hopped into the driver's side of the cab and Ari ushered Robert into the middle, climbing in after him.

Just as they were getting ready to pull out, Melanie rushed into the building, looking upset.

"Renee," Melanie called out, "get away from them! They don't work for Vostell!"

"Yes, I know that now." Renee rolled her eyes. "I'm going with them to make sure Robert and the submarine remain safe."

"But—"

"How did you know we don't work for Vostell?" Jordan asked quickly.

"I called them, and they said you're all fakes!"

I stared at Jordan. "Well, shit."

He turned to Renee. "We have to go now. Benedetti knows where we are now, and he's probably already on his way."

"Melanie, please wait until after we leave to call the police." Renee calmly hopped onto the trailer to ride it out into the parking lot.

"Renee!"

"I'll be fine! Take care of things here until I get back."

Renee insisted on checking the harnesses in the parking lot one last time while Jordan and Will got into the Jeep and Lex and David got into the Subaru.

"Renee?" I walked along to the back part of the trailer. The submarine only took up about half of the entire flatbed. "We appreciate you helping us."

"I'm not helping you, I'm helping Robert." She yanked on the last strap, pulling it tight. "You're doing something illegal and forcing me to do this to protect my life's work."

"I..." I trailed off as I saw two black Mercedes SUVs, three black Mercedes sedans, and a limo pull into the parking lot. "*Benedetti*!"

I pointed and everyone sprang into action. At the same time, the cars roared around the lot and rolled their windows down, pointing automatic rifles at us.

"Get down!" I grabbed Renee and we laid flat on the bed of the semi as Zeke floored it. Jordan and Lex got behind the semi as we exited the parking lot and got on the road.

The cars followed us, bullets flying the whole time. Jordan and Lex were taking the brunt of it, windows shattering into curtains of falling glass. David fired off a few lightning bolts, but they missed.

The narrow roads were proving difficult for Zeke to navigate as he pushed the semi to its limits.

"Ugh!" Renee cried out in frustration as the flatbed jolted hard after ramming into the back of a third parked car while turning the corner. "Where did he learn to drive?"

"Right here in California!" I conjured a large stone shield from my arm to protect us as Zeke hit a light pole, the sodium bulb shattering as the pole came crashing down over the top of the sub.

Some bullets hit the flatbed, getting dangerously close to hitting the front of the sub and causing Renee to yell out in anger again. "My sub! Do something!"

I stood, feet spread far apart to keep myself steady and produced a large round stone in my hands. I propelled it into the driver's side of the nearest Disciple windshield. It burst through and hit the driver square in the face. The sedan immediately swerved out of control and crashed into oncoming traffic. The others swerved around the wreckage and kept going.

This made Benedetti livid. I saw him pop his head out of the roof of the limo. We made eye contact, and I knew we were far from safe.

He held his hands out in front of him, conjuring up a hunk of diamond the size of my head.

"Look out!" I shoved Renee to the ground.

He fired off the huge diamond projectile, and I knew he was trying to disable the submarine. I reformed a shield with both my arms, catching the full force of the diamond as it smashed me into the sub. Pain screamed through my body as I collapsed onto the flatbed.

I groaned and stood, brushing myself off, anger roaring through me. *You want a fight? You've got one.*

Focusing, I ripped up a section of guard rail and slammed it down in front of the leading Mercedes sedan. I let go, and the metal got caught in the front wheels. There was a loud crunching noise and the car's rear end launched upward. It flew through the air, tumbling end over end several times before careening off the side of the road and into multiple parked cars.

People along the sidewalk ran out of the way, some screaming while others had their cell phones out, filming.

I had no idea what road we were on, but it quickly changed to some kind of freeway as we merged with traffic, their tires squealing as the drivers moved to get out of the way.

Zeke laid on the horn of the semi, and after sideswiping more than a dozen cars, the others ahead saw what was going on and hurried out of the way into the emergency lane. Their shocked faces as we drove by were almost amusing.

You had a large semi hauling a submarine with two people in business attire on top, hanging on for dear life, then a Jeep and a Subaru riddled with bullet holes, lightning flying from them to a bunch of sleek Mercedes, and rounded out by a limousine.

Jordan yelled something to Will, who said something and grinned, causing Jordan to roll his eyes. But Will began climbing out of the passenger window of the Jeep, then perched on top, holding his hands out.

He launched himself off the roof and began flying through the air, generating a miniature tornado under him.

He flew over the top of the nearest Mercedes, which lost control. Will sucked the car up and, with a kick, sent the SUV flying through the air and onto the adjacent road, where it rolled multiple times, stopping upside-down.

We were coming up on a bridge, though I didn't know which one. It stretched across the water and out of sight. Ahead, I could see two toll booths, one short, one tall. With cars still swerving to get out of our way, we were going to have a hard time getting into the farthest right lane to the tallest booth. It would be over.

But Zeke increased our speed. We careened toward the booths, and even the drivers scrambling to get out of our way were probably holding their breath. Zeke honked to try and get cars out of his way, but a few stubborn drivers refused to move out of the right lane. We passed by the tall booth before he was able to move over.

Jake and Lex saw what was happening and switched lanes so they weren't behind us.

Renee and I held on to each other as Zeke got closer... closer... too close...

A horrible metal-on-metal scraping sound filled the air as the top of the submarine caught the bottom of the toll booth and the metal supports. We covered our ears, but it was over quickly, and we had made it through the toll booth and were on the bridge.

The section we went under began to fold in on itself, raining debris on everyone behind us. Jordan and Lex had blown through three booths down, missing the collapse.

David popped his head out of the sunroof of the Subaru and began throwing lightning bolts at the Mercedes behind us.

Unfortunately, all this had caught the attention of law enforcement, and the sound of police sirens filled the air.

Benedetti was ready to join the fray now. He crawled on top of the limo along with about a dozen others. Then they started to use *their* powers.

"Spencer," I muttered, seeing him on the roof with his dad. I knew this was going to be a test for us all. Did we actually trust him? If we went soft on him, Benedetti might see that. If he went soft on us, Benedetti would know for sure.

Three of the Disciples leaped from the roof of the limo. A Terra guy tore off a concrete barrier and floated on it toward us. Another guy jumped on it while a Fortis used a mini tornado to get to the semi.

"Stay back, Renee!" She pressed herself against the glass of the submarine.

All three of them landed, and the guy controlling the concrete slab smirked as he let it go, right on top of the Jeep.

"Jordan!"

The barrier landed on top of the passenger side, crushing the roof and causing Jordan to almost lose control. Luckily, Lex had seen what was going on and pulled up beside him. He carefully positioned himself to crawl out of the driver's window and into the backseat of the Subaru.

Right as he let go of the steering wheel, the Jeep veered sharply into the side of the bridge and, with an explosive crunching sound, crashed through the concrete railing and fell into the bay below.

Jordan was left hanging on to the roof rack of the Subaru, feet scraping the roadway. He quickly hauled himself into the backseat and collapsed.

I turned and glared at the Terra Disciple.

He smirked at me. "Almost lost your boyfriend, huh? We'll make sure you're all nice and safe in cages if you just give up now."

"Whatever, red shirt."

"Huh?" He looked down at his black shirt, genuinely confused.

"Oh, come on." I frowned at the other two Disciples with him. "Does no one know that reference?"

The Fortis Disciple raised his hand. "I do. It's original Star Trek. All the people in red shirts were unimportant people who died."

I shook my head and muttered, "Well, it's not funny *now*."

"Oh." The Terra Disciple's face went from understanding to outraged in a blink. "Hey!"

He charged at me. I dodged to the side, sticking out my foot, and he tripped, falling off the semi and onto the roadway. Lex tried to swerve, but, with several sickening bumps, ran over him.

"Oh, fuck—I'm sorry!"

The remaining three Disciple transports and the limo didn't even stop.

Meanwhile, the other two guys had approached Renee. She stood with her hands up, looking unassuming. From the way she'd taken us all on earlier, I knew better.

Quick as a flash, she nailed the one on her left in the face with one of her well-placed high kicks.

The other guy grabbed her arm, and she used his weight to spin herself around and latch herself onto his neck with her legs. With another lightning-fast movement, she pulled him down and landed near the edge of the flatbed.

For one terrifying second, I thought she was rolling off the edge, but instead she did a quick spin on her hands and landed on her feet in front of the second guy. He punched, but she blocked and delivered a vicious blow to his face with her elbow.

He staggered backwards and tripped over one of the tie downs, falling over but stopping short of falling off.

As she turned her attention back to the other man, he swept his leg toward her and knocked her down. She landed hard and gave him a deadly look. Then she rocked backwards and launched herself back up, kicking him in the chest with both her feet, then landing on her back, only to shift her weight again and jump to her feet.

The guy flew past me and onto the hood of the Subaru, where Lex promptly swerved into the cement rail, scraping the side of the car and sending him flying off the side of the bridge.

Renee's other opponent shot a piece of rock at her. It hit her in the chest and she stumbled backward, looking furious. She picked it up and, looking like a shotput professional, spun and hurled it right back at him. He caught it and it crumbled in his hands.

"You're a real pain in the—"

She cut him off by delivering a spinning kick, catching him under the jaw. He fell on his knees toward the sub and caught himself, facing away from her.

"Pain in the *what*, now?" With a hard kick to his ass, she sent him flying off the flatbed and into the windshield of a slower-moving car, which slammed on the brakes.

She turned back to me and pointed. "Look out!"

I whirled around in time to see a figure flying at me. I felt intense pain in my face as they kicked me and sent me sprawling backwards, blood spraying out of my mouth.

"Long time no see, Jake." Vic stood straight, the scabbed hole where his right ear used to be twisting my stomach. I remembered trying to kill him in Sanctuary only two days ago.

"I wish it had been longer, traitor." I slowly stood, wiping my mouth with my sleeve.

He laughed. "You thought you could take one of Vostell's assets without Benedetti knowing about it?"

"No. But we hoped to be long gone before he figured it out. I mean, we made it all the way into Vostell's secret basement before he noticed."

Vic held his hand over where his right ear had been. "What was that? I can't hear you since someone mangled my ear."

"Well, you deserved it, so..."

He began forming a stone war hammer with his hands. "Give us our sub, and we'll make sure you at least eat while you're our prisoner."

"*The Ancora* isn't yours." Renee stepped forward to stand beside me.

"Damn straight." I nodded at her in solidarity.

"It isn't *yours*, either." She glared at me, then turned to Vic. "Leave now. I've seen what this young man can do."

"Me too, lady. I'm his teacher. Gotta tell ya, not that impressed."

"Then take me out." I held out my arms. "If you can."

His war hammer fully formed, he swung sideways, and I ducked. Just like we did in practice multiple times. I swept my leg forward, like he'd taught me, and he jumped, readjusting to bring the war hammer crashing down on me.

My instincts told me to roll back and out of harm's way. But he expected that. This time, he brought it down, and I was ready. I'd turned my hands to stone and caught the blow with my left hand. I quickly stood and jabbed my other hand forward, punching him in the neck.

His face turned purple, his hands turned to flesh, and he staggered back, clutching his throat.

"I believe this is where they say the student has surpassed the teacher."

My right arm still stone, I delivered a vicious uppercut to his stomach, sending him over the edge of the bridge and down into the bay. Since he couldn't scream, I was waiting to hear a splash. Unfortunately, my attention got diverted as Benedetti and Spencer flew over on chunks of road they had torn up, landing on the bed of the truck. I looked between them. Spencer was apprehensive. His father was pissed.

"Renee, think about what you're doing. I run a multi-billion dollar corporation, whereas this kid is a fugitive from justice. They have no right to your equipment. Hand over the sub now, and we'll say you were kidnapped against your will and get these kids thrown in jail!"

She folded her arms. "You're on the run from the law as well, Mark. So, either way, I'm giving my sub to someone. I'd rather be with the people who didn't hurt anyone until they were forced to."

"Stop and listen." Benedetti's fingers were like claws as he spoke to me. "You have something I need, Jake. More than that, you and your friends are something I need as well. We've gotten this far. I've seen your powers. With my resources and your determination, we could find the Omnia Fragment together!"

"You *still* want a partnership after all this?" I gestured around to the Disciples still fighting Jordan, Will, and David. "You're a real piece of work."

"I'm proposing the logical solution here." Benedetti looked over his shoulder at Will, who was coming away from his fight and landed next to me on the flatbed.

"Get out of here, Benedetti." Will moved to stand on Renee's other side. "The police are going to catch up to you. This has gotten visible to the public and fast."

"We've lost ten men so far, sir." Spencer shrank under his father's look.

"Cannon fodder." Benedetti smiled smugly at us. "We have numbers you can't even imagine. And we're not leaving without that submarine."

"Then, I guess it's your move, dic... tator." Will smiled, but Benedetti's jaw was set.

I knew this was going to get even worse. I needed a way to end this once and for all. I had to stop the police from following us and stop Benedetti from getting to the airport with us as well. It had to be something big.

The road had veered left, and we were driving up an incline. I had a plan.

"Let's get rid of some cannon fodder then, shall we?" I shot off a chunk of rock at Spencer. He barely had time to look shocked before he was sent flying off the bridge.

"No!" Benedetti gave me a poisonous look, then tore up another section of road to swoop down after him.

I focused on the road itself as the three Mercedes and limo continued to follow us. I could see the police lights approaching rapidly.

The bridge began to rumble, and the road cracked as pieces began to fall off and into the water underneath. The drivers seemed to see what I was doing and backed off, which is exactly what I was hoping for.

With a mighty tug, I pulled up, and fifty feet of our side of the road crumbled and began to fall away. Suddenly, with no road underneath them, the Mercedes fell the hundred or so feet into the water below.

I stopped using my powers, but the rumbling continued. I watched as the ripple effect of what I'd done took hold.

The road on both sides of the bridge began to fall away as the supports began to buckle. Cars on both sides began to fall in. Drivers were panicking, abandoning their cars and running, only to fall into the water below.

We made it onto land as the collapse stopped, and I was able to see the damage that had been done.

The two-mile stretch of the bridge that had been built to allow ships to pass underneath had completely collapsed. Only three supports were standing upright and holding onto a few cars. I had no idea how many innocent people had been caught in the destruction.

Renee and Will both stared at me in shock. I shook my head, eyes wide.

"I didn't mean... Oh my God, I didn't want..."

"We're... all clear," Will said softly.

As the wind whipped around my face and we exited the bridge toward the airport, I could feel the silent stares and judgment of my friends. I felt ashamed and defiant.

What other choices was I going to have to make to get Benedetti to leave us alone, especially after we got the Omnia Fragment?

How many would suffer because we refused to give up, and he refused to let us go?

Chapter 5: The Eye of the Shitstorm

We pulled directly onto the Oakland airport's tarmac near a large cargo plane. Members of the military were loading some stuff and, when we pulled in and parked, got to work loading the sub into the plane as well.

We did get many looks from them about the smoking, bullet-ridden Subaru, but they didn't say anything, and neither did we.

Lex parked and David and Jordan grabbed all our bags, including the small bag of fragments. No one spoke as we boarded the plane and found seats in the cargo bay. I could only wonder what the others were saying about me. What they were thinking about what I'd done on the bridge. All the people I'd likely killed.

"How did you get the military to help you out?" David asked Jordan.

"I can't really talk about it." He glanced quickly at me and then back to his feet.

Great. Another secret. This bullshit again.

Much more quickly than I imagined it would, the ramp closed, and the plane began to taxi. Soon, we were in the air and on our way to Hawai'i, our stop before heading to Saipan.

"There's a half dozen soldiers and two pilots on the plane." Zeke had to yell over the roar of the engines. "We'll need to layer up, since it can get pretty cold in the cargo bay."

We dug into our bags and grabbed additional clothes for ourselves and Robert and Renee. As we dressed, Robert broke the silence.

"What the fucking fuck was all that?"

Ari jerked their thumb at him. "He's speaking my language."

"Let's talk." Jordan gestured to the front of the plane.

"I'll come, too."

Jordan held out his hand to me.

"Don't. Just... don't."

And he walked away with Renee and Robert.

I unbuckled myself and made my way to a corner of the plane, where I sat down on the ground, put my arms on my knees, and tucked my head. I felt like a five-year-old being admonished.

I don't know how long I sat there before I felt a presence beside me.

"Tired?" David's voice was low.

"Yes."

"Wanna talk?"

"No."

"Then listen." David leaned closer so I could hear him better. "I'm not going to say what you did was right or wrong. It was a fight, and lives are at stake. We need people to make tough calls, and that was you at that moment. We have an important mission—"

"You know, I'm so done hearing how important this mission is." I lifted my head up to meet his eyes. "Do you think anyone on that bridge cared about our mission when I destroyed the road under them and sent them falling to their deaths? Someone's parent, or child died. Or their family. I could have just orphaned someone."

My eyes burned and I tore my eyes away again.

"We don't know that anybody died, though, West."

I shook my head. "Of course people died. Not only Disciples. My hands are, are wet with blood, and I..."

I couldn't go on. David scooted closer and wrapped his arm around me. I leaned into him and simply began to cry. And with each tear I felt the release of the pain and sorrow I'd been feeling since my first date with Jordan.

So much had happened over the last two months. And now, in the last few days, everyone we'd lost... I couldn't even feel that loss with the overwhelming guilt of what I'd done. The people on the bridge... all those innocent lives.

I kept repeating the word in my head. *Murderer. Murderer. Murderer.*

And yet, I felt a cold part of me I hadn't known was there speak up. *It was for the greater good.* I did my best to ignore that part of myself.

I don't know how long David held me while I sobbed. It was the kind of cry where I found it hard to breathe and I couldn't stop my nose from dripping.

Finally, I began to gain control of myself, wiping at David's coat, which had a wet spot from my facial leakage.

"Sorry about your coat." I sniffed.

"I'm sorry about your life."

"You know, it isn't that great right now, but it was alright before all this." I shrugged. "I mean, even after the explosion at the restaurant, I still felt like I was doing okay. Jordan had dinner with my family, and things went well there... I don't know how it's going to go now."

David shook his head. "Man, Jordan's not going to break up with you."

"Maybe he should." I wiped my eyes. "My parents like him. He's respectful, and real—at least, I thought he was. But I keep thinking about all the things I wanted, the things I could imagine with Jordan. But we can't have those things anymore."

"We talked about this back in Sanctuary, dude. You're not dead."

"That's not what I mean." I shook my head and sat up straight, continuing to cry. "I mean, let's say we're successful. We get the Omnia Fragment, find out who the Primarch is, and work together to make the world a better place. That's our life. We won't have weekends, or great health benefits, or even a union. We won't have kids, and soccer practice, and we won't begrudgingly buy a minivan. There... there won't be a wedding. Jordan won't have a mother-son dance. I mean, our powers keep pulling us apart. He lies. I kill innocent people. There won't be peace for us. We can't have a life together because our lives aren't ours to live."

He seemed to be considering everything I'd told him. "Fuck it."

"What?"

"Fuck all of that, West. You've given up. Life is going to be a fight, so you're refusing to fight for whatever you want."

"That's not what I—"

"Yes, it is. You're looking at all your responsibilities and choosing not to see Jordan as a place for support, but rather a burden. You see how hard it's going to be, so you're giving up." He stood as I stared at him in shock. He'd been so kind a moment before. "I thought you were a fighter. Someone who saw what they wanted and went for it. Someone who did what needed to be done and still worked for the things they want."

"I'm trying—"

"Shut the hell up." He held up a hand of dismissal. "You're taking the easy way out. The coward's way out. Fighting against bad people is easy. Fighting for love, for lifelong companionship with someone who loves you as fiercely as you love them... that's fucking hard. Jordan is willing. But it's too hard for you. You're a disappointment."

I stood, feeling angry. "Fuck you, David. I *am* a fighter."

He smirked, catching me off guard. "Then, as Will would say... prove it, bitch."

He stalked away across the plane, leaving me with my thoughts.

After a while, I climbed the ladder to the upper part of the plane. I found Jordan sitting on the floor reading the book on Saipan. He had a blanket draped around his shoulders.

As I moved to sit down next to him, he lifted the blanket and wrapped it around me as well, continuing to read. I scooted close, and he let me rest my head on his shoulder.

I immediately began to feel warmer, remembering Calors tended to have a slightly higher body temperature.

I let out a breath. "Are you okay?"

He closed the book and faced forward. "Are *you*?"

"Honestly, no. But I wanted to check on you."

"You mean about what you and David talked about?"

I felt a surge of annoyance. "Is he as gossipy as Will?"

"No. I sent him to check on you and report back to me."

The annoyance in my chest increased. "Why didn't you come check on me yourself?"

"Honestly, I had to think things through as well."

My heart twisted in my chest. "You did?"

He nodded. "I mean, I also figured you would come talk to me when you're ready."

I frowned. "You say that like you know me so well. We haven't even known each other a full two months."

"You learn a lot about a person when you almost die together several times."

"And? What did you learn about me in this latest situation?"

He paused, and I could tell he was choosing his words carefully. "You're... tactical. You see things that I refuse to see, because those things could hurt people. It's a little hard for me to deal with, because I don't know if you were always that way, or if all of this has made you that way."

I let out a dry laugh. "I wonder that myself."

Jordan squinted and carefully put his arm around me. "I wonder who I'd be if my parents and brother hadn't died. I mean, I was only four. I have no way of knowing what kind of child I was before Grace found me, or if I was a good big brother, or what my interests were. What was my first word? Did I cry a lot? Did we have any pets?" He sighed, and I could almost feel the longing in the heat emanating from him. "I'll never know who I would have been if my life wasn't changed by all this shit. All this pain, and loss. All I know is who I *have* to be. But... I can choose within that role. Who I am *now*, and who I want to be in the *future*."

"I guess I'm getting to a similar spot."

"I've had the time to adjust... for the most part." He frowned, stroking my shoulder with his thumb. "Losing Grace was... is... harder than losing my parents. I barely remember them, but Grace raised me. She was a mother. But she also had to balance being a mother with being a leader with immense responsibilities. As I got older, I realized she loved me *and* was an effective leader. She did both. It was hard, and I... I'll never figure out how she did it."

He squeezed me closer, and I blinked rapidly as his words washed over me.

"I hope you take this situation and remember how it went down. All I want to say is that..." He swallowed and clenched his jaw. "I can't have someone in my life who treats innocent people like collateral. And I certainly can't have someone like that in the Keepers."

Tears spilled again. "I swear, I'm not... I don't want to be that person, Jordan. It was all a big mistake. I don't have the control over my powers, and I knew it would take something extreme to get them off us, and—"

He waved the book at me, shaking his head. "I know, Jake. I... I can't help but think about what a giant hypocrite I am. There I was, back in San Francisco, talking about using Benedetti's tactics against him. And you did exactly that. I guess it took seeing it in real life to realize it. It helped me understand where you were coming from."

"That's not why I did it. I just didn't think things through and... and it got innocent people killed."

He nodded. "I know it wasn't on purpose. That's not my concern. My concern is how reckless we're going to have to be to stop Benedetti from getting us or the fragments again. I think... I think I'd like to be the one to make that decision in the future. I know it was an intense fight, but... I'd like you to take a backseat for a bit and focus on bettering your powers and your combat tactics, okay?"

I bit my lip. "I... I understand."

"Jordan?" We looked up to see Zeke, standing with a raised eyebrow and a smile. "I came to talk to Jordan. I was hoping to talk to him alone."

"Oh. Sure." I stood, missing the heat and the warmth of his embrace at once. "I'll head back down."

I descended the ladder and made my way back to my seat, avoiding the gaze of the others. A wave of exhaustion crashed over me. I buckled myself in my seat and closed my eyes. Thankfully, I fell into a dreamless sleep. When I woke up, it was to find the others all buckled in as well.

"Are we crashing?" I asked quickly, and Lex laughed.

"No, we're landing in Hawai'i. On Honolulu. And we're all going to change into the swimming stuff I bought for us, then head to the beach."

"Why aren't we staying with the plane?"

"It will take a little while for them to refuel. Which means, oh no, I have to sit on the beach."

I laughed, looking forward to doing the same. My mind, however, reflected the word *murderer* back at me one more time.

Soon, the plane had landed, and we were standing at the back of the cargo door, waiting for it to open. As soon as it did, a wave of hot, humid air hit us, and we shed our outer layers. Still, even in a button-up shirt, I was warm.

"Everyone has their own bag." Lex distributed them between us all. "Don't worry, I got the sizes right. And no peeking!"

"Let's go." Jordan looked exasperated as he grabbed his own bag. We all made our way off the tarmac in hopes we could find a shuttle that would fit the nine of us.

"How are Robert and Renee doing?" I asked Jordan as we walked through the airport to the front.

"As good as can be expected. The good news is that, after seeing everything Benedetti did, they're on our side and willing to help us get the fragment."

"Cool." The doors opened and we were once again bathed in the ultra-wet air and found several taxis waiting outside.

"Well, we're going to buy Robert a drink." Zeke, Will, and Robert split off to find a cab themselves. "We'll meet you at the beach."

The rest of us got into two cabs and made our way to Kahanamoku Beach, taking Lex's advice. Lex caught a cab with Jordan and me, once again leaving David alone.

"It's amazing." Lex pointed out the window at the expanse of water. "My mom and I came here on vacation every year until I was sixteen during the summer. But when she married my stepdad, we stopped traveling for fun. Oh, but don't walk barefoot on the sand. People leave so much junk on the beach, you could step on something."

We exited the cabs and made our way to the nearby buildings. It wasn't until I got into a bathroom stall and opened my bag that I felt a wave of relief wash over me. I'd been concerned Lex had picked out a thong or something for me, but the swim trunks were something I would totally wear.

I threw on the tank top with little flamingos on it, and stepped out to find Jordan only in his swimming suit, his bare broad shoulders complete with his defined chest and washboard abs.

"Enjoying the show?" he asked with a grin.

"Sorry, I didn't mean to stare."

He stepped toward me, gently placing his hand on cheek. "I know you're struggling right now, but try to relax, alright? Let's go get some drinks."

We stepped outside at the same time as Lex and David to find they had stripped to the bare minimum. I knew David was buff, but I was surprised to see how sculpted he was. And Lex's tiny two-piece suit was... tiny. I thought they were both really brave to be showing so much skin.

I watched Jordan checking them both out as they ran to the water.

"It's so interesting to watch you watch both guys and girls."

"I actually watch everyone." Jordan smiled as we made our way to a little outdoor bar. "I'm pan."

"Oh. I thought you were bi."

"Nope." He grinned. "Although, I've been assuming this whole time that you're gay. Is that true?"

I nodded. "I've never been attracted to women, or, I guess people with breasts. Although there was this one trans guy I was super into until I found out he was straight. I definitely think that makes me gay, still. I think."

"Gender and sexuality are fun." Jordan helped me settle onto a stool at the little bar. "I love how everything is about the person and not what's between their legs anymore. And you can call yourself whatever, ultimately."

An hour later, Jordan and I were working on our third drink each, and I had lost enough inhibitions to lost my tank top.

Ari and Renee seemed deep in discussion at the bar as well, so we didn't bother them. We made our way to the sand, and, holding hands, meandered along the beach, talking. Will and Zeke showed up a little later with Robert, whose face was rather red.

I had some fun with Will as he and Zeke made their way to the water by focusing my powers on the sand under his feet. He was genuinely alarmed that he had stepped in quicksand or something, but then turned and saw me giggling about thirty feet away. He blew me a kiss, but a second later, Jordan and I got a blast of sand to our faces.

After that, we decided to get more drinks. Oh no. Drink number four. Renee and Robert were watching us all, but mostly keeping an eye on Ari, who was flirting with a woman in a rubber one-piece.

We wandered down to the water and took off our sandals, sitting where the waves lapped at our feet. A ways away, Will and Zeke were playing chicken with Lex and David.

"Did you ever think you would end up with someone like me?"

I looked at Jordan. "Like, you as a Calor, or you as you?"

"Me. Jordan."

"Psh, no," I replied. "I thought I was going to end up with some guy that would deign to be with me. I never thought I would land a hottie like you."

"Oh, stop." He tried and failed to stop a bashful smile.

"I'm serious!" I sat up and rubbed his chest. "This is fantastic." I moved my hand to his face. "But add in that you're way too nice, and you like me for me, and you're noble and generous and all these other great things... I think I'm pretty lucky."

"But then, why were you going to end things?"

"I was just telling David how I felt. I had the thoughts, but it didn't mean I wanted to go through with them. I do want to see where this goes, even if it's hard."

"Well, it's not hard... yet." He gave me a wink and I felt a thrill in my stomach as my cheeks burned.

"You know, I, um, haven't. Ever."

"Haven't what? Haven't ever gone hiking? Haven't ever cheated on a test?"

I rolled my eyes. "I haven't ever had sex, Jordan."

He laughed. "I know that's what you meant. I mean, given the thing with your ex..."

"That's not the only thing." I sighed and told him what I'd told Zeke earlier about my sister being a survivor of sexual assault and how it affected me.

"Jesus." Jordan reached out and grabbed my hand in his. "I... wow. I'm so sorry. I can't imagine what that must have done to Kate, like, on such a deep level. And your parents. And you, of course. I hope you know you can trust me, and I don't ever want to push you."

"I know. And I do trust you." I took a deep breath. "I actually think I'm... I'm ready."

He nodded and leaned in to give me a soft kiss. As our lips met, he rested his hand on the back of my head, pulling me closer to him. Too soon, we broke apart. The beach, the drinks, everything was going to my head. I felt a wild desire to strip down and be with him right then and there. And I knew that wasn't me.

"What about you?"

"What *about* me?"

"Well, have you...?"

He nodded, raising an eyebrow. "Um, yeah."

"Like, a lot, or...?"

He smiled. "Does it matter?"

"I want to know whether to be intimidated by your experience."

He laughed. "I've been with four people. So, no. Plus, a little experience is a good thing, I think. Anal sex can be, um, messy if you don't properly prepare."

"Yeah, I imagine it's not like the porn I've seen where it's magically all clean and fresh back there."

Jordan smirked at me. "Oh? What kind of porn are we talking here?"

I immediately opened my mouth to lie, but Zeke approached from the beach. "It's been about two hours. We should get back so they aren't waiting on us."

Jordan gave me a saucy look, I smirked and shook my head, and we stood, brushing the sand off as best we could. Like in one of those classic movies, I had made out with a sexy man on a beach while waves lapped at our feet.

Of course, the glamorous feeling was quickly outweighed by reality as I began to feel the presence of sand in unwanted places.

As we got into our cab, I turned to Renee from the front seat.

"Did you have a nice time?"

She raised an eyebrow. "Surprisingly so, especially considering my whole world has been turned upside down."

"I hear that." I nodded vigorously. "Two months ago, I was preparing to start my senior year of college and go on my first date in years. It's been hard to adjust to all of this."

"You know, everybody gets so worked up when things change." Renee looked between Jordan and me. "I mean, I imagine the changes you've been through are a lot more than changing jobs or losing a loved one. But it always seems to catch people by surprise when those kinds of things happen, even though it's inevitable."

"Yeah, what's that about?"

"To me, it all comes down to one thing: fear. They're afraid of the unknown. I mean, who wouldn't be? But if you let that fear make your decisions, you're going to end up afraid *and* stuck. Or you could be afraid *and* fail. Either way, you're scared, but only one way lets you continue to live."

All I could do was smile at her as I turned back around, shifting uncomfortably due to sand. Of course, all this did was get me thinking about our current situation.

As we rode back to the airport, it felt like I had a moment of clarity. I was afraid of what had already changed. Was I still going to be afraid? Yes. Was that okay? Totally. But I couldn't let it dictate the decisions I make. Sure, my life had taken a drastic turn into Weirdville. Now, I was on the city council with an opportunity to become mayor. Either way, my life was going to keep moving forward, with or without my consent.

And that included hanging on to my guilt. I would always feel guilty about what I'd done. And I could still work harder and do better. And that meant—like Jordan had asked me to—I needed to sit in the back seat and let the others drive.

Once we got back to the airport, I used the bathroom to change clothes into the warmer stuff I'd need to wear for the flight to Saipan, as well as wipe some of the sand off my body and out of my crevices.

As I washed my hands, I looked in the mirror. I knew I'd changed physically, but even over the last week or so, I appeared harder, tougher. I hadn't lost weight, but I'd seemed to gain muscle. I could see my cheekbones a little.

As we walked up the ramp to get back on the plane, Jordan made an announcement. "I'd like to meet with everybody right after takeoff. We need to go over the details for the dive."

Once we were in the air and cleared to unhook ourselves, we all met in front of *The Ancora*. Jordan cleared his throat.

"Okay. I figured we should go over our plan for when we get to Saipan. We've got seven hours, so we should, um, have a plan." He cleared his throat as everyone waited expectantly. "Right. Okay. So, I guess the details we need to figure out are how to get the sub from the airport to the nearest dock. Then, get the sub to the Mariana Trench."

"It would take a long time for the submarine to get from Saipan to the Mariana Trench by itself," Renee said. "We need a boat. One that can haul a sub."

Jordan nodded. "Um, right. But we can't get it to the boat without transportation from the airport. Any ideas?"

"I'm fresh out of flatbeds." Zeke shoved his hands in his pockets. "All my contacts were in San Francisco for a reason."

"I have a friend in Guam." Lex met Jordan's gaze while David frowned at her, confused. "I could try to call ahead in the cockpit."

Jordan nodded. "Sounds good. Okay, so Lex can work to get the sub from the airport to a dock. Then, we need a boat. A big one."

Lex sighed, glancing quickly at David. "So, the friend in Guam is actually my ex-boyfriend, Mack. He has a yacht. Um, it's a big one that could easily carry the sub."

David frowned. "How did you know Mack was going to be in Guam?"

"Don't." Lex's tone was hard and took me by surprise.

"Don't... ask questions?" David replied.

She glowered at him, and he shrunk back. She turned back to us. "Anyway, he comes from money, so he's got a yacht big enough for all of us. It has staff and everything."

Jordan nodded, impressed. "Okay, you can make the call after we figure out who's going with Robert on the sub."

"There are three seats in the sub." Robert quickly drew a rough sketch of the inside of *The Ancora*. "Technically you can fit a fourth person, but they'd have to sit on the floor. That's if it's absolutely necessary."

"It makes sense that Ari and Lex go, but I'm not going to force anyone." Jordan shared a look with Lex and Ari, who both nodded. "And I can go with them."

"How about... no?" Ari raised an eyebrow at Jordan, who raised both of his in surprise. "I mean, I hate to say this, especially since I'll be in the thick of it, but if something goes wrong, we've lost the guy who's been keeping us together."

"But..." Jordan appealed to Lex for support with his hands out.

"What?" She crossed her arms over her chest. "I agree. Besides, what good is a Calor down there with all that water? It's water and earth down there. So, it should be a Terra."

Jordan looked at me, and I could see real fear in his eyes. In an instant, I understood both reasons why he didn't want me to go.

He couldn't trust me not to get others killed.

I could also be killed.

Fun.

"Well, what if there's an electrical problem?" Zeke asked. "I mean, maybe we do one of each? Ionis, Terra, and Aquis?"

"Any problems we experience down there probably wouldn't be helped with more electricity." Robert rubbed the back of his neck. "The biggest problem that far down is the water pressure, so it would make sense for both the, uh, the water superheroes to go."

"We're not—"

"Don't interrupt him, Ari." Will smiled at Robert, who knew Will well enough now to roll his eyes. I knew he enjoyed being called a superhero.

"Besides, with all that water and how deep it is, two Aquises would be best," David said. "I agree with Lex. It should be her and Ari, and it makes sense that Jake goes."

"No. Jake won't be going." Jordan's toned surprised everyone, but I nodded. "We can do the dives with Ari and Lex."

"Am I missing something?" Robert looked around at all of us.

"The freeway thing. Jordan doesn't trust the disaster that is Jake."

"Thank you for summing up the situation so delicately, Will." Jordan glowered at him.

"Jordan's right. I... I shouldn't be in the middle of things. I'm the newest one here. Besides, I've got my own shit to cope with." I met Renee's gaze. "I can't run away from what I've done, but I need time to learn to do better."

Chapter 6: Till Death Do You Part

Once we adjourned the meeting, Lex went to work making phone calls. While her ex-boyfriend, Mack, didn't have any contacts to gain access to a flatbed, he confirmed he would set sail immediately to provide us with transport and lodging for our search.

After the flatbed plan fell through, Robert and Renee decided to call in some of their NEMO contacts they thought could be trusted. Within a few hours, everything was prepared for when we landed.

"I'm just saying, an ex doesn't do that if there still isn't something there." Will was giving Zeke a shoulder rub as I sat playing cards with Ari.

"You're wrong, and it's also none of your business," Ari said.

"Oh, I'm not saying it's my business at all." Will kneaded his fingers along Zeke's neck. "I'm only saying it's interesting. I'm interested to see what happens once we land."

"Hopefully there's not another attack or something." Zeke rubbed his eyes. "Man, I'm tired as it is."

"What's really going to mess you up is that we crossed the International Date Line." Ari casually decimated me with a card demanding I draw four. "It was Wednesday afternoon in Hawaii. We lost a whole day."

"What?"

"It's going to be Thursday evening when we get off the plane in Saipan."

Will shot a pouty look at Zeke. "We've lost a whole other day to consummate our engagement."

Ari rolled their eyes. "We don't need to hear about your sex life."

"Well, that's good, because there hasn't been one since we left King. Thank God we'll be on a boat with a private cabin."

"Really?" I laid down a card, getting revenge on Ari.

"Yeah, I found out about the yacht. It's technically a mega yacht." Will ran his hands through Zeke's hair. Zeke's eyes were closed, obviously enjoying himself. "I mean, it has room for a submarine, so of course it's gigantic."

"I'm challenging you." Ari raised an eyebrow. "All those cards, you have to have something blue."

I scoffed and rolled my eyes. "I guess it makes sense. How many rooms does it have?" I drew six cards, sticking my tongue out at Ari.

"If it's like the one we read about, there's seven. And there's seven of us."

"There's actually nine, with Renee and Robert." Ari laid down three skip cards in a row. "Plus, with Mack and whoever he has on the boat with him. It could be a tight squeeze."

"'Tis what she proclaimed," Will quipped in a British accent, and Zeke, who was basically unconscious, raised his hand to lightly hit Will in the arm. "That's actually a good point. We don't know if Lex's ex-lovah has anybody with him."

"He doesn't anymore." Lex rounded the corner, arms folded. "He dropped his girlfriend and her friends off in Guam. They're at a hotel relaxing while we do a bunch of *work*."

She stalked off, leaving everybody but Ari speechless.

"Oh, I'm out." Ari laid down their last card. I had half the deck in my hand.

A little while later, the pilot came on the radio saying we were a few minutes away from landing. One unpleasant and (from what I understand) standard landing later, and the ramp was lowering once again to let in warm, sticky air. I thought it was good news that it was raining slightly, until they let us know it was ninety degrees and likely wouldn't get much cooler with the cloud cover.

"Okay, remember to be on the lookout for anyone suspicious, or any of the Disciples," Jordan said as we walked down the ramp. "Benedetti knows our destination, so we need to be careful from here on out."

Robert waved at a man who was standing near a flatbed. "Jakobe! It's so great to see you." Robert walked forward and they embraced, patting each other hard on the back. "How's Tina? And the boys?"

As they caught up and Robert explained what we needed, Jakobe pointed out one big problem.

"How're you gonna get the sub onto the bed of the truck?"

Robert looked at Jordan, who gave an easy smile. "We've got that. Why don't you two get out of this rain. We've got all the straps and stuff, so we can have you take a look when it's ready."

Jakobe shrugged, and he, Robert, and Renee made their way inside the airport with the soldiers to grab food. Once we were fairly certain nobody was watching, Lex and Ari used the falling rain to trickle inside the cargo plane and create a path for the sub to slide along. Then, once it was next to the flatbed, Will and I worked with Lex and Ari to lift the sub onto the flatbed.

Bam! The submarine settled onto the trailer and wobbled slightly. I put my hands up to stabilize it, looking around at Jordan's wide eyes. Luckily, nobody saw anything. Then, Lex went in to get the others, and they began the process of tying down the sub.

As they did, the military members that were on the plane with us came back out of the airport and began getting the plane ready for takeoff. I walked up to one of them.

"Thanks for helping us out," I said as he fastened several crates. "You have no idea how much we needed the help."

"Orders're orders." He held out his fist for me to pound. "We don't ask who or why, we make sure they get followed."

He turned around and got back to work, leaving me frowning. Who in the military had ordered them to help us? I thought Zeke had secured the plane. Did he have a service background he hadn't talked about? He seemed too young to have been in the armed forces long enough to have the pull to charter a cargo plane from San Francisco to Saipan.

I descended the ramp, looking for Zeke, but I couldn't see him anywhere.

"Mack's half an hour away." Lex hung up her phone and walked toward Jordan.

"Perfect." Jordan looked relieved. "Which dock is he meeting us at?"

She winced. "That's the thing... his yacht is too big for any of the docks here. But... he said there's space to load behind the two oil plants here. We need to be as quick as possible."

Jordan ran his hand through his hair. "If that's the worst complication, I'll be good with that." He waved his arms to get everyone's attention. "Jakobe, thank you so much for letting us borrow the truck. Are you good to drive us to oil plants from here?"

He nodded. "It should take us 'bout half an hour to get there with the truck."

"Great. Robert can ride with you. Lex, if you'll join them?" They nodded and made their way to the truck. Jordan lowered his voice. "Ari, I want you hiding out on the flatbed in case there's any trouble." Ari nodded, heading to the truck and disappearing from sight. "Zeke, the rest of us can take cabs and get there first to field any trouble at the loading site."

Zeke nodded and moved to make a call, but I followed him as he moved away.

"Hey."

"Hi."

"Didn't you arrange the military transport?"

He looked away. "Yeah. I can't talk about it, though."

"Why?"

His eyes narrowed as his gaze met mine. "Because I can't. I shouldn't have done it in the first place, and the less everyone knows about that particular thing, the better."

I sighed. "I... I thought we weren't going to do secrets like the council did. I thought this could maybe be a fresh start for the Keepers."

He tried and failed not to roll his eyes. "The council had secrets for a reason. Secrets exist for a reason. And this one is between me and Jordan until... until it's time for others to know. I can call the cabs on my own." He turned to walk away, then stopped. "I'm sorry. I'm just... this is all new to me. I never wanted this power, you know? And now I've got all these responsibilities and it's... well, it's tiring. I don't mean to take it out on you or anyone."

I smiled. "Thank you. I appreciate that. I'm sorry for prying."

He nodded and turned back to make his calls.

The semi pulled away from the airport, and a few minutes later, two taxis showed up. David, Will, and Zeke got into the second cab while Renee, Jordan and I got into the first one.

It almost seemed like a dream, driving through Saipan. Our driver stayed on the outer road the whole way, and we eventually caught up to and then passed the semi. To my left was the ocean, seemingly endless, with the sky rapidly darkening. To my right were several historical sights and points of interest our driver pointed out to us.

"Mount Carmel Cathedral!" He pointed off to the right, where a large church with a red brick courtyard stood. "My church."

I heard Renee tsk several times as she looked out of the left window. "Look. KFC and Taco Bell." I laughed and cracked the window slightly as we continued driving, making sure the drizzling rain wasn't getting in the car and basking in the air and noise of the island. It was hard not to think of this as a vacation when I'd never been outside of the continental United States, and definitely never anywhere with palm trees.

I loved seeing the different kinds of red bushes and trees. Some areas were like a miniature jungle, and the smell of the ocean combined with plants was intoxicating.

We passed by several other churches, as well as many other buildings advertising different kinds of Asian cuisine. We had a few Asian-style eateries in King, and most of them served food that was too spicy for my taste.

"This could almost be Florida," I said. "I mean, look. Gas station, Toyotas and Nissans—and recent road work here."

Renee laughed, but she wasn't smiling. "You must not travel. Look closer."

So, I did, looking for things I hadn't seen yet.

"I see... a lot of double signs." I wasn't sure what she wanted me to look at. "Like, signs in English and then signs in... an Asian language I don't know."

"Korean. What about the buildings?"

"Well, they're not like the ones in San Francisco, but they're still kind of pretty. And they don't have a lot of sidewalks."

Renee smiled patiently, but her explanation revealed it was a bitter smile. "The Northern Mariana Islands are a U.S. Commonwealth. Before that, these islands were conquered multiple times, and, because of that, the population was either decimated or forced to adhere to whatever country was in charge. For a long time, the people fought to remain true to who they once were, but their identity has all been but washed away. U.S. involvement here hasn't benefited the people. I mean, some of them live in metal shacks. There are a lot of different Asian cultures represented here, but you'll find the people are exploited for labor because they're so isolated. And, in recent years, there have been a lot of issues with drug trafficking."

"Wow." I let out a deep breath. "I seriously need to get out more. I mean, I don't know much about the real history of places. I mean, I know about the genocide of the Indigenous people in the U.S., but world history didn't cover what the U.S. has done in other places. I guess it makes sense why Americans are so hated in some places."

"You find bad people everywhere," our driver commented. "America seems to put them in charge all the time."

We laughed, though it wasn't that funny. Finally, we pulled into the oil plant entrance. We were stopped at the gate by a man in an official-looking uniform.

"He wants to know why you're here," the driver said to us.

Jordan leaned over in the passenger seat. "We're here to unload a submarine to head diving. We need to load up here and then—"

"No." The guard dismissed us. "Please leave."

Jordan blinked. "Our yacht is already waiting."

The guard sighed. "You can't use our property however you want."

Renee rolled down her window. "Excuse me? Sir. I'm wondering why you let other boats load and unload from your property that aren't directly related to oil production, but won't let us through?"

The guard looked alarmed. "We do no such thing."

"Uh-huh. I'm sure your bosses would tell you the same thing. But part of my work with the Naval Exploration, Mapping, and Oceanography Center had to do with researching this area and its companies. I've seen an awful lot of traffic through here."

"That doesn't mean you get to be a part of it."

The semi pulled in behind us just then, and Lex got out of the cab. The guard bristled at the action.

"Please get back in your vehicles and—"

"I'm sorry, are you not aware that we're working with the Department of Defense?" Lex folded her arms. "The yacht we're waiting for is called *Andromeda*. And it's U.S. Senator Tamara Ryder's personal yacht. Now, do you want to annoy the senator and get her interested in what goes on here, or will you let us unload the sub and go?"

Five minutes later, we pulled around a corner from some stacked cargo containers to find the largest yacht I'd ever seen, and an unfamiliar man descending the ramp.

He was dressed all in white: from a white captain's hat to his mostly unbuttoned long sleeve shirt with the sleeves rolled up, boardshorts, and boat shoes. And, because it was raining, the clothes were rather clingy and see-through. The man was built.

"Mack!" Lex stepped forward, waving.

"Alexandria Ophelia Grant!"

As he stepped forward to give her a hug, I noticed his face seemed too pretty to exist as well. Strong jawline, full lips, blond hair, and I felt like I could count his individual eyelashes from thirty feet away. When he smiled, his dazzlingly white teeth were perfectly straight.

Jordan, Will, Zeke, and I stood, observing Mack as he lifted Lex into the air and spun her around. Ari and David were paying the cab drivers.

"Sorry, Zekey. I've got to call this thing off between us until I determine that man's sexuality." Will unbuttoned one more of the buttons on his top while Zeke rolled his eyes.

"Are you kidding me? Of course he's straight." I gestured at him. "Obviously."

"Thank you so much for hosting us, Mack." Lex stepped back and held out her hands to introduce everyone. "This is Jordan, Will, Jake, and Zeke. This is Renee... and Robert. Ari's over there... oh, and here's David!"

David swaggered up and held out his hand to Mack who, instead of shaking it, brought him in for a bro hug. "Dude, it's great to meet you. I've heard nothin' but the best."

David smiled, but it didn't meet his eyes. "Nice to meet you, too. We all appreciate you taking us on last-minute."

"Eh, it's not like I had anythin' else goin'," Mack said, stepping forward and shaking everyone else's hands. Then, he stepped back and stood straight. "I officially invite you aboard *Andromeda*."

Nobody moved, and Mack laughed. "Aight, now, don't be shy, dawgs! Follow me!"

Renee and Robert stayed outside to help oversee the loading of the submarine onto the yacht while the rest of us walked up the ramp and into our new home for the next little while.

Andromeda was gargantuan. It was more like a miniature cruise ship than anything. As we followed him, Mack began to take us on a tour.

"There are a total of six luxury cabins on the main deck, not including the Captain's Cabin," he explained, giving a high-five to one of the crew members as they walked by. "The crew deck is below that. It's also where the kitchen is, and since there's a chef on-shift all the time, give 'em a call and they'll whip up somethin' for ya. Me casa is you casa. We got a crew of forty-six, so all y'all'll be well taken care of."

As we stepped onto the beautiful maple deck, I saw a few servers walking around with trays of champagne and beer bottles, hors d'oeuvres, and what was probably caviar, but I couldn't be sure because I'd never seen it in person.

"Have some refreshments, my friends." Mack gestured to the servers. I glanced tentatively at Zeke, but Will stepped forward and grabbed a glass and a small piece of bread covered in some kind of spread.

"This is exactly how I was meant to live." Will grabbed Zeke's hand in his. "Baby, please remember this and make me a lot of money."

"How did you get to afford all this, Mack?" Ari took a glass of champagne and popped a few meat-and-cheese concoctions into their mouth.

"My mom is the Senate Majority Leader. Senator Tamara Ryder," he said with a shrug. "We got this to celebrate her thirtieth year in the senate."

Ari froze, and their look turned from one of enjoyment to stone-cold rage. They set their flute of champagne down on a tray and walked away to another part of the boat, spitting their food into the ocean along the way.

Everyone watched them go. Mack looked around at us to explain.

"Yeaaaaaaah, Ari's super into politics." Will smiled weakly. "They're probably upset about the millions of corporate dollars your mother probably used to pay for this yacht and stay in office while her constituents suffer with a lack of affordable healthcare, education, and livable wages. Ari's probably also upset that your mom fought against marriage equality and sponsored that bill that targeted transgender people's rights to use public facilities."

"Oh." Mack shrugged again. "I've learned to stay out of Poly Sci. It brings me down, man. I prefer to live out on the open water, enjoyin' the ocean breeze an' a cold one."

"Yeaaaaaah, probably don't say any of that to Ari." Will drained his glass of champagne. "I'm sure Ari would argue that politics is the way the U.S. government makes any decisions regarding its citizens, and therefore everyone should be involved, and you're naive and entitled for living the way you do without thinking about how your mother got the money to do that."

Mack narrowed his eyes at Will.

"What? I'm saying that's what *Ari* would say. I didn't say it. Anyway, who's for some fancy drinks and eats?"

He grabbed another glass and made his way to a nearby lounge chair.

Meanwhile, the crew—along with Renee and Robert—had finished loading the submarine onto the yacht. Renee and Robert joined us aboard, and we were soon settled on a covered part of the deck into comfortable sofas and deck chairs. Evening had fallen, and we sat by lamplight, relaxing as we made our way into open water.

"Okay, folks, we're ready to go!" Mack raised his beer, and everyone did the same. "To adventures on the open seas!"

As we made our way away from the island and into open water, I felt an equal sense of one fear rising with another decreasing. It would be harder for Benedetti to find us as we made our way into the ocean.

But I'd never been in open water, and I'd never dived down into open water. The deepest pool I'd ever been in was twenty feet. And here we were, going to the deepest part of the ocean.

Everyone seemed to chill more with drinks, so I tried to do the same and cut my fearful thoughts.

"I'm Will. Wiiiiiiiillllllll-uh." Mack had, once again, confused Will for Zeke, and vice-versa. "I'm the Honduran hottie, and Zeke is the white boy imma marry!"

"What?" Mack put his beer down and sat up. "Dudes! You're takin' the vows? That's super dope? When? Where?"

"We don't know yet." Zeke gave a red-faced smile. "Once we get done with all this, I suppose."

"What about you two, Lex?" Mack turned to Lex and David.

"I asked her, and she said no." David shook his head, laughing, while Lex looked at him in disbelief.

"I can't believe you would tell everyone like that!" Lex stood and stormed off.

"What? What'd I say?"

He was slurring his words, having been drinking two beers to everyone's one.

"Sounds like she wasn't ready." Mack pulled up his shirt slightly to itch his abs. "I dunno, man. She... requires a better man than I am."

David sighed and set his drink down. "Better go talk to her." He stood and walked away.

"Yeah, we should probably head to bed." Renee set her drink down as well, eyeing Robert. "We've got a big day ahead of us tomorrow."

Robert and Renee bid everyone a farewell, and the party started to break up. Zeke had to rouse Will, who had fallen asleep with his head in Zeke's lap, and I told Jordan I was going to take a final walk around the boat before heading to our cabin.

He kissed me, and pulled away, gently rubbing my chin with his thumb. "I like this look on you. The unshaven thing looks good on you."

"I have a long way to go before being able to match your beard." I kissed him again. I began to meander, heading around the deck until I got to a more private seating area. There, I heard two voices.

"—sorry for telling everyone like that, but it was months ago, baby."

"They don't need to know about us like that, David," Lex said. "All it does is show that you don't respect my decision."

"I don't understand it is all. You know I—"

"No, I really don't think you do understand it or respect it. And I don't think you actually respect me since I told you I wasn't sure I was ready."

"Baby..." David's voice was a whisper.

"D, I don't know if I ever want to... to marry you." Lex's words caused David to inhale sharply, and I stood, silent, not wanting to interrupt but not wanting to be seen, either. "I love you, but I need more than that. Your life is the Keepers. Mine isn't. I wouldn't be here if I had a choice. I'm not going to change, and I'm not going to ask you to change, either. So... it's not going to work. It hasn't been working for a while. I think we both know that."

"So, that's it?" David's voice cracked. "We're... we're done?" Lex didn't say anything, but David spoke after a moment of silence. "I've loved you for three years, Lex."

"Love isn't always enough." Lex's words sounded final. "But I—David!"

I heard sudden movement and quickly ducked into a doorway as David hurried past, wiping his eyes. I heard Lex sniff.

I should go talk to one of them. No, it's none of your business. Let them be and you can deal with it tomorrow.

Instead of continuing my walk, I made my way below and ran into Ari sitting on the steps, rubbing their temples.

"Hey." I stepped down onto the lower deck and sat on the ground. "You okay?"

"Yeah. Headache from not eating anything."

I frowned. "Are you seriously going to protest Mack's ignorance by starving yourself?"

They met my eyes defiantly. "Maybe."

"Okay. Well, I don't know how long we're going to be out here, but I think you'll probably die of starvation before you make him become more politically involved. He was super supportive of Will and Zeke."

Ari rolled their eyes. "Good for fucking him. It's such bullshit."

"I know." I thought about what to say for a moment, but the words spilled out before I realized I'd even considered saying them. "Lex broke up with David."

They looked up at me, but I was surprised to find they weren't shocked like I was. "I've been wondering if that wasn't an impending decision. He proposed in March, and she turned him down. Since then, it sort of seemed like David was extra clingy and Lex was pulling away."

I nodded. "That makes sense. It sounded like she wanted to leave the Keepers and he wanted to make it his lifelong goal."

Their eyes went wide. "She... she said she wants to leave the Keepers?"

I nodded. "I mean, once this is all done, I wonder if there's any Keepers to get back together, you know?"

"No, I know, but you can't leave the Keepers."

"Why not?"

Ari groaned and beckoned me to follow them. They led me to their room, and when they closed the door behind us, they gestured for me to sit down.

"You remember Kevin, right? The Calor with the incel vibes?" I nodded, remembering how Benedetti had unceremoniously executed him. Ari continued. "So, one of the reasons I never got along with Kevin was because he was really into conspiracy theories about the Keepers. But one actually turned out to be true—his parents were killed by the Keepers."

"What? That's so crazy, though!"

"I know. I thought it was stupid, too. But I confirmed it with Jordan, who heard Grace talking about it with Blair. Apparently, they had arranged the whole thing because Kevin told his parents, and they kept trying to get him away from the Keepers until... they died of carbon monoxide poisoning. It turned out Kevin had actually made plans to run away, and his parents had set everything up in Canada."

"I... oh my God. No wonder he turned on the Keepers."

"I mean, I get that, too, but it's like disavowing agents who are caught, or assassinating people who are threats to national security. It all makes sense."

I frowned at them. "How can you say that? The U.S. government has become a Christo fascist oligarchical haven for straight, white men."

"Oh, I know it. Believe me. There's a lot of shitty things the government does, but assassinating people who could basically start a war and bring the entire system down is necessary. So, no, we can't 'leave the Keepers.' Lex is being selfish, and she knows better."

"Wow." I stared at them, trying to process what I was hearing. "I just... I mean, once we find the Omnia Fragment, who's to say what's going to happen?"

"I'll tell you what's going to happen." Ari faced me, arms crossed. "We're going to find a new home, recruit, and continue the work that's been done for thousands of years. This isn't about what we want. It's about what we *need* to do. We're the people with the power at this point, and we can't run away from that. If Lex presses the issue... maybe she'll get a visit from Jordan like Kevin's parents did."

I gasped. "What? You're saying he—"

"I don't know for sure, but I wouldn't be surprised. But if there's one person who's committed to the Keepers until death, it's him. His first priority will always be the Keepers."

They stood and gestured at the door, clearly done with the conversation. I was almost out of the door when they stopped me. "And Jake? Given the little stunt you pulled on the bridge, you should be aware that Keepers have also been known to eliminate people who are a threat to others' lives."

I nodded. "So, people like Vic and Benedetti."

They shook their head. "And people like you."

Chapter 7: Shaken, Stirred, and Screwed

Warning: This chapter contains discussion of suicide.

After I left Ari's cabin, I walked the short distance to the room I was sharing with Jordan, mind still reeling from our conversation.

As I stepped into the room, however, I was distracted by its beauty and luxury. The cabin was smaller than my room in Sanctuary but was clever in its spatial efficiency.

The bed was a queen, and the bedspread was a simple white with two large gold stripes near the bottom. The accent pillows were also gold and white, with a decorative long, round pillow with tassels on either end between them.

At the end of the bed was a combo bench/storage chest. Looking around the base of the bed, the frame was made entirely of drawers. The hull was at the head of the bed, where windows filled the entire wall but had screens pulled down for privacy.

To the left side of the bed was a couch with many decorative cushions and pillows, and to the left of that was a vanity, complete with sink, large mirror, stool, and nailed-down storage compartments for probably jewelry and makeup.

To the right of the bed was a built-in bedside table with a modern-looking lamp on top. Next to that was what I thought was a dresser, until Jordan opened it to reveal a mini-fridge.

"We must be the luckiest fugitives around." I closed the door behind me as Jordan sat down on the edge of the bed, opening a bottle of water.

"Yeah." He took a drink, staring straight ahead.

"You okay?" I walked over to stand by him and gently place my hand on his back.

He sighed. "I've been without my antidepressants since we left Sanctuary, and it's finally hitting me."

I frowned, rubbing his back. "I'm sorry. I didn't even know you were on them."

"Yeah. As long as I take them, I stay pretty level. Otherwise, I'm pretty down, and can get really low. Like, dangerous low."

I took a deep breath, my heartbeat quickening. I'd read through plenty of trainings and such after my first boyfriend completed suicide, and all those thoughts immediately moved to the priority center of my brain. "Do you want to kill yourself?"

"Oh, no." Jordan shook his head and squeezed my hand. "I promise, I'm okay for now. I mean, I did get to that point once about ten years ago. But Isaac was able to talk me through what he called a safety plan, and then I got on antidepressants. It took a few tries to find the right medication. But I've been on them ever since. Until now, that is."

I sat down next to him and leaned against him. "If you are thinking of doing anything... please tell me, okay? I'll try to be more aware, but please don't be afraid to ask me to sit with you or something, okay?"

He considered his feet. "I'm sure this is the last thing you wanted in a boyfriend, especially after Seth."

"Jordan, Seth didn't tell me he was experiencing suicidal ideation until he had decided to... well, to get in that car and drive to his death. I'm worried about you. I don't want you to make a decision based on what's happening right now that takes you from me. If you ever do get to that point, and I'm not around, think about me, okay? And how much I love you."

He smiled, holding my hand up to his mouth and kissing it softly. "They say love is all you need."

"Speaking of love..." I began to tell him about the conversation I heard between David and Lex, and the discussion with Ari after. I left out the part about Ari warning me that Jordan might, you know, kill me.

"Huh." He grunted softly and laid back on the bed with his arms above his head. "That's... a bit to process."

"I know." I scooted over and settled in next to him on my side. "I hope this doesn't affect things with the rest of the group."

"Oh, it's going to be awkward as fuck," Jordan said, laughing. "In my experience, Lex likes to pretend everything is fine and she's fine, and that hurts David and then he drinks. We'll have to monitor him, especially with Mack around—they'll probably bro out all over the place."

I laughed. "I'm glad I'm not the only one who saw the bro-ness of Mack."

"Is that the *only* thing you saw about him?"

"What, the fact that he's basically a model? Yeah, I noticed that. But he's, like, living in Broville. He's the Mayor of Broville."

Jordan smiled and put his arm around me. "This is why I love you."

"I'm sure there are more reasons, but I'll take that one for now." I bit my lip. "Is it true? What Ari said about Kevin's family?"

"I heard rumors along with the other Keepers, but I was basically able to confirm it by spying on Grace. I shouldn't have told anyone."

"So... you weren't the one who did it?"

His eyebrows shot up. "What? No. God, no. Grace would never have asked me to do that."

"Ari told me they wouldn't be surprised if you were the one who killed Kevin's parents."

He shook his head. "Ari needs to learn the difference between being able to do something and being willing to do something. I totally could have killed them, sure. But I never would have agreed to do it."

We laid in silence for a while. I closed my eyes, enjoying the feeling of rocking slightly in the water. Finally, Jordan spoke softly.

"What's your favorite color?"

"Blue. Yours?"

"Yellow."

I laughed a little. "I don't think I've ever met someone who likes the color yellow."

"Now you have."

"Favorite food?"

"Hmm... cheeseburgers."

Jordan rolled onto his side, and I opened my eyes. His expression was serious.

"What?"

"Big spoon or little spoon?"

I grinned. "Actually, I'm versatile. But I enjoyed being the little spoon with you."

He raised an eyebrow. "Versatile, huh?"

I smirked. "In more ways than one."

I rolled onto my other side and we both adjusted ourselves on the bed to where he was holding me, his hand gently running up and down my arm. We stayed like that until we fell asleep.

I woke up the next morning to Jordan lying in bed and cuddling up behind me. To my surprise, I felt *something* poke me slightly around my waist. I didn't want to embarrass him, but he was aware. He gently kissed my neck, breathing heavily.

I turned my face to his and began kissing him, tenderly at first, but then more urgently. I wrapped my arms around his neck, moaning softly into his lips. He responded by pressing his body against mine more fiercely.

We continued kissing while pressed against each other, hands exploring arms, waists, thighs. Finally, he pulled away, smiling at me. His cheeks were flushed. "Well. Good morning to you, too."

I thrust my hips into his, giving an impish grin. "It certainly *feels* like a good morning."

Jordan's cheeks darkened and he laughed. "Well, um, I am very *excited* to wake up next to you." He sat up, running a hand through his hair. "I decided to let everyone sleep in a little after everything that happened yesterday."

"Let me guess: you've been up since seven o'clock, went on a run on the deck of the yacht, cooked a magnificent feast for breakfast, saved a puppy, cured the common cold, and found the Omnia Fragment already."

He rolled his eyes. "Don't be ridiculous... it was a cat, not a puppy. Remember?"

I laughed, shaking my head. "You're adorable. Almost too adorable."

"I happen to think the same about you." He kissed my nose, then rolled away and stood. "Breakfast actually is ready, but I didn't cook it. We should also get a move on. Today's the big day."

"When do we get to the Mariana Trench?" I sat up, stretching and working my neck back and forth.

"We're already here."

A few minutes later, I was in the shower, noticing the scruff on my face and how long my hair had already gotten in the last few weeks. I styled it using a comb I found, then picked out a t-shirt and jeans.

I smiled a little as I dressed. It was like my first morning at Sanctuary. I didn't know what was going to happen, but I wanted to look my best. *Sure, Jake. Try and normalize the fact Lex and Ari are about to dive miles into the most unexplored parts of the ocean in search of a magic alien crystal. No big.*

Breakfast consisted of us eating on the deck while crew members told us what was available, then brought us what we chose. I felt like a celebrity.

However, it was tense. David looked like he hadn't slept as he mindlessly shoveled pancakes into his mouth, and Lex's eyes were puffy as she picked at her omelet. They were sitting on opposite sides of the seating area. To my surprise, even Will didn't say anything about the situation, which indicated to me how serious it actually was.

"Mornin'." Mack plopped down next to me, holding a cup of coffee and rubbing his eye. "How'd you sleep?"

"The rocking takes a bit to get used to." I had to push my pancakes into my cheek to talk. "But everything is incredible. I can't tell you how much we appreciate it all."

"I'm glad you like it." He heaved a sigh, then lowered his voice. "So, your group brings some baggage, huh, bro?"

I stared at him, wondering if he meant David and Lex or if someone had told him a man made of diamond tried to kill us all.

"I mean, here I was, birthday suitin' it in bed," he began, and I had to fight to keep control of my face, "when there's a knock at the door, and it's this super drunk dude blubbering about his babe. Of course, it was bro to the rescue, but still."

I laughed. "What, did you take him to the strip club on the yacht?"

He laughed loudly, nudging me in the side and knocking my fork to the floor. "You're hilarious, dude! And no. D-man is definitely feelin' a hangover. And if you can't beat 'em, join 'em."

He toasted with his coffee, then spoke in a normal voice. "So, Robert said y'all have superpowers or somethin'?"

I coughed on a bite and scrutinized Robert, wide eyed.

"I'm a chatty drunk." Robert raised his arms apologetically.

"You literally had two drinks," Renee said.

"I'm a chatty *lightweight* drunk."

I laughed and turned back to Mack. "Um, so I don't know about superpowers, but we can do stuff."

"So, are you, like, mutants? Will I get powers too? Is Jordan, like, the dude version of Jean Grey?"

"Not mutants. But we do totally move stuff with our minds. And as long as you don't touch any of the five fragments we have, you won't get powers."

"Oh." He blinked. "*Could* I touch them, though? I promise I'll only use them for good."

"No." Jordan stepped up and interrupted our conversation. "We need to get the sub prepped and ready to launch. Lex? Ari? Let's get this show on the road."

The show took an hour to actually get started, what with maneuvering the sub into the water, Robert and Renee micromanaging everything, and Mack trying to get someone to show off their abilities.

Meanwhile, Renee had also distributed wetsuits to Ari, Lex, and Robert.

"We should do a test dive or two before we head straight down," Robert told Jordan.

"The sooner we can actually get down to the bottom, the better," he said. "I trust you, but we probably only have a few days max before—"

"*Oh my God! Yes!*" We all turned as Will shouted the words and embraced Mack and Zeke together, Mack clapping them both hard on their backs.

"What?" I knew it wasn't an emergency, but it was definitely something of note.

"We're getting married, right here on the yacht, because Mack can perform weddings!"

Most everybody began to exclaim words of congratulations and happiness, but Lex took the opportunity to hurry away downstairs and David stalked off as well, probably looking for a drink.

I walked over to them both to hug them and congratulate them. A few minutes later we were toasting with drinks the crew seemed to whip up without any problems, and discussing what Will and Zeke wanted for their wedding.

"Thank you all for your wonderful support." Will held his hands up like he was directing a choir. "But no thank you for your input into our ceremony. We'll get it taken care of. In the meantime, do what we came here to do. Get the Omnia Fragment and save the world."

"Can I touch it once you get it?" Mack asked.

"No," said Jordan, Will, Zeke, Ari, Robert, Renee, and I at the same time.

That's the last thing we need: Mack Ryder, commander of, like, all the elements, bruh!

Ari went to retrieve Lex, and soon they, plus Robert and Jordan, were gathered by the rail, looking down at the sub bobbing in the water. I stood by, simply watching.

"We want to make sure we do this right, but we do it fast." Jordan stared intently into Robert's eyes to make sure he understood.

"It will take five hours to get down to the trench," Robert explained. "That's not to mention the time it takes to search for the prize."

Jordan nodded. "So, that means we can only dive once a day. We should start early."

"Not to mention take food with us." Ari had gotten over their aversion to privileged food quickly and now seemed to be trying to eat everything they were coming into contact with. "I'm not about to be five hours away from a snack."

Robert clapped his hands and grinned. "Okay, so this is a test run. We'll make sure everything's up to par then head on back. Shouldn't take more than eight hours."

"That's perfect." Will walked up to us with Mack and the others to see them off. "We come bearing snacks for the ride there and back. And don't worry—we won't start the ceremony without you."

"Wait, it's *tonight*?"

"What? No." Zeke looked at Will in alarm. "Right?"

"That's right." Will soothingly patted his arm. "We still have some things to do to get ready. We're thinking two days from now. That should be good."

"Sweet. Maybe we'll find the fragment by then, and then we can do a joint party."

Will stepped forward and grabbed Ari by the shoulders. "If you find the fragment in two days and steal my wedding celebration, I'll cut you."

He smiled a deadly sweet smile. I stared.

"Now, you toddle along and have fun." Will patted the top of their head. "And remember: I will murder anyone who gets in the way of my happiness."

Robert clapped his hands again. "Right, let's go!" He climbed down into *The Ancora* first. Jordan gave Ari and Lex a hug before they descended into the sub, and the sub slowly disappeared beneath the surface of the water.

Jordan and I shared a look. "You know..." Jordan smiled coyly.

"Yes, I know many things."

He rolled his eyes. "I was about to make a proposal, but if you'd rather I didn't..."

I laughed. "What are you going to propose?"

He leaned in and whispered in my ear, sending shivers down my spine. "We've got hours to wait, and I'd love you all to myself."

I felt my face heat up as I looked back at him. "Are you... prepared?"

He nodded. I sure hoped he knew what I meant. "Then, lead the way."

Hours later, we were lying in bed, my head nestled in the crook of his arm.

"So." He rubbed my bare shoulder with his thumb.

"So."

"How do you feel?"

I tilted my head back and forth. "I've never had a massage like that before. Well, I've never had a massage before. But I'm pretty sure they don't always go like that."

"With me they do."

I wiggled my eyebrows. "Then I might need to get a massage from you a lot."

He smiled. "You know, it doesn't always have to go like that."

"You mean, like instead you...?" I made a gesture with my hands, and he laughed.

"Yes. I would enjoy that."

Grinning, I ran my hand down his body, and he stretched, groaning slightly. "Would you enjoy that right now?"

He nodded, rolling with me and pressing my lips against his.

Hours later still, we found ourselves tangled in the sheets when there was a knock on the door.

"Don't come in!" I shouted.

"Wasn't going to," Will yelled back. "I was letting our fearless leader know they're back."

Jordan looked at me. "So soon?"

We scrambled to get dressed and made our way up to the deck, where everyone had gathered around the sub. Lex and Ari had already climbed out, looking grim, and as we approached, we heard Robert cursing up a storm inside.

"How was it?" Jordan asked eagerly, but Ari was shaking their head. Unfortunately, Robert heard and popped his head out of the top of the sub.

"We almost made it five miles before I pulled us out." Robert brushed his hands on his suit. "I'm going to do some work on the hull to make sure it's not going to fail on us since scraping the top of that goddamn toll booth in San Francisco. It should take the rest of the day."

Jordan nodded. "If you need any help, let us know. The sooner we get any repairs done, the better."

"We have another problem," Ari said. "The arm is busted."

"That's easy. Use your powers to grab the fragment when the time comes."

"How big is the cave, Jordan? It might be too big to fit inside."

"'Tis what she—"

"Fuck all the way off, Will." Ari's death glare change to a disgruntled frown as they looked from Will to Jordan.

Jordan bit his lip, considering. "One of you might end up swimming out of the sub, then."

"That's not going to work—" Lex began, but Jordan shook his head.

"Figure it out."

Lex and Ari stared at each other, clearly annoyed by Jordan's response. But we all understood: Jordan was refusing a situation where I ended up in the submarine.

Leaving Robert to his work, Jordan and I wandered around the deck. I immediately rounded on him.

"If they're saying it's not going to work, you should—"

"I'm not sending you down there, Jake. And that's final."

I shook my head. "I don't want to go. But if it ends up making sense, you should at least consider it."

He swallowed. "I *said* no." But I could feel his resolve wavering.

Hours later, it was dusk. I didn't know exactly what time it was, as I was trying to be present in the moment and not look at my phone. Lex and David both stayed shut in separate rooms, Will and Zeke were busy planning their ceremony, so Jordan, Ari, and I spent time lounging around with Mack, sparring in the gym, and even getting to know some of the crew members.

Mack was excited to learn some basic fighting skills, but we all made sure not to use powers around him. Not only was it not fair, but it was also embarrassing for me in an odd way.

That evening, Zeke and Will approached Jordan and me as we sat on the deck, enjoying a drink.

"Hey, Jordy. Hi, Jurassic Jake." Will sat down beside us. "We had a question for you."

"Shoot."

Zeke cleared his throat. "We were wondering if you would stand up there with us when we get married."

Jordan grinned. "I'd love to."

I nodded enthusiastically. "Absolutely."

"Oh... we meant just Jordan. Ari is going to stand up with us as well."

"Oh. Of course. Makes sense." I tried not to let my hurt show.

"Is there anything we can do to help?" Jordan asked.

Zeke presented Jordan with a piece of paper. I could see Will had written in little doodles around the edges.

"We're having you and Ari each do a reading," Will said. "Sorry about Zeke's handwriting."

"Bitch." Zeke smiled sweetly at Will, even through calling him a name.

That night, as we laid in bed, Jordan and I ended up chatting happily, and discussing what we might want a wedding to look like in our own future. We were vastly different. I wanted a big, fancy wedding, probably in the Episcopal church in King, and Jordan wanted a small, rustic ceremony outside.

It was fascinating to talk to him about why we wanted these things. For me, a lot of it came from childhood expectations of what a wedding should look like. For him, as he was raised with so many secrets, his desire to have a small ceremony was because it was more secure.

Spending this time together helped me realize just how much I cared about Jordan, and getting to know him as a person versus as a Keeper was what I needed to feel secure in our relationship. While I still wasn't entirely sure this was going to work out—we may end up being unalived at any moment—it was nice to talk and cuddle.

The next few days went by in a blur of waiting. Jordan and I continued to connect and get to know each other as we grew more intimate, while the crew prepared for the wedding. We continued honing our skills, and Jordan—much differently than the last time I'd trained with him—was helping me fine-tune my power usage, giving me tips and advice I found incredibly helpful.

Finally, the fourth day we were on the ocean, Lex and Ari approached Jordan and me with a problem while we were sparring in the gym.

"Lex and I have been experimenting—"

"Hot."

"Shut all the way up, Jake."

"Kidding. Anyway, you were saying?"

"We've been trying to figure out how we can make our powers work in the ocean, and we have a solution. But we don't think you're going to like it."

Their problem: Neither Lex nor Ari could work their powers well enough to compensate for the immense pressure of the water in the trench. Even working together, they couldn't support any object enough to get it into the basket of the sub.

Their solution? A mix of powers. Fortis, Aquis, and Terra. The Fortis could help control the pressure, the Aquis could help ensure the fragment wasn't crushed, and the Terra could focus on moving the object—again—without crushing it.

Jordan sighed, glancing at me. "Let's try it with Lex, Ari, and Will."

Will, of course, was on board at once.

"Oh, I get voluntold to go on a dangerous mission to the depths of the ocean before I get married? I'm an *air* person, people. I don't work well under pressure. Like, literally. I've never dealt with that much pressure. So, I hope you know I don't know what I'm doing."

"We believe in you, babe," Zeke said, giving him a kiss on the temple.

"Yeah, yeah."

Ari and Lex shared another look but didn't say anything.

One day later, we were back in the same spot, only Will wasn't afraid to tell Jordan how it was.

"Okay, so the three of us combined cannot work our powers enough to move a rock down there without it being crushed. There's only one way we can make this work. And it's the way you don't want it to work, but we don't have any other choice."

Jordan spun around and took a few steps away, clutching his head in his hands. Finally, in a moment of rage, he yelled, "*Fuck*!" And hurled a fireball into the air.

"Whoa." Mack raised his hands, concerned. "Is dude okay?"

Jordan turned to meet my gaze. Even without fire, it felt like his eyes were burning into my soul. "You better be aware of how shitty this is, Jake. If I have to send you down there and you end up getting yourself or one of the others killed—"

"I know. It won't be like San Francisco. I promise."

His jaw clenched. "Jake, if this goes bad in any way, I could lose the three of you, plus Robert, plus the sub. And who knows what Benedetti is doing right now while we're all on the run from the authorities?"

I nodded. "I... all I can say is that I'll do my best."

"I need better than your best. I need the best you can do, not the best you think you can do."

I bit my lips. "Okay."

We went to bed that night, Jordan clearly distraught. We didn't talk much, and barely touched each other.

Early the next morning, after a quick breakfast, Renee made sure I had a wet suit while Lex and Ari played rock paper scissors to see who would go with Will and me. I pulled and tugged at the crotch, feeling uncomfortable in the skin-tight material.

When I got back out to the deck, I found Ari and Lex having a heated discussion.

"I only played to make it seem like I wanted to go. I actually don't."

"Rules are rules, Lex. But if you don't give a flying fuck about anything with the Keepers anymore—"

Lex threw her hands in the air in frustration. "When did I say that?"

"Jake heard the whole thing between you and David!"

Lex's eyes went wide, and she turned to me. I didn't even have a chance to make an excuse.

"You have no idea what I'm going through, and you're going around gossiping behind my back? Thanks a lot, everyone. Here we are in this stupid situation trying to find the stupid fragment, and you're acting like a bunch of high schoolers! This is ridiculous. I'm out. Good luck with your diving mission. Hope Jake doesn't get you all killed."

She stalked off, leaving the rest of us looking awkwardly at each other.

"Well, if today's the day I die, so be it. Just make sure my headstone reads, 'died at his goal weight.'"

Ari shook their head at Will. "Everything's a fucking joke. Does no one get that this is the difference between life and death for all of us? Either we find the fragment or

Benedetti does. And if we're all unnecessary? We're all dead. *Dead*!"

Ari screamed the last word, then clambered into the sub and out of sight. Will sighed, seeming to be out of witty one-liners, and followed them. David was nowhere to be found, which left Jordan, Zeke, Renee, and me standing around.

"So... be safe." Zeke's smile indicated he knew how lame that sounded.

I nodded. "I promise, I'll... I'll do everything I can to keep everyone safe and bring the fragment back."

I gave Zeke a hug, Renee squeezed my shoulder, and I turned to Jordan, who was almost green with worry.

"Practice as much as you can, okay? And if you find the cave, take your time and focus on what needs to be done, alright?" He pulled me into a hug, kissing my neck multiple times. "I love you."

"I love you too."

And with that, I climbed down through the top of the sub, Robert sealed the hatch behind me, and my stomach churned as we descended beneath the surface of the water.

It took hours for us to get to the ocean floor

The light was minimal, our view was limited, and the propellers kept stirring up the ocean floor, adding a fog to the already difficult task of seeing. It felt like we were looking for a piece of dirt on a football field by walking a line from one end to the other, turning around, and walking a line next to that line all the way back. Only, the football field was forty miles wide at some parts.

The days seemed to blend together. We broke the monotony by using our powers to grab various interesting rocks and crystals off the seabed and put them in the little basket for study. We were getting a lot of practice for when we came across the Omnia Fragment.

We were nearing the end of our search for the day when I heard Will and Ari whispering to each other.

"What?" I asked.

"What?" Will asked.

"What did you say?"

"Nothing."

I frowned. "I could swear I heard whispering."

"Maybe there's a—"

"*Hang on*!" Robert jerked the controls hard, and I flew into the side of the sub. A boulder the size of a car had almost fallen on us.

"What's going on?" I stepped forward as Ari and Lex strapped themselves into their seats.

"I don't know!" Robert continued trying to dodge the falling rocks, some pebbles and some larger than the sub itself.

"Jake, do something!"

I began to steer some of the rocks away as best I could, hissing through my teeth with effort. "I can't get this one out of the way! Go right, Robert!"

"The trench wall is right!"

"We can scratch the paint job or die!"

He maneuvered the sub toward the wall, and Will and Ari both raised their arms to help guide the rocks away from the sub.

I felt a drop of water on my lip, sending a shot of fear through my stomach. *Oh, fuck, we're going to sink. No, Will and Ari won't let that happen. What if we can't dive again*?

A large boulder, bigger than the sub, was slowly descending toward us. *Move away. Fly away. Go. Goddammit, go*!

Will and Ari both helped with their powers to guide it away. It was slow working, getting closer and closer. It was about ten feet away when I felt more water on my lip and, oddly, by my earlobes, and put in extra effort. The boulder glided away, silent through the water and down, out of sight.

Robert was able to steer us away from the trench wall and into more open water, where no more rocks were falling.

"Jake, are you okay?" Ari looked at me with wide eyes.

I nodded, looking up and clutching at my jaw, where I felt liquid dripping. "I felt water."

"Jake, your nose... and your ears."

I frowned and inspected my hand. It was blood, not water. Ari reached into their bag and grabbed a napkin for me.

"That's new." My stomach clenched as my head felt like it was swelling.

"That means you overdid it," Ari said. "It happens sometimes. Take it easy for the next little bit. Robert, what was that? What caused the rocks to fall?"

"Maybe an earthquake." Robert was still looking around for any falling rocks. "An underwater earthquake, especially when you're underwater, can be hard to detect."

"Huh?" Ari asked.

Robert's eyes suddenly went wide, and he reached for the radio. "*Andromeda*, this is *The Ancora* requesting emergency response. Do you copy?"

There was nothing but static on the other end. Robert adjusted the knob back and forth, trying a few more times, but the last time it sparked and sizzled, and he jerked his hand back.

"I can't get a hold of them." Robert looked at us helplessly. "There's no way to warn anybody."

"Warn them about what?"

"Underwater quakes can cause massive damage on the surface." Robert was pressing buttons frantically.

"Like, how?"

He gave us a grave look. "Tsunamis."

Chapter 8: Shit Gets Really Real

Hours later, we finally surfaced, all of us craning around trying to find the yacht.

"Fire off a flare," Robert ordered, pointing to a yellow case near the hatch. I did as he ordered, opening the top of the sub and breathing in the fresh, salty air. Sunset was in full effect.

We waited. And waited. Four flares and two hours later, we finally saw a ship approaching. We were on high alert at first, as we weren't sure if it was the *Andromeda* or if it was someone else. As it grew closer, however, we realized it was definitely our friends.

Waving madly, we listened as they sounded their horn. Then, before we knew it, we were standing on the deck of the yacht.

"Is everyone okay?" I hugged Jordan tightly while Will and Zeke embraced. Ari and David fist-bumped. I couldn't see Lex anywhere.

Jordan pulled away, looking at me with his eyebrows knit together. "We're fine. We haven't been able to get a hold of you, which is why we were worried."

"You... there wasn't a tsunami?"

He shook his head, eyes wide. "No. Why? Jake, what did you do?"

I let out a noise of indignation. "*I* didn't do anything. There was an underwater earthquake that damaged the submarine!"

"Oh. I wasn't thinking—"

"Yes, you fucking were!" I crossed my arms. "You thought I caused it!"

Before I could hear his excuses, I stomped away, so angry I could actually hit him.

Now, that's not fair, Jake. What can he expect after the bridge in San Francisco?

That was a different situation. I'm not like that all the time!

Aren't you?

My rage-waddle in my wetsuit took me across the yacht where I spotted Lex leaning against the railing, head in her hands. I took a breath and approached.

"Hey."

"Hi."

"Care for some company?"

She nodded, and I stood next to her. We were silent for a bit before she spoke.

"Why didn't you stop when you heard me break up with David?"

I nodded. "I wanted to give you space, which is why I didn't stop. I'm sorry if that was the wrong choice."

She shook her head. "No. I needed to be alone then. But I'm ready to talk now, and I... well, I don't really have anyone."

I frowned in sympathy. "You can talk to me. I know we aren't super close, but... well, I'm here."

She took a deep breath and quickly wiped her eyes. "I miss Bree. I was always able to bounce ideas off of her, talk to her about all my relationship concerns and my problems with the Keepers. And... and to see her murdered right in front of me—"

She stopped suddenly, burying her face in her hands. I didn't know Bree very well, so I couldn't relate to Lex's loss. I had almost lost my dad, but he survived. Lex had this friend for... I didn't even know how long. All I could do was be here for her while she was mourning.

I wrapped my arm around her, giving her a squeeze. "I'm sorry, Lex. I can't imagine what you're going through."

She sniffed. "I don't even know if I made the right choice with David."

I let her go and continued standing next to her. "It sounded like you both wanted different things."

"I mean, only in one way. He wants to stay in the Keepers and I'm going to leave as soon as this is all done."

"Are you sure?"

She nodded. "I want to. And it's not like anyone can stop me."

"I heard stories from Ari," I began, but Lex waved her hand to cut me off.

"I've heard the stories as well. With the Keepers disbanded, there's no way anyone is coming after me. I'm not going to go around and use my powers in public. I'll probably never use them again."

I grinned. "I could totally see you becoming an Olympic swimmer or something. Only a little faster than everyone else."

She laughed. "Now, I could see that, too. But... no. Once I'm done, I'm done. I'm out. I don't want this kind of life."

"Who would you go back to?"

Lex shrugged. "I can't go back to my mom. She did the same thing David's asking me to do: resign myself to a life I don't want and try to find happiness in it. We got into it before I moved to King. She can't deal with the fact she has all this influence, wealth, and power—but no one who loves her."

"You don't love her?" I was shocked.

Lex sighed. "Not in the way she wants me to. When I told her I was moving to King, she tried to ship me off to school in Europe. She even switched my plane tickets so I'd end up in Paris instead. Like I wouldn't be able to tell at the airport. I got on the plane to King, told her I didn't need her, and she had a chunk of ice where her heart should be. When I got on at Vostell, I was promoted quickly. I think that was her as well."

"Wow."

"So, basically, once this is all done, I want to go live a normal life. Be with a normal guy. Have normal children."

"But you'll always have to lie," I said. "You can leave the Keepers, sure, but you'll still have the powers. And you'll have to lie to your future husband, and your kids."

"What I don't tell them will be to preserve the Keeper's secrets. I took an oath, and I took it seriously, even if I didn't know what it meant. So, no, I won't be actively lying."

"Isn't that called lying by omission? Don't you want to be with someone you can be completely honest with?"

"What, like how Jordan's been so honest with you?" She was getting defensive. So was I.

"Jordan and I definitely have our own issues. All I'm saying is that I'm not sure you'll be able to leave it all behind, even if you want to."

"What, are you going to take me out? Have my family killed, like Grace had Kevin's family killed?" She narrowed her eyes at me. "Would you really do it? If Jordan gave the order, would you find a way to kill me that looked like an accident? Kill me to protect a secret I want nothing more to do with?"

I shook my head. "I could never."

"I could." We turned to see Ari standing a short distance away. They slowly stepped forward. Although a head shorter than Lex, they were still acting like they were the toughest person around. "You have a responsibility, Lex."

"One I'm seeing through." Lex crossed her arms and glaring down at Ari. "I'm here, right? I made the trips in the sub and helped."

"That's not the end of this." Ari folded their arms, too. "What if you're the Primarch?"

"It's not me."

"It could be."

"I don't think it will be."

Ari scoffed. "So, because you *think* it won't be, makes it magically so?"

"Just because I could be doesn't mean it will be me, either."

"No, it doesn't. But here's the thing." Ari stepped away and sat on a nearby chair. "There aren't that many Keepers left. And if you think any of us, after everything we've sacrificed, would let someone jeopardize our future... you've got another thing coming."

Lex shook her head in disgust. "So you would do it."

"Whether I was ordered to or not."

"I thought we were friends."

"We are." Ari gave a rather twisted smile as they stood and got in Lex's face again. "But anyone who betrays me is my enemy. And you've seen what I can do to my enemies. So, don't become one."

Lex held Ari's gaze. "So, either I'm held hostage as a friend, or I'm free as an enemy. What to do, what to do..."

I stepped forward. "You two, it doesn't have to be like this. I'm sure if we all talked to Jordan—"

"Oh, whose side are you on?" Ari burst out. "After everything you've been through, you'd let her leave? She's being a selfish bitch!"

"I'd rather be selfish than be like you. You're exactly like Benedetti—you'd probably kill your mom if asked."

Ari slapped Lex across the face hard enough to send her sprawling across the deck.

"Ari!" I tried to get between them, but Lex had already rolled forward and, with a powerful kick to the stomach, sent Ari flying through the air and into the ocean below.

"No!" I ran to the railing in time to see Ari rocketing from the water, both feet planting squarely into Lex's chest, then landing on the deck. Lex stumbled backward into a window, cracking it but not falling through.

"*Enough*!" I shot vines out of my hands and wrapped them around Ari's and Lex's hands. They were both breathing hard, Ari struggling against the vines while Lex screamed in rage. "We're not doing this. You're both better than this. You've said what you wanted to say. That's as far as it's going."

"Ari threatened to kill me!" Lex yelled. "I can't trust them."

"Neither of you has to trust each other. You have to work together." I unwrapped the vines from them, but neither Ari nor Lex looked inclined to start anything again. "We need to deal with what *is*, not what could be. Nobody's killing anybody. Except for Will, if you ruin his wedding day with your drama."

Nobody laughed at my lame attempt at a joke—though I wasn't convinced it wasn't entirely true.

Lex shook her head. "Whatever." She turned and stalked off across the yacht.

Ari crossed their arms and glared at me. "You know I'm right."

"I know you sound bloodthirsty. Killing Lex won't bring your mom or Logan back."

It was my turn for a slap. "Fuck you."

They turned and walked in the opposite direction of Lex. As they walked, I called out after them. "You're not going to keep friends if you keep hitting them and threatening to kill them, you know."

They turned and raised their arms, walking backward. "I don't need friends."

I didn't believe them.

Jordan, who had heard the noise of their fight, came jogging around the corner.

"What the hell was that?"

"What?"

"I heard fighting, and—"

I rounded on him. "And you immediately thought it was me?"

He sighed and laughed. "Jesus Christ, can you stop jumping down my throat for a second? I came to find you to apologize, not accuse you of fighting."

"Oh. So, you didn't think it was me?"

He rolled his eyes. "I heard your voice, and I wondered, but I ran into Lex, and she said you tried to stop it. What happened?"

"It's the same thing I talked to you about. Lex wants to leave and Ari's willing to kill her to protect the secret."

He shook his head. "I need to have a talk with Ari. I know they've talked a lot about preparing for war with the Disciples, but they seem... eager."

"*Some*body has anger issues." I quirked my eyebrow, and he nodded.

"And it's only gotten worse since losing her mom. Which I totally get. It explains it. Doesn't excuse it." He sighed. "Like it doesn't excuse me jumping to the conclusion that you had caused the underwater earthquake."

"I accept your apology and your plan to make it up to me later."

He grinned slyly. "Oh?"

I pulled him to me by the front of his pants as he gasped in delight. "Oh, yeah."

Jordan laughed, kissing me then pulling away. "The other thing I wanted to tell you is Zeke and Will decided, with diving suspended until the sub gets patched up, they're getting married today at sunset."

I squealed with excitement. "This will be my first gay wedding. I can't wait."

A little while later, Jordan and I checked in on Robert and Renee at the sub, who were hard at work fixing the fried radio and the sub arm. Luckily, Mack had some extra electronic parts they were able to adapt.

"How's it going, Robert?"

Robert gave a tired smile as he finished connecting a few wires together, then turned to his snacks. "It's fine. I got some sleep, but I got started as early as I could this morning. I know how important this is to get done."

"We appreciate it," Jordan said while Renee wiped her forehead. "Seriously, you both are indispensable. We are forever in your debt."

"Hey, we've seen a whole other side to this world." Robert shoved a cracker with cheese on it in his mouth and continued talking. "We're going to see this through."

We had hours to wait for the ceremony, so Jordan and I spent more time alone in the cabin. We easily found what we enjoyed, and I realized quickly that Jordan and I weren't only having sex. It meant so much more to me, and to him as well.

Finally, we made our way to the bow of the ship.

Chairs were set up facing the front of the ship, where Mack stood in front of the sunset, wearing an official captain's uniform, all buttoned up and everything. Will and Zeke wore flowy white shirts with the sleeves rolled up. Jordan was wearing the suit he'd worn to break into NEMO.

Interestingly, Lex and Renee had found fancy dresses that Mack had been saving for a 'friend' that they 'left behind' after a 'party.' Even more interestingly, I found several men's dress shirts and pants that were way too small for Mack that had me questioning who exactly he was 'partying' with.

David and I sat together on one side of the aisle, while Lex, Renee, and Robert sat on the other, along with many of the crew members.

"Weddings bring us together in love," Mack read from some sheets of printed paper, "but the marriage is what we're truly here for. Making these vows is an act of trust, hope, and determination, as well as a sign of commitment to share your life with one another until the end."

Mack nodded at Jordan, who pulled a piece of paper out of his pocket and began to read an original poem Will had written for Zeke.

Life is hard.
There is pain, and loss, and strife.
Life is cold.
There is death, and hunger, and betrayal.
Life is empty.
There is no one, no thing, no love.
Life is unexpected.
There is discovery, and power, and secrets.
Life is surprising.
There is a man, and a past, and a wound.
Life is circumstantial.
There is a connection, and friendship, and laughter.
Life is giving.

There is a man, and his heart, and his soul.
Life is kind.
There is solace, and trust, and a home.
Life is love.
There is desire, and bliss, and beauty.
Life is you.
My love, my companion, my strength.
Life is me.
My doubts, my defenses, my passion.
Life is us.
Our hearts. Our minds. Our souls.

As I glanced around, I saw Lex look away. She had clearly been looking at David, and she wiped at her eyes inconspicuously.

I met Jordan's gaze as he finished reading. This was so freaking romantic.

Ari read Zeke's poem to Will next.

You are mine, and I am yours. We belong to each other, yet we are not property.

You make me steady, yet, everything in our lives exists as sand in the wind.

You are patient. You are the drying of my tears, the muscles of my smile, the heart of my soul.

I am excited. I am terrified. I am prepared. I am unsure. I am struggling. I am steady.

I am in love. I am all the feelings, the thoughts, the desires that have existed and ever will.

You are brave, strong, smart. You are with me, and I am with you.

"Next, the vows." Mack was taking this surprisingly seriously.

The two recited a new spin on traditional vows, but I honestly wasn't paying much attention because I kept staring at Jordan.

Then, it was time for the rings.

Zeke reached to Jordan, and Will reached to Ari. Jordan grinned widely at Zeke, and they briefly squeezed hands.

Ari, meanwhile, patted themselves down in fake panic before pulling the ring out. Will pinched their cheek, leaving it rather red. I was surprised he didn't murder them right then and there.

They exchanged rings, they kissed, and were married. It was the most beautiful and simple ceremony I'd ever seen. Mack didn't even say, 'my dudes' once.

Once Jordan and Ari signed the marriage certificate and everyone had taken pictures, we began to dance, drink, and eat. The events blurred together in a beautiful swirl closely dancing with Jordan, kissing him many, many times, and his coy smile when I removed his tie and beckoned him to follow me back to our cabin.

The next morning, I woke with a smile on my face from a dreamless sleep. I rolled over and, of course, Jordan was already out of bed. There was a note on his pillow, however.

You were too peaceful to wake up, so I let you sleep. Sub is fixed. I have a feeling that today's the day. See you upstairs.

~ Me

P.S. You're everything I've ever wished for and dreamed of.

Heart full and goofy smile on my face, I got out of bed, picked my scattered clothes up off the floor, and changed once more into the red diving suit.

Once I got to the submarine, it was already loaded in the water, and Jordan and Ari were passing snacks to Will for us to take with us. I heard Robert's voice call from inside, requesting more dark chocolate.

"The radio's distance is compromised, but the *Andromeda* can track us with the radio on." Renee nodded to me as she explained the situation to Mack and a few members of the crew.

I walked up to Jordan, and we hugged. I didn't want to say anything that could possibly ruin the night we'd had.

"I love you. Be careful down there, okay?"

"Always. And, about your note... you are, too."

He grinned, and, with a final kiss, I descended into the sub and into the deep, dark waters below.

As before, the trip down took about five hours. Ari, Will, and I played a card game while getting distracted looking at the scenery.

"What's that?" I pointed to something orange among the dark rock.

"It's a Dumbo Octopus." Robert pointed excitedly to the small creature that was like a blob with ears. "I've seen pictures."

"Do you think there's anything down here that's all prehistoric and can swallow the sub?" Ari asked.

"If there is, it hasn't been—shit, hang on!"

Bam! Everything stopped moving suddenly and I was forced hard onto the floor of the sub as we hit the bottom of the trench, hitting my head on a hard object. An alarm began to sound, and I hurriedly looked around to see if we had sprung a leak, or the glass had cracked. Luckily, nothing seemed to have happened.

"What the hell was that?" I sat up and felt my forehead, where I had a bleeding gash.

"Sorry, sorry, so sorry!" Robert rubbed his neck. "I got distracted. Everything's okay. We're good."

"Jake's not." Ari got out of their seat, fetching the bag with the fragments in it. "Here. We can't have you gushing blood all over the place."

I healed, and Robert suggested we continue the search.

A few hours in, Will let out an odd shriek and pointed at a small source of light in the distance.

"Oh. That's a Barreleye Fish. Also known as a Spookfish."

I could see why it was called a Spookfish. It was like a larger version of a regular fish, but it had a dome-shaped head that was transparent. In the dome, you could see two barrel-shaped things that faced upward, looking slightly green.

"Those things are its eyes." Robert pointed as it drifted lazily along. "Those things in its head. The things there that look like eyes are actually nostrils."

"I feel like we're on another planet." Will shook his head in wonder.

"Does it hum as well?" I asked.

Robert gave me a funny look. "I don't think so. Why?"

"I hear humming."

"I don't hear anything."

"Wait, I hear it, too." Ari turned their head, listening for the source.

Everyone fell silent, and Will raised an eyebrow. "Me, too."

"Maybe it's a broken gauge or something."

I walked farther back, the humming getting louder. "Wait! It's back here. It's... it's the fragments."

Will and Ari both unbuckled themselves and made their way back into the cramped space with me. I pulled out the Fragment of Terra, which was glowing, its insides swirling.

"What the hell?" Ari grabbed the Fragment of Aquis.

"Maybe it means we're close to the Omnia Fragment!" I said excitedly. "Robert, let's keep going the way we are and see what happens."

So, we did. The humming and glowing kept growing. While it was loud, it also didn't seem like we were hearing it with our ears. My insides were vibrating. It felt like my DNA was shivering.

Hours later, as the vibration in my chest seemed to reach the maximum frequency, Robert called out. "We found it! We found it!"

With a soft bump, we came to rest at the bottom of the trench, looking at the glittering entrance to a cave, complete with five shards above the top that stood out in the lights.

"This is definitely it. This is exactly like the picture Jordan showed me."

"There's a problem." Robert made a curvy gesture with his hands. "We're too big to fit in the hole."

"'Tis what she proclaimed."

"Let's use the arm, then." I completely ignored Will. "We can start picking through the crystals."

"Are you kidding?" Will looked at me like I was crazy. "It looks like there are thousands of crystals here! And there's no guarantee we'd know which one it is."

"Maybe it's, like, the rock that's glowing and humming?"

"Hey. That was sassy. Stay in your lane, Jake."

Robert began maneuvering the arm and getting as close to the cave entrance as possible. He grabbed the first shard, and, one by one, started filling the basket in front of the sub.

"I mean, we don't need to keep them *all*." Ari raised their eyebrow as we discovered the first load was a dud. Robert, however, started loading some into his own bag.

"Are you kidding? Some of these may be worth a fortune!"

Ari rolled their eyes, but we didn't say anything as Robert brought in loads two through ten. It took nearly three hours to get the ten loads into the sub, and we were all getting tired. We'd packed enough food, but we'd been in the trench for fourteen hours already. But now that we were here, none of us wanted to leave.

"You know, I wonder if we shouldn't put the fragments in the basket and send them out into the cave to see if one of the crystals out there lights up or something."

"Are we legit going to let one of the fragments out of our reach?" Will frowned at Ari, concerned.

"I mean, if Robert keeps a hold of it with the arm, it should work, right? There's no other way to find the fragment."

"We could—"

"Not yet, Ari."

Will and Ari shared a look, quickly glanced at me, then away.

"What?"

"Nothing. Don't worry about it."

I opened my mouth to protest, but Robert called out from the front. "Let's get this done, people."

We decided on using the Fragment of Terra to lure the Omnia Fragment out. I don't know why we all agreed that was best, but we did. A few minutes later, the submarine arm was dangling the fragment out into the cave.

"Yeah, folks, I don't see anything happening up here. No fancy lights or anything. The lights don't get all the way to the back of the cave, though."

I rubbed my forehead. "Maybe I can focus my powers and bring the crystals in the cave forward."

"Would that apply to the Omnia Fragment, though? I mean, it's technically the body of a dead alien, right? Do our powers work on them?"

I shrugged. "I've never tried to float the Fragment of Terra anywhere."

"Shit!" Robert called out and we watched as the arm released the Fragment of Terra. It dropped to the floor of the cave, getting lost in the sea of other shards. "It's alright. I can pick it up. Well, if the stupid... arm... will... work!" Robert hit the controls in frustration, but nothing happened. The arm had just stopped working.

"What a piece of junk," Will joked.

"It's a prototype for a reason." Robert raised his voice. "The sub wasn't supposed to even be this deep for years until we'd perfected everything. But you changed all that when you kidnapped us and stole it."

"I know, I know. I was kidding. I'm sorry, Robert."

He let out a deep breath. "Well, kids, we're stuck. I don't know what to do."

"Well, shit," Ari turned to Will, who nodded. "Now that really *does* only leave us with one option."

They looked at me.

"What?"

"Well, it's pretty basic." Ari clapped their hands together. "You, uh... you go swimming."

Robert turned in his seat, eyebrows raised. "No. That's not simple."

"I mean, we'll use our powers to deal with the water around you—"

"The water's not the problem." Robert gestured to the darkness outside the window. "It's the pressure of the water."

"We can take care of that." Will rolled his eyes.

"You're going to die, Jake."

We all stared at him. "But if Ari and Will can take care of the pressure—"

"Have they ever had to take care of thousands of pounds of water pressure on a person?" I glanced at them. They both shook their heads. Robert continued. "Then, they won't know what to expect and you'll die."

"Like, is there a way—"

"Standard atmospheric pressure is about fifteen pounds per square inch." Robert used his hands to explain the science. "If you were to be out there, by yourself, you're at sixteen-thousand pounds per square inch. That's five times the pressure exerted by a high-power bullet as it strikes a bulletproof object. Your organs would collapse and fail, you would likely compress physically. And you wouldn't feel a thing because it would all happen at once and you would die."

I blinked a few times, then turned to Ari and Will.

"This is a *terrible* plan."

Chapter 9: Am I in an RPG or Something?

"Trust us." Will was trying to be soothing as he shoved me in the back area of the sub. "We are connected to water and gravity. With the two of us, we can definitely make sure you're okay. Besides, there may be an air pocket or something inside the cave."

I sighed at Ari, who nodded encouragingly. "Do I at least get a helmet?"

"We don't have any diving gear." Robert approached with a bulky radio. "The best we have is our short-range radio system. Here."

Robert began outfitting me with a headset and testing the radio.

"Yeah, I can hear you. But you are right next to me, so..."

"...Can you hear me in the radio?"

"Yes."

"Good. So, we can hear everything that happens when you're out there." Robert twisted a few knobs on the radio panel.

"Yeah. You can hear me gurgling and crunching as I die."

Robert frowned. "You won't have time to gurgle."

I punched him on the arm, then turned to Will and Ari. "Are you sure you two can't come with me?"

"If all three of us were out there, it would require a lot more power to keep all of us safe. More of a chance for something to go wrong."

I nodded. "Okay. I'm ready, I guess. My life is literally in your hands. No pressure."

Will laughed. "That's funny, 'cause the goal is literally to not let the pressure get to you."

I continued staring accusingly at Will as I stepped away from the door and the two of them closed me in. I had the bag with the fragments, a headlamp, the headset, and a flashlight. Plus, the flippers on my feet.

"Okay, Jake." Robert's voice sounded over the intercom. "We're as close as we can get to the cave, so here's to hoping all you have to do is swim in and grab it."

"Great. You jinxed it." Will's voice was carrying from where I could see them in the hatch's tiny window. "Now he's going to have to swim for hours."

"Now *you* jinxed it." Robert sounded offended.

"You'll be great, Jake," Ari called out, giving me a well-intentioned thumbs up.

I took a deep breath and shook out my limbs, trying to psych myself up and not freak myself out.

Submerged in water. It's fine. You've got this. They've got you. You did this with Ari before, and you were just fine. I mean, there was that moment you almost died, but that really wasn't so bad. You lived. And there's two of them now. You'll be fine!

There was a hissing noise as the compartment began to slowly decompress. I felt intense pressure on my entire body at once.

"Will—"

"I'm on it," he grunted, holding both his hands toward me, fingers flexing through the tiny glass window.

"How's that, Jake?"

I nodded. "It's manageable. How's Will?"

"Will's fucking fantastic, thanks for fucking asking. He'd appreciate it if you hurry the fuck up." His teeth were gritted with effort.

"Time for the water." Robert pushed another button, and ocean water began flooding the compartment.

"Oh. Oh! Jesus, that's cold!"

"We can't do anything about the temperature." Ari also sounded highly grumpy. "Buck up. You have to tell us how the pressure is."

"My ankles feel a lot of pressure," I said as the water quickly filled the chamber. A moment later, it went away. "Okay. I'm good now."

I tried to control my chattering teeth as the water made its way up to my chest.

"Chest is tight." Then it wasn't. "Okay, thank you."

Then, the water was up to my neck. I took a deep breath, just in case. Then, I closed my eyes. I could feel the cold radiating from the water, but it wasn't making direct contact with my face.

"The water's over his face now." Ari's voice was distorted as the water went past my ears. "He closed his eyes and he's holding his breath, though."

"Jake, you can breathe." Will's tone was as annoyed as it was comforting.

"We've got you, Jake."

I opened one eye, then the other. They didn't sting. I blinked several times. Then, I let out some air. No bubbles formed in the water because the water wasn't touching my face. I took a tentative breath in and didn't die. *Cool.* I began to breathe normally and gave Will and Ari a tentative smile.

"I'm still cold, but I'm okay."

"Good, good." Robert's voice sounded in my headset. "Now, I'm going to open the bay doors behind you. You'll have to swim around to get to the front of the sub, and then into the cave."

"Got it." I tightened my grip on the flashlight.

I heard a mechanical whirring, and the back of the sub fully opened, the door retracting up. I steeled myself, then waddled forward, landing on the ocean floor silently, stirring up some of the sand. My headlamp and flashlight couldn't penetrate the endless darkness in front of me, so I focused on looking at the ocean floor.

"I am now standing on the bottom of the Mariana Trench," I reported. "That's one small step for... well, you know the rest."

"Yeah, yeah. Get a move on." Ari didn't sound worried about sparing my feelings. So nothing new there. "We're not stopping you from dying without major effort. Let's go."

"Swimming to the cave now." Kicking my legs, I surged toward the front of the sub.

"Don't worry. We'll be right here and watching the whole time." Robert probably thought he sounded soothing instead of ominous.

"Well, it would be kind of a dick move if you left, since A, you're my ride, and B, I'll literally die without your help." I swam until I spotted the Fragment of Terra lying on the cave floor, shining among duller crystals. "Gotcha. Okay, I've got all five fragments now and will continue on. And if I die in this cave because you left me, I'll be pissed and come back to haunt you."

"You could always hitch a ride with a giant squid."

"Nah. They're all... tentacley."

I got to the front of the sub and found Ari and Will, still with their hands out, looks of fierce concentration on their faces.

"Okay. I'm entering the cave now. I'll grab some crystals farther back as well, so you can study them, Robert. And then we'll sell them and make a fortune to rebuild Sanctuary."

"Can we rebuild it somewhere it doesn't snow?" Will asked as the sub slowly faded from view.

I swam farther into the cave and met the end rather quickly. I used my lights to look around and saw the cave continued upward.

"Okay, it looks like I can swim up. I'll be going out of sight."

"Wait, Jake." Robert's voice rang through my headset. "If you run into any problems, or the headset gives out, just flash us."

"I will do no such thing."

"With the *flashlight*, Jake."

"Oh. I can do that."

I swam up for about a minute, until I could definitely see what appeared to be an air pocket.

"I can see open space," I said excitedly. "I'm about to—"

As I was about to surface, my head bonked into something that felt like it was as hard as rock. Yet, I could see nothing in the way.

"Jake?"

"Son of a… I'm okay. I hit my head on an invisible barrier blocking the way."

"An invisible barrier?" Robert sounded fascinated.

"Yeah. It's solid. I can't surface."

"Is there a way around?" Will's voice sounded tight. "Not that we don't love keeping tens of thousands of pounds of water pressure from killing you, but please hurry."

"Maybe… maybe I use a fragment or something to get through." I fished around in the bag and grabbed the likely key, the Fragment of Aquis. Then, I took a deep breath. "Here's to hoping."

I pressed the fragment upward, and it broke the surface, sending a small shockwave through the water.

"Yes!" I swam upward and broke the surface, only to gasp a moment later.

The Fragment of Aquis, which had been shining a brilliant blue, had cracked and dimmed. Then, as if it were dust… it simply dissolved away.

"Oh, shit."

"What? Jake, what's wrong?"

"Oh, fuck." I wiped my gloved hands, only to find it was like brushing sand off them.

"Jake, what the hell is going on?"

"The fragment! It… it's gone."

"What do you mean? Did you drop it?"

"No, it's like it... I broke through the surface and the Fragment of Aquis ... it like turned to dust."

"What the fuck did you do?" Ari once again sounded like they were eating the microphone with how close they were to it.

"I'm sorry." I continued to apologize as I climbed out of the water and pulled myself up to the ledge that opened into a cave glowing with bioluminescent moss and algae. "I'm out of the water now. It dissolved. There was nothing I could do."

"Oh my God," Ari and Will said together.

"What? What does that mean?" Robert sounded anxious.

"With the Fragment of Aquis destroyed, it means nobody can gain power over water again. This... nothing like this has ever happened before."

I heard something slam in the headset.

"Ari, it's okay." Will's voice was gentle. "If you and Lex're the last people with these powers and the Keepers die out, that is what it is. It will be a relief."

"The powers are all supposed to work together, Will. If there aren't any people with water powers, the whole balance is thrown off. It will mean all the Keepers are done."

There was silence in the sub as I looked around the cavern.

"Well, I... I guess I will make our sacrifice worthwhile." I couldn't think of anything else to say. "I should... I should keep going. That's probably what Jordan would want."

"I agree." Ari sniffed. "If this is what we have to do to get to the Omnia Fragment, then so be it."

"Okay." I removed the flippers from my feet and put on the shoes that Will and Ari had kept dry in the bag I was carrying. "Here I go."

I took a steadying breath and stood, beginning the walk through a passageway. It turned to the right and kept going forward after that, until I got to an empty chamber. The air felt different, and as I felt my hair, I realized why: it was highly electrified. My hair was sticking straight out from my head.

Across the chamber I saw the entrance to another area that appeared to be faintly glowing.

"Okay, I'm in the second chamber. Can you still hear me?"

"Barely." Robert's voice came through with a lot of static. "Keep going, even if you can't hear us."

"Okay. Maybe if I—"

I was *going* to say 'take a few steps in,' but I got interrupted by lightning arcing across the room and hitting me. I flew backward and landed a few feet away, my shoes smoking and body aching. Lightning began to shoot across the chamber in every direction like in one of those plasma lamps.

"Ow..." I sat up slowly, letting out a groan and stretching my neck. "I mean, I'm okay, but ow. I totally got struck by lightning."

Nobody said anything in reply.

"Okay, sorry." I stood and brushed myself off. "I mean, I'm okay, but I'll stop whining."

Again, there was no reply.

"Hello?" Nothing. "Robert? Ari? Will? Can you hear me?"

No answer. I inspected the headset and everything appeared to be fine. Of course, being struck by lightning probably didn't help it work better.

"Okay, well, I'm going to keep talking to you, just in case you can hear me." I took the Fragment of Ionis out of the bag. "I can't enter the room, so I'm going to toss the Fragment of Ionis into the room and see what happens."

A little upset about being struck by lightning, I chucked the fragment into the room. Immediately, I knew it was the right thing to do. All the lightning began striking the fragment at once, bathing the room in a painfully bright light. I shielded my eyes as they began to dissipate and, with one final, painfully loud strike, the Fragment of Ionis burst, leaving nothing but ash.

"If it turns out we're the last people to have these powers and the Primarch ends up with all of them... that's actually really going to suck. Whoever set this up should have known what they were doing."

For the first time, I allowed myself to consciously think about the vision I'd had on the plane to California. The being with four arms, four eyes, a sideways mouth, and cool dreadlocks. What if that being was still alive? What if the Primarch had to transfer power person to person, or alien to alien, only there were no more aliens to transfer it to?

What if I was going to find an actual alien instead of a fragment of one?

I stepped into the chamber and continued to walk forward, this time without being struck by lightning. *Yay.*

"So, it's like a test. One fragment given or sacrificed to get to the Omnia Fragment."

I made it to the next hallway and, like walking out of an air-conditioned building into hundred-degree heat, felt the temperature begin to rise. While it was nice to not be freezing, it was soon almost too hot to handle. With each step, it grew brighter until I was standing before a massive pool of lava, shielding my face from the heat.

I quickly snagged the Fragment of Calor out of the bag and looked at its swirling insides for a moment.

What if it's sentient? Does it know it's about to die? Has it experienced life for all these millions of years just to be tossed into a pool of lava by a dude who thinks cats are assholes?

I sighed. "You're probably overthinking things, Jake."

Or, you're being compassionate before throwing a living being into a pool of lava, you monster.

"Sorry." *What a lame apology.* I hurled the Fragment of Calor into the center of the lava. It landed with a plop and quickly sank.

Nothing seemed to be happening. For a terrifying moment, I thought maybe I was supposed to use the Fragment of Aquis, but then I remembered it was destroyed.

Then, the lava began swirling in the center, and I backed away as the heat intensified. I could swear I had first-degree burns on my face.

The lava rose and twisted, forming a sort of spire that seemed to extend upward into the darkness. I stared in awe at all that was taking place. The sound was deafening—like a waterfall or a landslide.

Then, it hardened, and I was left in the darkness with only my headlamp and flashlight. The room was still warm.

"I guess I cross the hardened lava now and hope I don't fall in?"

Since there was no one but me to answer my question, I struck out, carefully putting my left foot onto the newly-made floor and testing its strength. It seemed like it was going to hold me, so I quickly began crossing to the other side of the room.

Only there was no other way out. The only way in and out of the room was through the chamber I'd come through.

Unless... I gulped and looked up, where the spire had ascended into darkness.

I continued keeping myself company. "Nobody's going to believe this. I wish I'd brought my cell phone. Stupid Will. 'Are you attached to your cell phone, Jake? Do you love it, Jake? Gonna marry it, Jakey-poo?' I'm going to tell everyone it's Will's fault that no one will ever see what I'm seeing."

I approached the spire, put the flashlight away, and found some hand and footholds. Carefully, I started to climb, but I couldn't get a good grip with my gloves. I took them off and stowed them in my bag as well.

"*A-climbing I will go, a-climbing I will go.*" I began to sing as I ascended the surprisingly cool formation. "*Hi-ho, this hurts my toe, a climbing I will go.*"

The spire continued to get more and more narrow as I made my way higher and higher. Pretty soon, it felt like I was climbing a rope.

"*My God this hurts my hands, my God this hurts my hands... hi-ho, don't look below, my God this hurts my hands.*"

The spire started to curve, and I began climbing horizontally. I couldn't see anything farther than my headlamp would let me.

"*I really need to pee, I really need to pee, hi-ho, why didn't I go when I was in the sea*?"

Fully hanging upside-down, my feet were crossed over each other as I occupied myself with lyrics and not with thoughts of falling into the darkness below.

"*Of course, you are alone, of course you are alone. Hi-ho, just pee yourself, of course you are—*"

Crack.

The thin piece of volcanic rock that was my lifeline broke, crumbling in my hand.

And I fell.

"Aaaaaaahhhhhh!"

Falling! *Death*! *You're gonna fucking die*!

"Aaaaaahhhhhhh!"

Still falling... still screaming... falling... falling... falling... when am I going to land?

I stopped screaming, still squirming around in the air as I fell.

I don't know how long passed. It felt like hours. I could have been falling to the center of the planet for all I knew.

Suspense won't kill me dead, suspense won't kill me dead. Hi-ho, the fall will though, suspense won't kill me dead.

All I could think of was making up lyrics about my death to that annoying tune as I waited for the ground to turn me into a Jake-flavored pancake.

Or maybe I am dead, and this is in my head. Hi-ho, death is real slow, or maybe I am dead.

After a longer amount of time, a thought occurred to me. *Jake, maybe you're not falling. Maybe you're... floating?*

I sighed. "This isn't the worst thing ever." I pulled the flashlight out of the bag and tried to wiggle around to get my feet pointed downward. You know, just in case the ground was still coming. I could survive broken legs and a possible broken spine long enough to heal with the Fragment of Terra. Sure.

"Okay, see, if I pretend I'm cool, calm, and collected, I actually am. Yep. Everything's totally fine and normal."

I couldn't see any sign of the ground or walls of any kind. I was hovering in darkness.

Uh, Jake? You still have two fragments. Maybe pick the one that has to do with air, dumbass.

Be nicer to yourself, Jake. But... yeah, you could have considered that hours ago, too.

I pulled the Fragment of Fortis out of my bag, and immediately knew it was the right thing to do, no matter how much I hated it.

A violent wind whipped around me, swirling in random directions and flipping me ass over tea kettle. I had no idea which way was which until the wind settled on a direction: up.

Story time. When I was a child, I saw the cover of a book which apparently told some story about a kid falling into the sky. I never read it, because the cover was enough to give me nightmares.

I dreamed I was in a wide-open space and gravity shifted, and I fell, getting higher and higher until I began suffocating.

Then, I would begin to burn alive in the atmosphere and wake up, limbs flailing around in my bed.

My brain is weird. I know. But I needed to explain that to explain why falling up was probably the absolute scariest thing I'd ever experienced, even more so than falling down.

Instead of thinking of lyrics to that tune, I was screaming myself hoarse. Every atom in my body was thinking the same thing at the same time: "*Aaaaaaaahhhhhhhhhhh!*"

I was still screaming when I began to see the ceiling quickly approaching. I hit it, not as hard as I could, but hard enough to knock the air out of my lungs.

The fragment and I both hit at the same time, and the fragment, like I assumed it would, burst into nothingness.

I laid there for a moment, desperately trying to get in a breath. Finally, I was able to take in a shaky, gasping breath and think.

"What do you want me to do?" I shouted over the howling of the wind. I crawled around on the ceiling, but there was no way out. It was a six-by-six round room, and I couldn't see down far enough to where the walls ended.

"Use the Fragment of Terra!" I shouted back at myself.

I pulled the fragment out of the bag and, with a final look at it, slammed it into the ceiling.

There was an immediate explosion like none I'd experienced—and I can say that because I've experienced several. I wasn't blown back, but I knew there had been a lot of force applied to me. I wasn't burned or frozen, but I was hot and cold. I hadn't been electrocuted, but I was tingling all over. And I could feel the earth. Not dirt—the planet. It was like I was in tune with it all.

"Greetings, Jake."

I blinked, realizing I was staring at a bright light. I blinked again, and the light was receding. As it did, I could see the fragments—all five of them, surrounding a person.

Me. But it wasn't me. I was standing several feet away from the circle of fragments. Another version of me was standing in the center of them, holding... the Omnia Fragment.

It was like all the fragments put together, both in size and in color. I could see a rainbow of swirls inside it, a cloud of all the colors.

"You don't have to be afraid."

As I stared at the person in the center of the fragments, I realized I was hearing my voice, but not with my ears. It was in my head. Plus, his mouth wasn't moving.

"You... would prefer I not look like you."

Suddenly, I wasn't there. It was Jordan standing in the center of the fragments, holding the Omnia Fragment, which was about the size of my backpack.

"Is this real?"

"Define 'real.'" Now it was Jordan's voice I was hearing.

"Am I imagining this? Is this a vision, or... am I dead?"

Jordan shook his head. "No. You are not dead. And, yes, this is a vision, one that is truly happening."

I frowned. "Before... when you said I didn't want you to look like me... did you read my mind?"

"Yes." Jordan was speaking still, though his lips weren't moving. "It is the way I communicate."

"I... would prefer you didn't read my mind." I regretted the words as soon as they were out of my mouth. "I mean...

I'm sorry. I don't want to offend you, it's... something I'm not used to."

"You find it obtrusive. You are not at ease." Jordan spoke again, but this time he spoke through his mouth, and I could hear him through my ears. "I will no longer respond to your thoughts. I will also use my mouth to communicate. Forgive me if I find it difficult to do both. This way of communicating is ancient."

"Are you... human?"

"No." He smiled. "If you would like, I can show you my true form."

I nodded eagerly. Slowly, Jordan dissolved and, sure enough, it was a being like the one from my vision. A blue alien with four arms, four eyes, and a sideways mouth. Their cool hair tendrils fell to the floor.

"Are we descended from you?"

The alien nodded.

"Do you have a name? What is your species called?"

"Luriana. My people are called the Voranah."

"Are you the Primarch?"

Luriana smiled—at least, I think it was a smile, as it was literally sideways. "In the way you that call yourselves Keepers understand it, yes and no. I *was* the Primarch. There was one other after me. There has not been one for thousands of years."

"That's why I'm here. We need the Omnia Fragment to stop someone from destroying our world."

Luriana cocked an eyebrow. Well, the skin around their forehead moved. "But Sebastian Benedetti does not want to destroy your world. He wants to save it."

I frowned. "I know. So he says. But he's killed an awful lot of people trying to save it. And the way he wants to do things will probably result in some huge war."

They tilted their head to the side. "What will you do with the power you possess?"

"I guess I'll continue to keep it a secret. From what I understand, the Keepers have only managed to survive by making sure no one knows about the powers."

"The Keepers have killed as well."

I nodded. "To stop people like Benedetti from showing off their powers to the rest of the world. He wants to create an army of powered people."

"Similar to the four-hundred combat-trained Keepers?"

I stared, mouth open. "I'm not saying it right. You make it sound like we've done something wrong."

"How have you helped the planet?"

Frowning, I stepped forward. "The way it was explained to me, we've had to stay secret because of people like Benedetti who want to take over. I've only been here, like, three weeks."

"And you have followed their rules unquestioningly."

"No. If you can read my mind, you know I've questioned a lot of stuff."

"Forgive me. I mean you have not questioned the rules in a way that would bring about change. You have... complained about how unfair the rules are to you personally."

I let out a noise of impatience. "Uh, yeah. You know what they did to me. To my family. I was dragged into this thing because of other people's decisions."

"And yet, given the power to change the circumstances, you chose to secretly find the power over all the elements with Jordan. You chose to go along with his plan, instead of questioning him."

I could feel my heartbeat quicken. "Jordan lied about why he wanted the fragment?"

Luriana nodded. "Deep down, Jordan is interested in resurrecting his family. He believes the person with this power can do so."

"But you're saying that's not possible."

"Correct."

I sighed. "I didn't know that's what he wanted."

"You did not ask. Of course, had you asked, he would have lied to you. Jordan has become many things he was not destined to become. That has created many... difficulties."

"What kind of difficulties?"

"The kind that changes the course of everyone's lives on the planet."

"Does that mean your people can predict the future?"

Luriana smiled again. "Because I am deceased, I am able to view time in a non-linear fashion."

"Is that the case with all Voranah?"

"No. Only those who become the Primarch exist here with me in this afterlife."

"Is... is there an afterlife for everyone else?"

Luriana shrugged. "I do not know. However, the Voranah are not that different from humans. At least, they were not when I left our home planet all those millions of years ago."

I frowned. "But Earth has been around for billions of years."

Laughing, Luriana opened two of their arms wide. "The planet existed before we arrived. Even we do not know about the origin of the universe."

"Oh. Um, okay. Does that mean you died and left behind the Omnia Fragment?"

Luriana shook their head. "I passed along my powers and essence into a woman more than two-thousand years ago. But her child left behind the fragment that will grant the next Primarch power."

"You know who it is. Who is it?"

"I should not say."

I nodded. "But if I touch it, will I find out if it's me?"

Luriana slowly nodded. "However, there is a problem."

"What?"

"The Omnia Fragment was removed from this place years ago by a spy from my planet. It is now with them."

"So, that's what it looks like, but it's not actually here." I groaned. "So we came down here for nothing."

"You came down here for answers. And I have them."

"Does that mean this spy is the Primarch?"

"No. They do not have the power. In fact, the power may never be gained by anyone."

I stared at Luriana. "What does that mean?"

"The group of people you came with... none of them are the Primarch."

I gasped. "Does that mean... is it Benedetti?"

They paused. "No. It is not Benedetti."

"So, it's not the people I came with, and it's not Benedetti." My stomach lurched. "Does that mean... am *I* the Primarch?"

All four of Luriana's eyes fixed on me.

"No."

Chapter 10: Sharkbait – Ooh Ha Ha!

In that moment, I felt my eyes well up with tears from several different emotions.

"Why do you cry?"

"I guess... I'm sorry. I had hoped it was me in a way, but I'm also... relieved. It's a big job, with a lot of responsibility."

Luriana nodded as I sat down on the edge of the circle of fragments. They followed suit and sat down across from me.

"So, does that mean Jordan was wrong? He did his DNA stuff wrong?"

"No, he was correct." Luriana fell silent, looking thoughtful. "The one with the potential to wield the power does not currently exist because they are not ready. They have not made the decision to accept the power is theirs."

Lex. "Oh. So, it's like a self-belief kind of deal. How do we know when we're ready?"

"You must find the fragment."

"Okay. But... what do we do, then? Do we... start using our powers to save the world? Like, grow crops and stop famine, stop natural disasters and stuff?"

"You must trust the judgment of the Primarch when they are revealed. They will determine how best to proceed with the challenges that face you."

I let out a noise of protest. "You're saying we should trust Sebastian Benedetti if he ends up being the Primarch?"

"Yes."

"Fuck that."

Luriana crossed their arms. It wasn't in the way humans do, and it was quite beautiful. But when they spoke, their voice was crisp and severe. "If you do not trust the Primarch, your species will end up like mine."

"We're already not doing that great, if you haven't noticed."

"Yes, your planet is becoming like mine when I fled. There was war, hatred, rampant diseases, and distrust of everyone who didn't think like us. And fear. So much pain and fear. It consumed our race and led to multiple wars using what you refer to as weapons of mass destruction. So, I gathered The Dietat and their families, and we fled."

I frowned. "I thought there were only six of you."

Luriana looked down. "We were pursued off the planet. I had obligations to my people that I was fleeing from, and they wanted justice. Only those of us with the powers survived."

"Not every Voranah has powers?"

"No. Powers are gifts. The woman I gave my power to was a remarkable woman. Your stories tell so little of her life before and after the birth of the man who used the powers openly."

"You mean... Jesus Christ."

"I mean Mary, the mother of Jesus." Luriana smiled. "Mary was ahead of her time. She would be considered an incredible advocate in today's world. She was powerful and fierce in her own right. She would raise the boy who would eventually become one of the most famous people in the world. But I chose her because I'd seen her remarkable spirit."

I took a deep breath. "Is Jesus… is he actually the son of God?"

Luriana considered me, thoughtful. "Mary and I conceived Jesus. But I was near death and ultimately sacrificed my remaining time to transfer my power to her. She had the original power over all the elements, but her firstborn, Jesus, absorbed that power from her. The rest of her children, had they touched the Omnia Fragment, would have had the chance to gain the power as well."

I stared, mouth open in shock. "So… she wasn't a virgin?"

Looking bemused, Luriana uncrossed their arms and stood.

"Physically, our way of reproducing is much different. By human standards, she was still a virgin."

"Wow. So, did you, like, pretend to be God and stuff?"

"She did have beliefs I exploited, yes."

I frowned. "But… why? Why did you decide to impregnate an underage girl and give her your powers?"

"I was dying. And while we long had beliefs about an afterlife, I was still scared that I would not be allowed to enter, because I had betrayed my people. So, I chose to end my life and continue the line of potential power in humanity. In Mary, and in the child we created. I knew that, when he died, he would form into what you know as the Omnia Fragment. Once I died, however, I was able to appear to him several times and tell him where the other fragments were found after the War of the Elements."

"I've seen those memories," I said. "When someone gains the power from the fragments, they see the war."

"Yes. I... I manipulated the beliefs of humanity. And I did so selfishly."

"You're basically the reason Christianity exists, then."

They let out a soft chuckle. "I did not come to anyone else besides Jesus in visions either before or after Mary. Other Voranah may have interfered over the years. After all, they knew which planet we came to. Those on the home world—if it still exists, and I assume it does—never lost track of the planet we fled to."

"You know, there have always been rumors about alien sightings and stuff. Abductions and that kind of thing."

Luriana laughed. "That is humorous. After all, we can modify our appearance to look like humans. Or animals, of course. Humans are easier because we look like you. However, unless the culture of Oriach has changed dramatically, we would never abduct humans."

"Are there other aliens out there that *would*?"

"Yes."

I took a big breath. "That's intense. Wait, real fast—what was that you said? Oriach?"

"Yes, that's the name of my home planet."

"Wow. I mean, knowing we're descended from aliens is one thing, but to know we're not alone in the universe... wow."

Luriana smiled. "You previously thought you were the only species in the universe?"

"Some humans do. They also think the God who created our planet also created our entire universe."

"Ah. Again, even we do not know how the universe formed."

I racked my brain. "So, going back to the whole Jesus thing... did his disciples have powers?"

"Yes. In fact, the story of Judas betraying Jesus for thirty silver coins is a little more complicated. Judas handed over the fragments to the Romans. He believed that using their powers so openly, helping people, and performing what the people considered miracles was dangerous. That is why the Romans were so threatened by Jesus. He and the disciples had powers they could only dream of."

"But, did he perform those miracles?" I frowned, trying to recall biblical stories. "Like, turning water into wine, healing people, walking on water, feeding the five-thousand...?"

Luriana shrugged. "The Primarch cannot heal the sick, cure the blind, or perform exorcisms—if demonic possession even exists. However, walking on water, turning water into wine, creating more food out of food that already exists... yes. Those things are all possible with the power. They take years to master, however, which is why Jesus's story is fragmented—if you will forgive the term—in your Bible."

"So, where was Jesus when the Bible doesn't talk about him? It was like, from twelve to thirty there's no information on him."

"He was the only Primarch to never touch what you call the Omnia Fragment. He was born with the power over all the elements. Some of the fragments had been found by others over the ages—most notably Noah and Moses—but Jesus was the first to gather all the fragments together. He traveled all over Europe and Asia to find them and shared the power with his disciples."

"So..." I took a deep breath, trying to sort out my thoughts. The most popular belief system in the world was based on the lie an alien told a young girl before knocking her up with a baby that had power over all the elements. "What happened when Jesus died?"

"The disciples knew Jesus's body would crystalize. The disciples who had the power of Terra moved the rock from in front of the tomb and found the Omnia Fragment. Thus began the journey of hiding the fragment from the world."

"But, Jesus's siblings could have used the power! Why'd the disciples hide it away?"

"Jesus's siblings all agreed to not use it. It was still too dangerous for them to consider using it with the Romans in power. That is why they hid it here, creating obstacles that could only be completed by one with a complete set of fragments. Then, the one who was worthy would find the fragment and gain the power."

I tsked. "So, the holy grail isn't the cup Jesus drank out of. It's Jesus himself, in a way. The fragment that used to be him."

Luriana nodded, then tilted their head to the side as I thought of another question to ask. "May I ask you one more question, Luriana?"

"Of course."

"Have you been trying to contact me?"

"What do you mean?" Luriana frowned.

"I mean, I had a vision a few days ago. It told me to find someone. It sounded like Sam-something."

Luriana seemed alarmed. "I have not communicated with you, no. Can you remember the name of the person you are supposed to find?"

"You can't read my mind and tell me?"

"I cannot read memories. I can read thoughts."

"Oh. Then, I'm sorry. I don't know. They also have a title that started with a P, but I can't remember."

"Primarch?" Luriana drummed the fingers of their front left hand on their face. I noticed they had a thumb with three fingers, instead of four like a human.

"No."

"Prefect?"

"Hmm-mmm."

"Praetorian?"

Something clicked. "Yes. Yes, that sounds right."

That definitely meant something to them. "If they sent the Praetorian... no. No, they wouldn't."

"What?"

Luriana's eyes focused on mine, shining brightly. "You must find the Omnia Fragment. It is vital. We must be done here. The more time we waste, the more dangerous it becomes."

"But I—"

A rushing sound filled my ears and the light brightened. Suddenly, I had the feeling of falling again, and I hit solid ground. My head jerked back, sending a spasm of pain through my neck and shoulders.

"Ugh." I sat up, rubbing my neck gently. "That... um, wow."

I looked to my right and gasped. There they were... the fragments. Whole and complete. In a circle. I stood and walked over to them and picked up the Fragment of Terra. I don't know what I expected, but it was definitely not nothing.

There was no vision, no glowing, no shattering. It was like it had been before we found the cave.

I put the fragments in my bag, traded my shoes for flippers, and put my gloves back on.

"Okay, I'm ready to come back," I reported into the headset.

There was no reply.

"Check, check? Check, one, two. Check, one, two. Checkity check?"

Nothing. I rolled my eyes and took it off. Then, I grabbed the flashlight out of my bag and held it out over the hole. Then, I flashed it a few times, trying to remember what the code was that Robert had established.

There were no flashes in response. I clicked the flashlight on and off a few more times and waited.

Then, the sub's lights blared through the cave twice.

"Yes!" I put everything in the bag and sealed it tight. Then, I slowly began to let myself down into the freezing water.

I didn't feel a lot of pressure on my body until my head descended into the water, where it felt like it was being squeezed like a melon. And I couldn't communicate to anyone that it hurt. I'd have to deal.

I let myself float down to the bottom of the cave. They decided to only turn on a few lights—thank God, otherwise it would have been like looking in the sun after being in dark spaces for so long.

They had moved the sub away from the entrance, so I had an easier time swimming out. The lights they had on were shining right in my face, and it wasn't until I got close to them, I could see them waving. It wasn't a very clear view, as I had swum into a school of fish.

"Hey, look! Shiny rocks. I'll just grab these..." I began taking all the crystals Robert had in the little basket in front and putting them in the backpack while they waved.

"Hey! You won't believe..."

I trailed off. They weren't waving to say hi. Their faces were panicked. And they began pointing behind me. I turned in time to see its cold, black eyes.

Shark.

But it was one I'd never seen before. It had a protruding, flat nose, probably about three feet long. The shark itself was huge—at least fifteen feet, and I couldn't see its mouth. It was an off-white color—probably because of the lack of sunlight. For a wild moment, I thought it might have been the Primarch following me out of the cave, mimicking a shark form.

But as it darted forward, I knew it wasn't there to talk. It was there to eat.

It opened its mouth, and its jaws literally *flew out of its mouth*. But I realized it wasn't going for me—it was going for the fish floating around me. But the fish dodged, and the shark's jaws latched onto my left arm.

"Augh!" I cried out in pain and horror as its many two or three inch long needle-like teeth burrowed through my suit and began to tear at my skin. I jerked away in reflex, but that only made it worse. Combined with the shark pulling this way and that, it felt like it was tearing my forearm off.

Defend yourself, Jake!

I began looking for any weaknesses, trying to remember anything and everything I knew about sharks. I couldn't blow it up. I didn't have a gun or a harpoon. What was their weakest part?

Gills! *Go for the gills*! I reached out with my right arm toward the slits on the side of its body and tried to grab the gills. I got a slight grip and pulled, causing some of its own blood to ooze out. But it still didn't let go and continued tearing up my arm.

"No-ho-ho!" I surprised myself with how whiney I sounded, tears streaming down my face. I met its gaze. It felt like it was tearing down to the bone at this point. It knew it had me.

Acting on pure instinct, I jabbed my finger in its eye.

That got it. It let go of my arm and its jaws retracted back into its head, looking like a beak with teeth. I tried to gauge whether it was done or not, and it wasn't. It began to swim toward me again and I tried to flipper away as fast as I could, trying to get to the back of the submarine. I was halfway along the sub's body when I looked back to see where the shark was.

It caught up to me easily, because the fish it was going for were swimming with me. I tried to wave and kick them away and was getting ready to latch onto my flipper. Now, I was getting pissed.

"Get the fuck off me!" I shot a stone fist out of my hand, shredding my glove. I hit it in the gills. The shark jerked back and, after seeming to think about it for a moment, came back again. One of the little fish was hanging out near my right foot, and the shark went for it. Dodging out of the way again, the shark latched onto my flipper instead.

"Mother fucker!" It began pulling again. I violently tried shaking my foot this way and that, but it didn't let go. So, I tried my best to combine my movement with the shark's and tear the fin off.

It worked. It was stuck with a huge part of my rubber flipper. It chewed as I began to work my way around to the back, where the sub's doors were still open. My movement was slowed, however, and the shark was still following the little school of fish that wouldn't leave me the fuck alone.

I made it to the cargo bay and swam inside, but it followed. It moved lazily, like a serial killer in a movie that doesn't need to run and somehow still catches up to their victim.

My anger was getting the best of me. I formed my fist into hard rock and, as soon as the shark struck out with its jaws once more, I punched it right in the mouth. It didn't make any noise of pain, but definitely reeled backward. It gave one last look before swimming away.

I hesitated for a moment, seeing a few things floating in the water after it. I grabbed at them with my hand as it returned to normal skin and saw several of its teeth.

Trophies. I felt a surge of pride and strength. I'd just survived a shark attack. Sure, maybe my arm was almost torn off, but I survived.

"It's gone." I heard Ari's distorted voice come through the speaker. "Hurry and close the doors just in case it decides to come back, though."

I swam to the door and pressed the button to close the cargo bay. Then, I heard a rushing sound, and the water began to drain out. I swam to the top and broke the surface, taking a look at the damage on my arm. The cargo bay was also repressurizing.

I couldn't even see where the suit and skin were separated. The shark had ground them together in a bloody mix.

Gritting my teeth, I hardened my finger into a stone blade and began to cut the suit around my wounded arm, pulling off the shredded material. Finally, the water was completely drained, and my ears were popping as I stood there in one flipper, trembling and holding my bleeding arm.

With a creak and a groan, the hatch to the cockpit opened, and Ari and Will rushed in, holding towels. Will wrapped one around my arm, while Ari put one around my shivering shoulders.

"Where the hell were you?" Ari sounded angry. "You've been gone for twelve hours. We were just planning to go after you."

"Fuck all the way off," I snapped. "Was that thing even from this planet? Did you see its jaws? I hate it!"

"It's a goblin shark," Robert explained as he stepped out of the chair and began examining my wound. "Yikes. Also known as a vampire shark."

"Well, I didn't think it was called a fluffy love shark," I said through clenched teeth. I shrugged the bag of fragments off my shoulders, moaning as it slid along my half-eaten arm. "I didn't even know sharks could be down this deep."

"Oh, yeah. Goblin sharks, frilled sharks, telescope octopi, angler fish, zombie worms. They all live in the Mariana Trench. Everyone is looking to space to find the unknown, but they aren't looking in the ocean."

"We're coming back to the zombie worms. But first..."

I pulled the Fragment of Terra out of the bag to heal myself.

"Oh, so glad your fragment survived the journey," Ari spat.

"They all did. I don't know how, but they did. Check the bag, bitch."

They did. Meanwhile, the space filled with a green glow as light began forming around my body, beautiful greens and browns. I watched with fascination as my wounded arm—which looked like ground beef—glowed green and, when all the light receded, revealed healthy-looking, completely uninjured skin.

I took a steadying breath. "Well. That's done. Now, we need to get back to the boat. I'm sure they're wondering where we are."

Robert nodded. "And on the way, you can tell us all about what happened to you in there."

He got in the pilot's seat, and we began our ascent.

"I don't see the trophy in here." Ari sifted through the bag.

"The Omnia Fragment wasn't there."

"*What*?"

"The Primarch said the fragment was stolen years ago."

Will glanced at Ari, then back at me. "The Primarch? As in, the one and only?"

I sighed and explained the ways in which I had to use the fragments to progress until I met Luriana, who had been the Primarch when the Voranah came to planet Earth millions of years ago.

"If it wasn't in the cave, why were the fragments glowing, then?" Ari asked, frowning.

"Maybe it has something to do with the location, not the Omnia Fragment. I don't know."

"Wait, so... they're officially alien?" We were sitting on the floor around the bag of fragments while we spoke. "We aren't descended from them like they're the original humans or something?"

"No. They came here from their planet, Oriach."

Ari's jaw dropped. "So, wait... then is it really true that we're all descended from the Jesus's siblings?"

I nodded. "The thing is, Luriana lied and exploited Mary's beliefs. They posed as an angel—or the Holy Spirit, I guess—and that was when they transferred their power to Mary."

"Wait, *Mary* could control all the elements?"

"Yes, but when she gave birth to Jesus, she lost the power and he gained it. Then, when he died, his body turned into the Omnia Fragment." I frowned at Ari, who started grinning. "What?"

"So... Jesus, Christianity... those beliefs I was raised with... they're all bullshit?" They let out a gleeful whoop, punching the air. "I can't wait to tell my dad and step-mom that Christianity's a fucking lie. Lex, too."

"Don't." Will's serious tone surprised me. "Just because the organization is a lie doesn't mean the teachings of Christ are a lie."

"But the very idea that Christ was the son of God—"

"That doesn't change what Christ taught." I had never heard Will talk about religion other than that once last week in the pub in San Francisco. "He was all about forgiveness and loving our neighbor. He still performed those miracles. He still preached peace and kindness. Even though his origin is different doesn't mean his teachings aren't valid."

"Whatever." Ari rolled their eyes, then looked at me expectantly. "So? Where are we going next?"

"I... I don't know." I ran my hands through my hair. "I mean, I talked with Luriana, and they told me a spy from Oriach took the fragment, but they don't know where the spy went."

Ari flipped their hands in the air. "Well, that's a bunch of bullshit. We kidnapped Robert and Renee for nothing?"

"I second that bullshit," Robert called from the front.

"I mean, I guess."

"Well, but when did the spy take it?"

I shrugged. "Don't know."

"You didn't ask?"

"It's not like I had a list of questions written down for when I met a million-year-old alien today, Ari."

They scoffed. "It seems like a pretty obvious question to ask."

"Well, I'm sorry it wasn't to me."

"Then maybe we should have sent someone who could ask the right questions."

"Hey, it wasn't *my* idea to go into the cave, Ari."

"Stop." Will held his hands up to us both. "What's done is done. Obviously, we all would have handled it differently. There's no right or wrong way to meet the alien that created life on the planet."

We all fell silent for a long while. I laid back, trying to get as comfortable as I could. Apparently, I could get fairly comfortable and was exhausted, as I fell asleep for a few hours. When I woke, it was to the sound of Robert on the radio.

"Yacht *Andromeda*, this is submarine *Ancora* requesting location. Do you copy?"

Static silence filled the sub after Robert's words.

"We may only be out of range."

"We're normally able to get in contact with them this far away. Wait..."

We looked to Robert, expecting him to say something more. But he didn't.

"Wait for what?"

"Um, we're getting close to the surface, and I can't see the yacht on radar. But I can see about a dozen other ships, and several of them are much bigger than the yacht."

"What kind are they? Are we in danger?"

Robert's eyes were dark as he stared at me. "Jake, any large fleet of ships gathered in our general vicinity is probably not a good sign for us."

"Are we in international waters?"

He shook his head. "The Mariana Trench was established as a U.S. National Monument clear back in 2009. But I haven't known them to monitor it or anything."

"Maybe it's Jordan calling in the military to search for us because we've been gone a whole day?" Ari looked hopefully at us. "I mean, he had the military connections to get us here."

"Well, if it's Benedetti, he's going to kill us." Will wrinkled his nose, like the thought smelled highly unpleasant.

"If it's our government, they're going to for sure capture us," Ari said. "Maybe kill us."

"If it's any other government, they'll also capture us, but *definitely* kill us," Robert added.

I sighed. "Well, there's only one thing to do, apparently. Surface... and see how we die."

Chapter 11: *Mockingly* That's Classified

"It looks like we've got some company down here, too." Robert pointed out the front of the sub where we could see a much larger, even more penis-like submarine slowly coming into view.

We all jumped as the radio crackled. "Submarine *Ancora*, this is General Scott McCormack of the United States Air Force. We have you surrounded. You will surface at once, surrender your vessel and all of your belongings. You will be removed from your vessel to our command ship, the *USS Ashland*. Any sign of aggression will be met with the full force of our artillery. Respond."

Robert fumbled for the radio.

"Uh, General McCormack, this is Robert Friedley, pilot of *The Ancora* of the Naval Exploration, Mapping, and Oceanography Center. We are here on a research mission with the yacht *Andromeda*. Please, don't shoot us. Um, over."

There were a few moments of silence where we all looked at each other apprehensively. Then, the radio came back to life.

"Your friends aboard the *Andromeda* have already been taken into custody, and the vessel has been impounded. You are trespassing at a historical monument of the United States of America. You must surrender, or we will be forced to open fire. Do you understand?"

Robert smiled sadly at all of us. "I guess this is the end of the line for our little adventure." He pressed the button on the radio. "General, we will surrender peacefully. We have no weapons aboard the submarine and will comply. Repeat, we surrender. Please, don't shoot us."

The general came back and gave us coordinates to meet with him and the rest of apparently the entire navy stationed near the Northern Mariana Islands, and Robert began moving us into position toward a large ship. I had no idea what kind. Big, with lots of guns.

"Open the hatch and disembark with your hands above your head. Do you understand?"

"Yes." Robert glanced at us. "There are only four of us in the sub. We'll leave everything and come out with bare hands."

"I'm taking the fragments with me." Ari stepped back as we all jumped down their throat at once.

"Do you *want* to die?"

"You're going to get us all killed!"

"Then you can go out first!"

"Okay, okay!" Ari set the bag down and holding their hands up defensively. "But we can't let them get the fragments. We have to hide them somewhere they won't find them."

"It's a submarine. They'll tear it apart to find anything we hide." Robert shrugged apologetically. "I'm really sorry, but—"

"Wait. Maybe they won't know about the fragments because there's all the other crystals in the bag." I opened the bag and began to shove the fragments in unceremoniously, then shook the bag up, the fragments, crystals, and shards of whatever all clinking together. "There. Now they're cool crystals we found while exploring. That's why we're out here. We're out here with friends collecting cool crystals from the deepest part of the ocean to, you know, sell and make us rich."

"If they buy that, our government is probably the stupidest government around," Ari paused, looking thoughtful. "Hm. Maybe there's a chance."

Robert piloted us alongside the *USS Ashland* and a hook descended, capturing our little sub with a thunderous metal-on-metal sound. There was moment of silence, then another, softer thud. Finally, we all heard a loud banging noise on the hatch.

"Come out with your hands up!"

"We're with white people, so they won't shoot us, right?" Will whispered to Robert, who shrugged.

"We'll go first," I offered, and Ari nodded.

Neither of us moved.

There was another knock. "*Ancora* crew, come out with your hands up or we will come in there and get you. This is your final warning."

Ari stared at me, eyebrows raised expectantly.

"Fine." I stepped forward. "But I'm going to remember that you made me go first."

I stepped to the short ladder and climbed up, grabbing the hatch and turning.

"I'm coming out! I'm super unarmed and compliant."

Opening the round hatch and, squinting in the harsh sunlight, I was met with the barrels of three guns pointed right at me.

"Hands where we can see them," the nearest uniformed man ordered. "Now, up the ladder, sir."

I began climbing the side of the ship and found a bunch more sailors with weapons pointed at me. One was holding handcuffs, and another was holding a radio, describing everything I was doing to someone on the other end.

I stepped onto the deck of the ship and held my hands out slightly, making sure it was obvious I was following their rules. A few of the sailors exchanged looks at the sight of me. I realized I looked like a tattered mess. The whole left arm of my wetsuit was torn away while also being singed in a few places from being hit by lightning. Plus, I was barefoot.

I let out a shaky breath as I scanned the faces of the people staring me down behind their weapons. That was when I noticed one person I recognized. My eyes widened in shock, but he shook his head slightly and gazed to his right.

"Are you the pilot?" I looked around to see a man walking forward in sharp green fatigues. I was able to match a scary face to the scary man over the radio.

I shook my head. "No. My name is, uh... well, my name is Jake West. The pilot is Robert Friedley."

"Whom you kidnapped, along with Renee Lloyd. You also stole the submarine. And destroyed the San Mateo-Hayward Bridge in your escape to the airport, where you boarded a military transport with a forged authorization." He straightened up a little more, something I didn't think was possible. "*My* forged authorization."

"Sir, *I* am Robert Friedley." Robert clambered off the ladder. "I can assure you I was *not* kidnapped."

I locked eyes with the sailor I recognized, and realized his eyes kept darting to the right for a reason.

"Sir, we're all willing to cooperate, but your ranks have been compromised."

The general looked at me like I was out of my mind. "Excuse me?"

"That man, there. He's not a sailor." I pointed at Spencer, who stepped out of ranks, slowly setting his gun down.

"He's correct, sir. But I'm not alone."

"You son of a bitch!" One of the other sailors turned her gun on me and opened fire. Luckily, Spencer was close enough to her that he managed to redirect her bullets. I dodged but felt a searing pain in my face as I launched myself to the ground. The sailors next to the woman roughly secured her and the weapon away from her.

"Fuck!" I felt my right cheek, blood oozing from where the bullet had grazed me.

The Disciple was screaming like a wounded hyena. "After everything your father has done for you? He will hear of this, I swear it!"

"Take her away!" General McCormack put his own gun away. I hadn't even seen him draw it. "This is my ship, goddammit, and I will not have people here who aren't supposed to be. Take them all to the brig. And begin extraction of their vessel. Orders are to search the sub."

We were all handcuffed. Then, the four of us and Spencer were hauled off. At one point, I was separated from them and taken to the medical area, where the doctor there hastily slapped some kind of ointment on my face and a few bandages.

Then, I was escorted through a maze of corridors and doors, down several sets of stairs, and arrived in a cramped area that had six different doors.

Doors with bars. I was steered into the first one, and the door closed behind me.

It was a cell. There was a bed and a toilet-sink combo.

I've never even been in detention.

"You will be here for twenty-four hours." the guard closed my door, and I heard the others begin shouting questions.

"Where are the others?" Will banged on the bars of his cell door.

"What about Mack?" Ari asked.

"And Renee?" Robert sounded angry. "If you think we were kidnapped why the hell am I in a cell?"

"If we have any questions, we will come to you." The guard walked away.

I looked into the cell across from me. Spencer stood by the door of his cell.

Our eyes met. "Hey."

He nodded. "Hey. I'm glad you didn't get shot worse."

"Thanks for stopping her. At least we're all safe from your dad in here."

"No, we're not." His expression was grim. "The military basically shut down Vostell and seized all of its assets. My dad is becoming more desperate by the hour, doing everything he can to avoid capture."

"Oh." I sat down on the bed. "By the way, I'm sorry I knocked you off a bridge. I'm glad you didn't die."

"Oh, I wasn't going to die. Yeah, it hurt, but Dad was actually angrier that you hurt me. Which is kind of nice. Makes me think he might care."

"Does that mean you're going to turn on us?" Ari asked.

"What? No. He needs to be held accountable for what he's done."

I laid back on the bed, overcome by exhaustion. I hadn't been in a bed for a day.

"I'm going to sleep."

"Same." Robert let out a yawn. "I'm exhausted. And there's nothing to do but wait, apparently."

I don't know that I've ever fallen asleep so quickly or woken so suddenly. But the sound of a brig door slamming brought me out of my slumber. I sat up, my back cracking slightly.

"Jake!" Robert's voice sounded out. "They're taking me somewhere. I don't know where."

I hastily stood and went to the barred door. "Hey! Where are you taking him?"

"Quiet." The guard shot me an annoyed look as he took Robert out of the room.

"Hey!" But shouting once more did nothing. I sat back down on the cot. "Well, shit. How long have I been asleep?"

"A while," Will said. "No clocks, so we don't know."

"Did anything else happen while I was asleep?"

"They came down to tell us we were going to be moved to the general population cells." Ari's voice sounded like it was in the cell next to me. "We might get to see everyone again."

"Cool."

"Also, Ari pooped." I gaped at Spencer and could see he was suppressing a giggle. "It... it smelled *so* bad."

"Everybody poops, Spencer," Ari said hotly. "*You* try eating junk food and being stuck in a submarine for a day! God! Are you six?"

I started laughing, and Spencer and Will joined in.

"Quiet in there." A different guard poked his head in, and we stifled our laughter.

For a moment.

"You can't even smell it, Jake," Ari whispered.

"*I* could. All the sudden, there were loud, wet explosions and then the smell. I'm surprised Jake didn't wake up choking."

"Shut up, Spencer!"

"All of you, quiet!" The guard stepped into view, causing us all to shrink away slightly.

A while later, another sailor entered the room carrying a tray with four plates and four glasses of water.

"Don't eat too much of the bread," the guard advised as I eagerly took the plate. "It will swell once it's in your stomach. This is enough to tide you over until... later."

"What's later?" I asked.

They didn't answer. Big surprise.

However, hours later, there was a surprise. The general from earlier, holding a simple manilla folder, stepped into the room and motioned for the guard to open my cell door. I normally would have stood, but I decided to stay seated for a reason.

If I had to look up to him, he had the power. I didn't want to give him the wrong ideas about me and the fact I could bend the bars of the cage I was in.

The others were silent as they were all escorted out behind him.

"Jacob Anthony West." He flipped through some of the papers. "Born in King, Idaho. You turn twenty-three on May 21st. Youngest child to Paul and Angie West. Attended King State University until... hm." He closed the folder and looked me straight in the eyes. "Until you died."

I swallowed. "Um, about that—"

General McCormack held up a hand to interrupt me. "The others are being taken to the general population. That's where we're holding some friends of yours who claim they were simply cruising around on a yacht, having a party."

"Are they okay?"

His eyebrow arched slightly. "I have yet to see them. However, we were able to determine they were hitching a ride with the, ah, rather unknowing host. We've let him and his crew go."

I nodded. Mack was okay, but everyone else was on the ship with us. I felt bad. I didn't get to say goodbye to him. He'd been chill about our superpowers.

"What I need to find out is why you're considered dead—legally, with a grave and everything—yet, you're sitting here in front of me. I'd also like to know about this whole Marley Wagner who works for Vostell business."

He paused, staring at me.

"Do… do you want me to answer a question?"

"I asked you a question."

"It didn't sound like a question."

"The question was implied." He gritted his teeth. "Why are you here and alive, diving in the Mariana Trench?"

"Oh." I took in a breath, trying to think of a lie as quickly as I could. "Um, it was all just a big misunderstanding."

"Oh?"

"Yeah, so… there was a school shooting in King, Idaho. Don't know if you heard about it."

"The shooting at King State University."

"That one." I nodded, licking my lips. "And it was reported I was dead because I had some, uh, friends and family that were told I was dead, even though I wasn't dead, I was … unconscious."

He blinked. "You are a terrible liar."

I sighed. "I know, but you put me on the spot."

He slammed his hand down on the sink. "Why are you diving in the Mariana Trench?"

"We're looking for crystals. That's why we have a bag full of them."

"And that required kidnapping, felony theft, forgery, impersonating an officer—I could go on."

"I mean, you know when it's someone's birthday and you go to their house and force them to go somewhere, right? It was like that. We knew Renee and Robert loved diving and loved gems and stuff."

He blinked again. "I shouldn't even bother talking to you if all you're going to do is lie."

I opened my mouth to speak, but the door to the brig opened, and a sailor stepped through.

"General?"

"Not now."

"Sir... there's someone who requested to see you."

General McCormack wheeled around. "I said *not now*."

"It's one of the people from the *Andromeda*. He claims to be your son."

The general seemed to deflate. "Well, that would make a lot of sense." He turned back to me. "If you're spending time with my son, you're in the wrong crowd. I'll be back."

"Wait, who's your son?"

"I am."

Zeke stepped through the doorway and folded his arms across his chest.

"Zeke!"

He gave a small smile. "Hey, Jake. Hi... Dad."

It all made sense in a flash. General Scott McCormack. The forged credentials. How we were able to get military transport. And Jordan knew. He'd protected Zeke's secret. Jordan had to have known the military was going to catch up to us.

"Zeke? What are you doing here, son?" The general took a step forward, then hesitated. He spoke again, this time with more force. "What are you doing here?"

"Jake is with me. We all came on this trip together."

"You forged my signature and used my rank to elicit a military transport of stolen goods and kidnapped people out of the continental United States, Ezekiel Alexander! What the hell were you thinking?"

"Can we not talk about this in front of Jake, please?" Zeke looked highly uncomfortable.

General McCormack waved his hand at me. "He's dead. He can wait."

"Hey!"

The general continued. "You've got a lot of nerve using taxpayer dollars allocated for the defense of our nation for a personal treasure hunt, young man!"

"It's a lot more than that, Dad. We're in danger. Someone's trying to kill us."

"What?" Zeke's dad sounded concerned and angry, very much like my own parents when I'd been busted sneaking back in after going to a party with my high school boyfriend. "Why didn't you call, then? You know I could have helped if you—"

"*What*, Dad?" Zeke's face flushed, and his voice cracked. "I tried talking to you years ago. You never wanted to listen. And the last time I talked to you, you told me I deserved to rot in prison and get my... my fudge packed there like the fairy I was."

The sailor and I met eyes. This was definitely a conversation we couldn't escape from.

"I..." Zeke's dad seemed to deflate. "You're... you're still my son. If you're in danger, I want to help."

"Maybe make it clear next time," Zeke said. "Say something like, 'I care enough about you to be alive, but beyond that, I don't give a rat's ass.' Something like that?"

The sailor cleared his throat. "Sir, I can escort West here to—"

"Do it. Take him to general holding. Zeke... walk with me, please."

"No." Zeke stepped back. "I'd rather go back to general holding."

I couldn't see his face, but the general nodded at the sailor. He stepped out of my cell with a backward glance at me. "We're not done, Mr. West. I'll talk to you later."

The general quickly retreated.

Left alone with the sailor, Zeke and I were escorted back through the ship. As we walked, I was dying to ask Zeke what their story was, but I didn't want the sailor to report to the general we were all lying.

"So... you really died?" the sailor asked out of the blue.

"There was a shooting, I went underground—it's on my to-do list."

We made it to a larger cell, where our friends were waiting, but minus Renee, Robert, and Spencer.

The sailor opened the door and Jordan and Will rushed forward. My whole body felt like it was floating as I embraced Jordan. The sailor closed the door, and we were left alone.

"What happened to you?" Jordan asked as he led me to the nearest cot. They were stacked three high for a total of eighteen beds in the general population brig.

"There's so much to explain, I don't even know where to start." I looked around. "Where's Spencer?"

Jordan stared at Ari and Will. "Spencer's here? Why didn't you say anything?"

"We thought you knew!"

"How could I possibly know that?" He slapped his hands to his thighs. "Whatever. Doesn't matter. Did you find it?"

I was about to answer when I saw the camera in the corner of the room. I cleared my throat. "Oh, yeah. We found all sorts of amazing crystals. We can make a fortune, if they ever give them back to us."

Jordan was confused for a moment but followed my line of sight to the camera.

"Yeah, that would be a real bummer if they didn't give us back all our crystals," he said slowly. "You know, I was super worried with how long you were down there. They only caught us a few hours before they caught you."

"Mack says hi." David waved from the cot across the way. "He says he hopes you're okay, and, uh, 'you're one hilarious dude, bruh.'"

I rolled my eyes. "Thanks. Um, where's Renee and Robert?"

"They separated us from Renee when we got here. But she was livid she was taken against her will."

I gasped. "She told them we kidnapped her?"

"No. She was mad at the Navy. She said she was going to work her hardest to get us all out of here."

"Well, she may not be our best bet." Zeke sighed. "I met my dad down in the brig, and he seemed amenable to talking. I don't know how much good it will do, but I can try to see if he'll see me again. I wanted to check with you first, Jordan."

I looked at Will. "Wait, you knew about this?"

Will shrugged and inspected his fingernails. "Yeah, I knew." He glanced up, taking in our shocked faces. "Everyone's surprised I can keep a secret. Don't die or anything."

I looked around. Our group was the definition of over it. David especially, as he was unshaven and his hair was unkempt. "How long has it been since we got on this ship?"

"Almost two days, I think."

I thought quickly. I wanted to tell them all about what had happened down in the cave, but I couldn't.

"Huh, you know, I had the craziest dream." I wet my lips, trying to be cool. "When I was sleeping down in the brig. I dreamed I was back looking for the crystals, but I couldn't find the one I was looking for."

Jordan caught on. "Really? Like, there was a big, important one you were looking for and you couldn't find?"

"Nope. Guess what? An alien took it." I forced a laugh, and everyone quickly panic-laughed along. "Yeah, it was the weirdest thing. I met this alien who was all like, "Oh, yeah, by the way, I totally got Mary, the mother of Jesus pregnant through alien sex, and when Jesus died, he actually turned into a crystal that's considered the holy grail!"

Everyone fell silent. Finally, David spoke. "That's a fucked up dream."

"I still can't believe you didn't find what you were looking for." Will fluttered his eyelashes. "Maybe it's a sign you're searching for something in real life. Any ideas where you think you should be searching for, um, something?"

I shrugged. "Maybe the dream means I am supposed to search somewhere else. But there's no point because it said all the people who I was with weren't ready to be in charge."

"In charge?" David was confused.

"Yeah, like they weren't chosen yet because they weren't ready to be chosen to have some crazy alien power."

"Huh." Jordan's eyes were intense. "So, if it wasn't one of us, is it... someone else?"

I shook my head. "No. From what I understand, the alien was sure it was one of us. But the person wasn't ready yet."

David shrugged. "I mean, is anybody ready to have the power over all the elements?"

Everyone glared at him.

"I mean, in your dream," he added, as if that fixed his slip-up.

The door opened at that moment, and General McCormack stepped into the room, accompanied by a squad of sailors.

"Attention." None of us moved. Zeke put his hands in his pockets. Zeke's dad cleared his throat. "I'd like you to gather closer to me."

Slowly, we all moved toward him.

"Are you finally going to let us go?" Ari asked.

The general's jaw tightened. "I don't know what planet you live on, missy, but you have about a dozen felony charges leveled against all of you."

"So, we're under arrest," Zeke said. "Funny. I don't remember us being read our rights."

"Oh, we're far beyond that." He snapped his fingers and the soldiers stepped forward, each pulling out a pair of handcuffs and some sort of black cloth along with them. "In response to a clear threat to the United States of America, you are hereby being transported to a secure facility to be interrogated regarding anti-American activities."

We all began protesting, but Jordan held up his hands. "We'll be okay, everyone."

But even he couldn't stop me from freaking out internally the moment I realized what those black cloths in their hands were.

Hoods.

Chapter 12: Governments... They Know Shit

Even though Jordan had said we would cooperate, David swung at the nearest sailor. General McCormack himself took David down, hard, and two sailors put the hood over his head and handcuffs on him before I could blink.

"Fuck you!" David shouted, though his voice was slightly muffled.

"Anyone else wanna dance?" General McCormack cracked his knuckles, looking around.

Zeke sighed. "Fine." He stepped forward and put his hands together. "Take us outta here."

One by one, we were handcuffed and hooded. I was the last one. Before a sailor put a hood on me, I held up my hands. "Please promise me that Robert and Renee are okay. And..." I lowered my voice. "Please don't hurt Jordan."

Zeke's dad glanced at Jordan's hooded figure being escorted away, then turned back to me. "You are all in for a world of trouble. I can't promise that."

The hood went over my head, and I tried to calm my breathing, thinking back to the days of pandemics and masks. Two sailors gripped my arms tightly and proceeded to help guide me through the doors. I kept banging my feet and tripping, as I wasn't used to stepping so high over door frames.

Soon, I felt fresh air on my skin, and knew we were on the deck of the ship. I was walked down a ramp and across hard ground for several minutes, before I was told to step up on a platform. I stepped up once more, then was pushed to sit. The world around me shifted, and I realized I was in a vehicle.

Someone's shoulder bumped into mine as the vehicle began to move.

"Hello?"

"Jake?"

"Will?"

"Yeah. You okay?"

"I mean, no. Not really. You?"

"Same." He let out a whine. "This is totally messing up my hair."

"Quiet!"

Will and I fell silent. However, Ari spoke up. "We are citizens of the United States." They sounded outraged. "We have rights, you fuckfaces! How dare you!"

"I *said,* quiet!" I heard the sound of a muffled slap, and Ari cried out in pain.

I struggled to stand, but someone kicked me in the chest and sent me sprawling back into the seat. "Hey! Don't you hurt anyone!" My outburst also earned me a slap to the face.

We all fell silent for what felt like maybe five minutes. Then, the vehicle stopped, and we were escorted back out into the salty air. It felt like we were on solid ground, but after days of being on a ship, it was hard to tell.

We were walked across more hard ground, then escorted up a ramp that sounded metal. I was pushed into a seat, and straps were put over my shoulders. I felt like I was probably on a plane.

"Hello?"

"Quiet." Another order. But we were all bad at following directions.

One by one, everyone checked in. Except for Zeke.

"Where's Zeke?" Will sounded panicked. "Where's my husband?"

"He's with the general." A woman's crisp voice sounded. "He's in safe hands, I assure you."

"If you've met the general, you know he's not," Will snapped back.

"He wouldn't hurt his own son, would he?" I asked. "He seemed kind of sad that Zeke didn't trust him to tell him he was in major trouble."

'Well, the fact that Zeke is a wanted felon is probably a reason as well, Jake."

"We'll be okay, right?" Jordan gently rubbed his shoulder on mine in reply to my question.

"Ladies and gentlemen, my name is Dr. Stokes." A woman's voice sounded out. I could hear footsteps, so it sounded like she was pacing back and forth. The loud roar of engines confirmed we were indeed on a plane. I guess we must have docked somewhere and been driven to the airport.

Dr. Stokes continued. "We have reason to believe you may have been exposed to a biochemical weapon, or some kind of contagion. We're going to be taking blood samples from all of you."

"The fuck you are," Ari said. "You have no right to take our blood. And I'm not a lady or a gentleman, so use more inclusive language, bitch."

"We have every right to determine if you are spreading a disease to others," Dr. Stokes replied. "Please hold still while we draw blood."

I felt the plane begin to taxi. *Is now really the best time to be taking our blood?* But she went ahead.

She got to me, and I felt a cool swab on my left arm. She tied the band around my arm and began poking with her fingers for my veins.

"They're shy." I was trying to keep the mood as light as possible. "People usually have a hard time finding my veins. My right arm is better."

"I can't get to your right arm in your wetsuit." But, after a few moments of her trying to find my vein, she sighed. "I'm going to need you to unzip your suit and show me your right arm."

"You know, it would actually be lovely if I could get out of it entirely. It's... chaffing."

I heard her mutter to someone, and footsteps receded.

"I'll get back to you."

She moved along, and I heard Spencer suck in air to calm himself.

"I hate needles," Spencer's whine almost sounded like a five-year-old's.

"I hear it's better if you don't see it," I said.

"I can still feel it. Noooooooo."

"Just breathe." Dr. Stokes tried to sound soothing, and I heard Spencer moan slightly.

"You better not be working with Vostell on any of this," Jordan warned. "The CEO wants us captured. You're playing right into his hands if you're giving him what he wants."

Nobody responded as the plane sped up and took off. I hated not being able to see what was happening. It's not like I enjoyed looking out of the window of the plane anyway, but still.

I don't know how long went by before I heard two soldiers approach.

"You. In the wetsuit. We have new clothes for you."

"Awesome. Um, how's that going to work with me wearing a hood and handcuffs?"

"Yeah, you gonna at least buy him a drink, first?" Will's voice sounded from nearby. "He doesn't undress for just anyone, you know."

"Quiet!"

The soldiers unstrapped me from the seat and helped me walk somewhere else on the plane. It wasn't until we got several steps away that they removed my hood and handcuffs.

The soldiers standing in front of me were blocking most of my view, but they were both decidedly... large. They were taller than me, sure, but they filled the space they'd brought me to very well.

Great. The strong, muscular army men were going to watch me strip down to my underwear and put on...

"A hospital gown?" I held up the folded cloth they offered me. "Please tell me you're not expecting me to sit on this freezing cold plane in nothing but my underwear and a paper gown?"

"It's all I could find."

"Please. There's got to be scrubs or an extra uniform or something that's a little warmer, right?"

The soldiers glanced at each other, then the one with the darker hair rolled his eyes. "I *do* have some civvies he could borrow."

"I mean, I'm sure Ari and Will would also like to change out of their wetsuits if you have anything."

The dark-haired soldier cleared his throat. "Look, I've got some extra uniforms I can see about, but we're really not supposed to be talking to you guys or helping you out. Wait here."

"Thank you."

The soldier left, leaving me with the other one, who had dark eyes.

"So... where we goin'?" I asked casually.

"I'll put this on again." He held up the hood.

I fell silent. Soon, the soldier returned with a pair of jeans and a red t-shirt.

"Thank you." I stared at them for a moment. "Um, could I get some privacy?"

"No. We're not taking out eyes off you."

I sighed and began stripping. It wasn't as bad as I thought it would be. I still felt humiliated to be undressing in front of some buff soldiers who were probably judging my body.

Or, more likely, they didn't care, and all the judgment was in my head.

Once I was wearing the soldier's civilian clothes, they immediately handcuffed me and hooded me again, taking me back to the others.

"Which one is Will, and which one is Ari?"

They both responded, and the guards took them away to change out of their wetsuits. Minutes later, we heard more footsteps, and they came back.

"Everybody okay?"

We all responded we were. Then, we were all silent. All we could do was wait. Wait to live, or wait to die, I guess.

I found that if I tilted my head back, a little light came through the neck of the hood, which allowed me to differentiate between having my eyes open and having them closed.

I didn't remember falling asleep. But I was suddenly unhooded, back in the cave with who I thought was Luriana. But, looking at them, I noticed they were different. The end of the tendrils on their head weren't white, but vivid, emerald green. And while they had four eyes, they also were a different shape than Luriana's.

We were sitting across from each other, the five fragments in a circle between us, with the sixth fragment in the middle of them.

"You. You're the one I saw before. On the plane. You told me to find you."

They shrugged. "I gave you my best directions. I told you sand and human buildings."

I held out my hands pleadingly. "There are so many places on the planet that have sand and human buildings. I could literally spend the rest of my life searching for you."

"You could if you are content with Benedetti getting to the Omnia Fragment before you."

I leaned forward. "He knows where it is?"

"He is much physically closer to it than you are."

"How can you tell?"

The being tapped their head with one of their three fingers. So odd to see a human motion performed by an alien. "I have been reaching out to him, just as I have been reaching out to you."

I gasped. "Why? Why in the world would you do that? He wants the fragment for the power he can have over others!"

"The people on the planet need someone with this power who can lead, and who can do so effectively."

I let out a noise of disgust. "Sure, if by 'lead,' you mean 'be a tyrant.' We've seen the type of leading he does. He kills people who get in his way."

"Yet, he is closer to the goal than you are."

I flipped my hands in the air. "What the fuck ever. We're supposed to accept the fact that he could get the Omnia Fragment before us?"

They tilted their head to the side. "So, *you* desire the power."

"No. I want the power kept away from him."

It was the alien's turn to look frustrated. "Humans divided this power in the first place. You have broken yourselves into factions over it, yet the power is the same. You must find a way to work together to prepare for the challenges to come."

"We can never work together. He murdered Jordan's parents."

The alien sat up straight. "Then you have already lost. Benedetti has at least offered to work with you."

"Under *his* conditions."

Closing their eyes, they shook their head. "You have no idea what is to come."

"Then tell me!"

They opened their eyes at once, the black hourglass pupils seeming to suck me into the darkness. "The end."

And I was suddenly in complete, pitch-black nothingness. Except... no. Stars. I was in... outer space? I was floating in space with the alien.

Then, just as I realized I was in space, I saw Earth.

"Tell me what you see."

I focused. "Ocean, continents, clouds... I see how beautiful the planet is."

"You are realizing the bigger picture. Good. You are one of eight billion people on this planet. Benedetti is another. So are Jordan, and Lex. Ari. Will. David. Zeke. You all have so much in common. More than you realize. Your squabbles between each other are all meaningless except for one—the fight over who gets the Omnia Fragment."

Looking at it, I found myself realizing how small I was in the grand scheme of things. Our fight with Benedetti is one of millions—billions of fights on a daily basis.

Some of the fights have been wars that involved the entire world. Some are between lovers, friends, or family. Some were stupid, like when my parents used to bicker over who an actor was in a movie. But even those kinds of arguments tell us something about ourselves.

It's not that we want to be right. It's that we want to matter. We want our voice, our opinion, our very existence, to make a difference.

I turned to the alien. "I… I guess I don't understand. Why are you helping Benedetti if he wants the power for himself?"

"He wants the power to change the world," they said softly. "Those with the power to help have a responsibility to do so. Otherwise, what is the meaning of your lives? Having the most money? Having the biggest armies? Being the mightiest warrior? Those with power on Earth wield it over others, instead of reaching out to others. Benedetti's methods are cruel, but his ultimate intention is to indeed make the world a better place. Would you do the same with that power, or would you lock it away, hide it, ensure no one ever discovers it?"

I was at a loss for words. They were saying Benedetti was right, and that I was wrong? But… Benedetti talked about wanting to plant crops, stop severe storms. But he also talked about military might, and I didn't agree with that. The Keepers shouldn't be used as pawns of the government to go to war against other countries. We should be reaching out to them.

"So, you're saying… if Benedetti becomes the Primarch, we should follow him because he has better intentions than we do?"

"Yes."

I inhaled deeply. "If one of us was the Primarch, would he follow us?"

"No."

I shook my head. "The hypocrisy. It's ... unreal. Don't you get it? He's evil!"

"His actions are morally questionable. As have been yours."

"Only because he forced my hand!"

"You could not have found an alternative to destroying the bridge?"

"I..." There were no words that could explain my decisions, other than fear.

The alien seemed to know what I was thinking. "The solution is not peace, and it is not domination over the other—however you define 'the other.' It is unity as a race. You need a leader that will bring all of humankind together as never before. It is essential."

"Jake."

My eyes snapped open, and I was suddenly aware that I was still in a seat, strapped in, and hooded. It was like I'd had a shot of adrenaline rush through me.

"Gah! What?"

"You've been out for hours. You didn't even wake up when we landed the first time. We're about to land again." Jordan's voice had an edge to it. "I think that's our final stop. Are you okay?"

"I... I had another vision."

I heard Spencer gasp. "You have visions, too? My dad—"

"What did you see?"

I sighed. "Benedetti's close to the fragment. And, the being said if... if he gets it, we should follow him."

The others chimed in with their own thoughts.

"Fuck that."

"Not gonna happen."

"That alien can literally kiss my ass."

"Listen up." A woman's voice rang out and we all fell silent. *You know, we should probably scrap the alien talk in front of all the government officials.* "We're back in the continental United States. It is now eight o'clock Saturday morning. This is your last chance for a bathroom break or questions."

"I have a question." Will spoke quickly. "If I got married on top of the Mariana Trench by someone who can legally perform weddings in the United States, is that marriage legal, or do I have to plan all that shit again?"

I heard a few snickers, and I don't think they were from our group.

"That's not something I know, but congratulations," she replied. "Now, bathroom breaks. Let's go. And you. I still need a blood sample."

The soldiers began to escort everyone who needed it to the bathroom while the doctor began trying to find a visible vein on my arms again. I nudged Spencer to my right.

"You said your dad had visions?" He didn't say anything. "Spencer?"

"Oh, sorry. I was nodding, but you obviously can't see. Yeah. He kept saying a being was calling to him, but he didn't know from where."

"I wish I knew." I wet my lips. "How have things been with your dad since all this started?"

He was silent for a moment. "You know, I've heard Jordan's name for years. Dad made him sound like some pompous, punk know-it-all who was always one step ahead. It pissed him off, especially because his company was basically funding the Keepers and Dad still didn't have the fragments to show for it. Then, when you came along, it was Jake, destroyer of all the plans, ruiner of everything. But... when we met in San Francisco, you were kind. And I've... I've never really had that."

"You don't talk about your mom. Oooooh, you got me." The doctor had successfully found a vein and pierced my flesh.

"I don't have a mom. He said she died giving birth to me. He's had plenty of women try to get close to him, but he didn't want any of them. The closest thing I had to a mom growing up was a live-in babysitter, and he would replace them every few years, so I didn't get too attached."

"I'm surprised you didn't rebel against him," Ari commented. "You know, spend his money and go out partying and stuff."

Spencer laughed bitterly. "I guess... I thought if I tried to be who he wanted me to be, he would... well, whatever. I thought... it doesn't matter. Either he'll find out I betrayed him, or he'll find out if we ever get out of here. I'm not going back. I knew sending me to infiltrate *The Ashland* was a one-way trip."

"Really?" I was shocked at what I was hearing. "I mean, he didn't have a plan for you and what's-her-face to escape?"

"No. He told us we'd be able to escape on our own if we did our jobs right."

"That's some bullshit," I heard David say. "He doesn't care about the people who work for him, but you're his kid. Didn't he expect you to take over for him once he was too old?"

"I think he expected to get..." Spencer seemed to remember soldiers were listening to everything we were saying. "I think he was expecting a miracle to occur, and he'd never have to worry about it."

I knew what he meant. Benedetti expected to be the Primarch, and apparently become immortal or something.

"We're gearing up for take-off," the woman called out. "Last chance for the bathroom."

"I'll go," I said. I didn't need to go, but it would be nice to walk around for a minute, even if I was being escorted everywhere.

Once I'd dribbled out some pee, and was settled back in my seat, we took off again. I don't know how long we flew. Hours. We could have been flying in circles for all I knew.

I was surprised with how calm I felt. I guess I still felt a sense of comfort that, somehow, the U.S. government was going to get things figured out. Maybe that was my privilege talking.

Finally, the plane landed—no idea where. We could have been anywhere. As we were marched off the plane, all I could tell was that the air was dry and hot, and even the breeze seemed to be superheated.

We were walked inside somewhere, our footsteps echoing off the walls. We stopped, there was a ding sound, and I was directed forward, hearing other footsteps shuffling around me. There was another ding, and I felt the pull in my stomach that told me we were in an elevator, going down.

"So, what's everyone's favorite color?" Will had apparently decided to break the tense silence.

No one answered for a moment, then I shrugged. "I like blue. Not dark blue, but light blue."

"Purple." I was surprised Lex chose now to say anything, given how silent she'd been the whole trip.

"Green." The voice was unfamiliar, and I heard a motion like somebody hitting somebody else. "Ow. What?"

"We're not supposed to talk to them, Collins," Dr. Stokes admonished.

"Sorry."

The elevator dinged, and we were marched out again. The air was cool, and the floor was shiny and smooth. We walked up and down a few ramps, went through some doors, turned a bunch of different ways, and then, just as I was getting annoyed that they were disorienting us on purpose, I heard the footsteps of the others fade away, and it was me and maybe one or two people walking down hallways.

"Where's everyone else?" I asked, but no one answered this time.

Finally, we walked through a final door, which made a sort of hissing noise as it opened. I was guided inside and forced to sit down on a hard surface. Something poked my sides. It was a chair with arms.

The handcuffs around my hands were undone, then both of my wrists were handcuffed to the chair arms.

I'd had this done once before, and a jolt of fear ran through me that we were actually flown to some secret government torture facility, and I was going to be tortured again. I wasn't a fan of the first time, and there was no way the Keepers could break in and rescue me.

Finally, my hood was removed.

I squinted as I took in a bright light shining in my face. I could make out a big window I couldn't see through, and a table with a chair on the other side.

An interrogation room. Great.

"Wait here." Collins and the other soldier walked out of the room, closing the door behind them.

It's not like I can go anywhere. "Thank you." Maybe using my manners would get me less tortured?

I started thinking about all the movies I'd seen where there had been interrogations. Would there be a good cop and a bad cop? Someone who chats with me like a friend? Would there be food? Could I ask for some? Should I?

My thoughts were interrupted as the door opened, and an older man with a lot of decorations on his dark green uniform entered and sat down across from me, holding several folders. He had a dark grey moustache, but his hair was white.

As he sat down, I could make out that he was shuffling papers around in a folder until he found the one he was looking for, then closed the folder and set the paper carefully on top.

"Jake." His slight southern accent seemed right on par with his weathered skin and small scar on his forehead. I don't know why that made sense to me, but it did. "My name is General Eric Breckenridge. I'm in charge here."

I nodded and gave a small smile. "Nice to meet you."

"Bullshit," he said, leaning back and intertwining his hands on the table. "You're scared, alone, and completely at my mercy. You are not happy to see me."

I shrugged. "True. I guess it's just a habit to be nice."

He didn't say anything to that. "So. I imagine you've got some questions. But we've got some questions for you, too. How do you think we can help each other?"

I fought the urge to roll my eyes. He was talking to me like a kid, and I *hated* when people did that. Probably because I'd been treated like a kid all my life as the youngest.

I cleared my throat. "Um, how about we take turns asking questions?"

He tilted his head to the side. "You know, that's not a half-bad idea. Of course, the important part of questions is that they have answers. And, since I think we're both fairly busy, we should probably be honest in how we respond, right? Save us some time and hassle."

Again, I didn't roll my eyes, but it was close. "Like you said, I'm at your mercy, so whatever you think is best."

"Mighty kind of you. And, since you seem like you have good manners, I'll use mine and let you have the first question."

I looked around, as if the walls would tell me which of my many questions to ask first. "Um... all the people I came here with—Zeke, Ari, Will, Spencer, Lex, David, and... and Jordan. Are they all okay?"

"They're unharmed. My turn. Says here that you're dead, son. But since I don't believe in ghosts, how is it possible we're having this conversation?"

I sighed. "I was involved in a shooting on the campus of King State University. I was shot, a group of friends took care of me, but other friends didn't know that, and reported me dead. I couldn't do anything about it because I was unconscious. I was going to fix all of it after I got back from vacation. Basically, it's a big misunderstanding."

You really need to get better at lying, Jake.

I couldn't see his face because of the stupid light, but I saw him nod. "A misunderstanding. Hm. Jake, can I ask a follow-up question?"

"Uh, sure."

"Do you expect me to believe that horseshit?"

"Um... yes?"

"Oh, okay." His condescending tone made me feel exactly like a kid when my parents knew I was lying, but were waiting to see what sort of crazy story I could come up with. He wanted to see how stupid I thought he was.

"Now, go ahead and ask me your question."

I didn't know how many questions I'd get, so I'd better make them count.

"Where am I?"

He gave a slight laugh. "You're in an interrogation room."

"I... was thinking a bit less specific?"

"The United States."

"A bit... more specific?"

"Well, that's all the specifics I can give." He leaned forward on one arm. "Next question. What do you know about those artifacts you got in the Mariana Trench?"

I shrugged, knowing he could probably see on my face that I was going to lie again. "I found them on a dive with friends. I thought they were pretty and could be worth money."

"Did you touch them with your bare hands?"

You should point out that you don't have to answer that because it's your turn to ask a question, Jake. No, that would probably be even more idiotic than your story. Play along.

"Yes."

"Anybody else touch 'em?"

"I... I don't know. We surfaced and the Navy confiscated everything."

"Okay, so the fact that you and all your friends have traces of the material those crystals are made up of in your blood is... coincidence?"

Well, no. But I can't talk about that. "Um, I had no idea that was even a thing."

He sniffed theatrically. "Man, it kind of stinks in here, doesn't it? Can you smell that?"

I knew what he was getting at, and I wasn't impressed. "No. Can't smell a thing."

"So, you're not ready to cut through all this bullshit?"

"I thought it was horseshit, sir. And, you've asked four questions in a row, so I feel like I get to do the same."

He laughed. "Oh, you *are* a little smartass. Alright. Go ahead."

His comments had clued me in that maybe, just maybe, he knew exactly what was happening in our DNA and that maybe, just maybe, there was a special place in the U.S. where they dealt with people like us.

"What are some of your daily tasks at this facility?"

He raised an eyebrow. "File paperwork. Give orders. Shower. Shit. Shave. Interrogate people."

There it was. The way he said 'people' answered all my other questions. He knew everything. He knew there was something off about those crystals. Something off about us.

"My turn. Why don't you tell me about yourself? The basics of your birth, where you grew up, what your family and friends might say about you."

He probably thought I was a body snatcher or something. He probably thought I'm an alien dressed up in a Jake West skin suit.

I sighed. "Okay, yeah, the smell of shit is really getting to me. Can I just... confirm some things you probably already know?"

He brought both arms forward, staring intently at me. "Glad you decided to cut through all the shit, bull and horse. What are you?"

"Oh, I'm a human. Like everybody else in our group. Like you. Only... a little different after touching the fragments."

"What are your intentions?"

I spoke before thinking. "Well, I majored in English, and I was almost done with that degree, but then—"

"Smartass gets old after a while. What are your intentions with the humans on planet Earth?"

I thought carefully. "Well, since I was born and raised as a human, and have only known about the fragments and the... differences they create for a few weeks now, I'd say I want to make sure my friends and I aren't accused of being something we're not."

He stroked his mustache. "What differences are we talking about here?"

"You're going to think I'm nuts."

"Don't lie and don't fuck around. Then I'll believe you."

I took a deep breath. "Okay. So, this all starts back in August. There was an explosion, and Jordan saved my life."

I didn't hold back. I talked about everything that had happened up to the point where I entered the cave under the sea where life was, in fact, not better down where it's wetter.

"I had a vision. In the vision, I met one of the aliens responsible for the creation of life on our planet. I think I'm going to get a sixth fragment, instead I get attacked by a piece of shit goblin shark. Our sub gets captured by the Navy, someone posing as a sailor tries to kill me, and now... here we are."

He stared at me for a long time. I tried to maintain unblinking eye contact, but I was too nervous. Finally, he spoke.

"I've spent my life dedicated to this—to finding out if aliens exist." He wasn't talking to me, but more to himself. "And you're telling me that, yes, they do... and we're the aliens?"

I shrugged. "I mean, I guess life after all the dinosaurs are like colonizers. Our creators came to the planet and settled it, but we were born here, so we're technically native, even though our ancestry can be traced back to a whole other planet."

"And how is it you know this?"

"The vision. In the cave."

"Ah, yes, the cave in the Mariana Trench."

I swallowed. "You know about that cave."

Our eyes met, and in that instant, I knew—where the Omnia Fragment was, and who was in possession of it.

The U.S. Government had the Omnia Fragment.

Chapter 13: Parental Choices and Their Effects

"You have it!"

Breckenridge folded his arms across his chest. "I think I'm going to have to be done answering any of your questions. However, you mentioned you gained powers. What exactly does that mean?"

"Power over earth. Others have fire or lightning. Water or air. Do you want me to tell you, or show you?"

He squinted at me. "Seeing is believing, but I also expect to live through the experience."

"Okay... just... don't shoot me or something," I said.

I focused on making vines slowly come out of my fingers. The general watched, waiting, then stood as the vines, like living tendrils, made their way over to the desk between us. He made his way closer to me, grabbing my hand and examining the vines himself.

"Insane... this is insanity!"

"There's also this." The vines receded into my hands as my arms began to grow, larger and larger, until the handcuffs snapped off my hands, which had formed into a sword and shield.

Breckenridge stepped back, and I knew he was threatened. I quickly let my hands revert back to normal hands. I sat there, staring, waiting.

"You broke out of your restraints."

I drummed my fingers. "That's true. That means you know this whole time, I've been able to fight back. All of us have. But, we haven't. Because we're not the enemy. But I can tell you who is."

"And who's that?"

"Sebastian Benedetti. You might know him as Mark Buchanan, the CEO of Vostell. He has powers, too."

"Vostell?" That seemed to get his attention.

"Yeah. From what I understand, he has a lot of close friends in the military. And I also understand he's in some trouble. You might want to watch out for him."

He seemed to ignore me, then moved to the table and began neatly gathering the folders and papers in front of him.

"What are you doing? Is that it?"

"What else is there?" He looked down at me. "You may not like it, but you have alien capabilities that look pretty substantial. I can only imagine what your friends with fire or water can do. That makes you all dangerous. And it's my job to keep dangerous people as far away from our nation's people as possible."

"But... we have lives outside of here! People know who we are, care about us. They'll wonder where we are!"

"Some of you, sure," Breckenridge said. "That can be taken care of. As for you... you're already dead. Makes my job a hell of a lot easier."

"This is bullshit!" I stood up, and in a flash, Breckenridge had his gun pointed at my head.

"Don't make me use this."

I let out a shaky breath. "I mean, please don't. But also, we're not the dangerous ones! Benedetti is. He's the one who wants to use the Omnia Fragment to control the world. We just want to live our lives."

"I've heard enough." Breckenridge turned and opened the door, still pointing his gun at me. "You will get to live your lives. Here. Welcome home."

He slammed the door after him. I stood, stunned.

"Well, shit."

I sat down in the chair again, fidgeting. What were they going to do with us? Did we seriously mean 'welcome home?' I had no idea where 'here' was. And what was he going to do with Benedetti?

Please don't let him bring Benedetti here. Please don't be a friend of his or something.

I jumped when the door opened, and guards came in to escort me to another room. The fact I told the truth had apparently earned me a heavily-armed escort of six. *What fun.*

Now that I didn't have a hood on, I could see the facility in greater detail. The floor and hallways were all made of the same large, white square tiles.

As we walked, I realized the facility was likely underground, but also rectangular in shape. To my right, about every fifty feet, there was a hallway, but the hallways were fairly short and ended at what looked like an identical hallway to the one I was being walked down.

This all seems so excessive. Did my tax dollars really pay for all this expensive lighting? I'm definitely going to be writing to... well, a bunch of political people when... well, if *I ever get out of here.*

As we turned a corner, a sliding door opened with a hiss, and General McCormack walked out, flanked by more riot-gear guards and—

"Zeke!"

He turned and wrapped his arms around me. He seemed like he was okay, but exhausted. His dad held up his hands to calm the guards, who all tightened their grips on their weapons as we embraced.

"It's so good to see you." I took a deep, shuddering breath. "I was worried."

"It's good to see you, too." He gave a sideways look at his dad. "I've been talking with Dad about everything. There's a lot more at play here, Jake."

"I told everything to the general I was questioned by. Like, *everything*."

Zeke nodded. "The truth seems to be the way to go. My dad didn't believe me until I showed him what I could do."

"If you'd prefer, we can take you somewhere else to chat," Zeke's dad said.

I deferred to Zeke, who nodded. General McCormack smiled, a real, genuine smile, and I realized how much he looked like Zeke when he did.

"Follow me."

Zeke and I followed the general and six guards, while the other six followed me and Zeke. I heard a musical theme from one of my favorite movies in my head as I was escorted by the men dressed all in black, with large, black helmets.

Of course, that definitely made me the princess in this situation. So, yay.

As we marched, General McCormack spoke, his voice echoing, yet sounding strangely close in the tight quarters.

"Jake, this facility is home to the most advanced technology available. That means we're able to make a lot of scientific and military breakthroughs right here. In fact, this is where we first discovered the existence of what you call the fragments."

We walked through a door on the left, a huge storage room with a rather low ceiling. The floor was made of marbled concrete, and the lighting was more minimalistic. I couldn't see where the room ended.

There were some things in glass cases—papers, what looked like a few journals, some rocks, and—

"Oh my God."

Zeke's dad beckoned us forward to see what was in one of the glass cases. Supported by several spindly metal rods, was a piece of green, swirling crystal about the size of a half-dollar.

"This thing has been in the government's possession since 1863," he said. "It was found during the construction of the Transcontinental Railroad."

"I never knew the Fragment of Terra had a piece missing." I took in Zeke's expression, which said he didn't, either.

"We have the larger piece in a safe place now, but our tests confirm they're exactly the same. This appears to be a piece of the larger fragment."

"Where are they?" I asked. "We need to know they're safe."

"They're safe." General McCormack was being vague on purpose. "When we found your bag of crystals, we identified the one, and four more like it. They've been sealed with only top-level security clearance. But right now, we're looking at unraveling one of the biggest mysteries of all time."

"Next, we get to figure out who *actually* killed JFK." I laughed but quickly stopped as a few of the men behind us bristled, and only Zeke smiled. McCormack led us out the room and continued talking.

"After your meeting with Breckenridge, we met with our commanders. As far as we can figure out, you are all one-hundred percent human, only with fantastic genetics."

"You don't think we're aliens?"

"I'm not sure about the others, but I don't." He shot a quick glance at Zeke. "I know my son isn't some kind of alien. I taught him how to ride a bike and raised him alone after his mother died."

Zeke seemed to bite his tongue. I had no idea how difficult this was for him.

"What's going to happen from here?" I asked. "Do we seriously have to stay here? And where *is* here, anyway?"

"That's classified."

"What is?"

"Everything you just asked me."

"You literally can't tell me what you're going to do with me?"

He shook his head. "No."

"Well, that's... fucking bullshit. Sir."

Zeke gave me an 'are you crazy' look.

"Mr. West, you're lucky you're not bound and gagged with a hood over your face in a noiseless room." He clenched his jaw.

"I mean, yeah, but that's not my point. You can find us all up. Social media. Pictures, Emails. Credit scores. Dick pics, I'm sure in some cases." I glanced at Zeke, knowing we were both thinking of Will. "I mean, we were all born and raised with families and friends. You can't take us away from our lives and expect there not to be consequences."

"We're fully prepared to deal with any backlash." His voice was more of a growl. "You may have been harmless before, but now that we know you've been in contact with alien artifacts that have given you powers, we don't have the luxury of assuming non-hostility."

I stopped walking and everyone else followed suit. "What, am I supposed to say, 'take me to your leader, earthling?'"

General McCormack sighed and folded his arms across his chest.

"'Cause I will."

"Don't."

I mirrored his posture, and we stared each other down.

"Oh, let's play nice, shall we?" Zeke patted each of us on the shoulder. "Jake, we *are* lucky to be able to talk without bags over our faces. Dad? Think about it logically. The only one in our group who's a wanted felon is me. And that was for stuff before I even came into contact with the fragments. So, we're not all dangerous criminals, and we shouldn't be treated like it."

His father unfolded his arms and seemed to resign himself.

"Look, you can understand why we're taking precautions, right?"

"Absolutely. I totally get it." I put my hands out in a sort of pleading gesture. "This is all new to me, too. So, what I'd love most of all is to be trusted when I say that Sebastian Benedetti is a dangerous man, and everyone in this facility needs to be put on alert."

"So, Benedetti is the threat? He's the one who caused the collapse in King, Idaho? The bridge collapse in San Francisco?"

"I mean, the bridge thing in San Francisco was us being attacked and defending ourselves from him. But he totally did cause the cave-in of our home in King, which caused the... the collapse."

But as I said it, I knew it wasn't that simple. I had caused the collapse of Sanctuary by bringing the ceiling down. Vic had done it too, so I knew it wasn't all me, but I was at least partly to blame for the sinkhole.

He frowned. "So, you're saying this Benedetti is the CEO of Vostell? And he's the dangerous one?"

"Yes. He has powers like me, but they're way more advanced. He can turn his whole body into diamond and stuff. I know that Vostell has worked with the military in the past, and I wouldn't be surprised if he has connections in Washington or something."

"I'm sure he's donated to plenty of senate and presidential campaigns, but that doesn't influence my work."

"You sure? Or does it actually make sense to you to send a dozen heavily-armed Navy warships and submarines after a tiny sub with no weapons?"

The general let out a noise of complaint and looked at Zeke. "Is he always like this?"

Zeke shrugged. "I've known him for a month. But... I think he's right, and I think you know that. When he's right, he does tend to get a little... bitchy."

I tsked at Zeke's comment but didn't deny it. "Anyway, I'm also concerned about my friends. You're not running tests on them, are you?"

"No. On their blood samples, sure, but not on them. Your friends have all been returned to a dormitory while we conclude the tests. That's where we're heading now. Zeke, if you'd like, we can continue to talk." Zeke inhaled slowly, then nodded. His dad smiled. "These men will take you from here."

"Thanks, Zeke." I pulled him into another hug. "It sounds like you're saving the day."

He barked out a laugh. "Yeah, we'll see."

We split up, the six Machine Gun Vaders walking me to another door down the hallway and several more sloping ramps down. When we arrived at our destination, one of the guards pressed a keycard or something against a panel, and the door hissed and slid open.

I caught a glimpse of twelve beds and a few people in the room before I was crushed into a hug.

"Jake! Oh my God, are you okay? We thought they were torturing you or something."

Jordan pulled away, holding me at arm's length, his eyes watery. Lex, David, Will, Spencer, and Ari all gathered behind him.

"I'm okay. They didn't torture me. But I told them everything."

"You gave up our secrets without even a little bit of torture?" Will raised an eyebrow and pursed his lips. "Even I would have lasted under some pressure."

"They already knew. The one general thinks we're all aliens or something, but Zeke's dad knows we're not and they're running tests on our blood to confirm it."

"You ran into Zeke's dad? Was Zeke with him?" All of Will's attitude was gone.

I nodded. "He's okay. They're talking."

"He should be with me instead. He's probably trying to get us all released. He shouldn't have to do that alone. We even said we'd tell his dad we got married when we got back. Somehow."

"Zeke's not alone. He knows you're there with him in spirit."

Will began pacing. "I bet we could break out of here. David could fry all their electronics, or if I built up enough—"

"Stop." Lex looked at the camera in the corner significantly.

"I don't care." Will spoke through gritted teeth. "They can't lock us up. We didn't do anything wrong!"

"Dude, you know that's not true." David walked over to him and sympathetically patted his back. "I mean, Zeke sort of forged his father's credentials. That's a big military breach. He should answer for—"

But Will had heard enough. Clasping his hands together, he spun quickly with his arms outstretched. His fists connected with David's face, sending him flying backward and crashing into a wall.

"*Puta Perra*! Zeke has already answered to his father enough! He threw him through a plate glass window and down the stairs after he found out he was gay. Zeke spent a month in the hospital recovering. And because his father is a military man, nothing happened. He was fifteen years old and could never go home. So, he lived on the streets of San Francisco, dealing, stealing, and tricking to finish school. His dad didn't even show up to his graduation, or court when he got busted. *Don't* tell me what he has to answer for. He's already been through enough."

He glared around, breathing hard, as if challenging anyone to make him feel better. But as much as he was staring at all of us in anger, it became clear it was fueled by pain. His eyes began to water, and he burst into tears, coving his face with his hands.

David stood, wiping his bloody nose and walking toward him. To my surprise, he gathered Will into a hug. Will stiffened at first, then wrapped his arms around him. David patted him on the back soothingly.

"I'm sorry, Davey," Will muttered into David's chest.

"'S'all good." David's face already bruising.

Will pulled away, dabbing at his eyes and trying to compose himself. Then, he looked around at all of us staring.

"What? You've never seen a queen cry before?" We all laughed a little.

"If Stonewall taught us anything, it's to never piss of a minority queen," David said.

Will laughed in amazement. "You know about Stonewall?"

David nodded and shrugged. Will stared at him for a moment, then turned to Lex, who was standing next to me. "Lex, I love you honey, but you're a fucking *idiota*."

Lex looked between David and Will, clearly torn, but then turned away.

"So... what do we do now?" I asked. I walked over to the nearest bed and sat slowly. "I mean, do we wait?"

"We could play I-Spy," Will suggested. "I spy with my little eye... something scared shitless."

We laughed nervously.

"Did you find out anything about the Omnia Fragment?" Spencer asked.

"Not really," I said, "but I know they have the other fragments here, and the general I talked to knew about the cave in the Mariana Trench. So, I think they know the location of the fragment. The general got all dodgy when I told him I thought the fragment was here."

Jordan's jaw dropped. "What if... what if it *is* here?"

"When we got to the cave, the fragments started humming and being all swirly and stuff." Then, it hit me. "Wait—the Fragment of Terra! They already had a piece of it. I saw it! And it was all glowy and swirly and stuff. I think that means the Omnia Fragment is nearby."

"We need to find it." Ari looked at all of us. "Benedetti has connections with a lot of government people. Vostell has been contracted by the government a lot. Wherever we are, he could already be on his way here."

Spencer nodded in agreement, then turned to me. "Back before we got here, you said something about visions. What were they about?"

I frowned. "They all involve an alien. Like, I'm having a dream but the alien interrupts to tell me to come find it. When we were in the trench, it told me I was far away, and Benedetti was closer."

"Closer to what?"

"It. The alien."

Jordan sighed and sat down. "Maybe we've been going about this all wrong. Maybe we need to find this alien before we can find the fragment."

"It's a Voranah."

"What?"

"That's what the alien race is called. The Voranah. And, from what Luriana said, they wouldn't send Voranah to Earth to, like, capture or abduct people or something. Other aliens would, sure, but not the Voranah."

Spencer blinked and shook his head. "Other aliens? Like, there are more aliens that exist out there besides the Voranah?"

I nodded. "We didn't get into it much because Luriana freaked out when I said the Praetorian had been trying to contact me."

"What's a Praetorian?"

"Dunno."

We fell silent, thinking. Finally, as I mulled over the conversation, bits and pieces began to surface. I snapped my fingers. "They fled a war on their planet. There were a lot of them, but only the six with powers survived. What if the war resolved, but the power over all the elements was lost to them? What if they sent someone from their planet to ours to get the fragment and reclaim the power?"

Spencer frowned. "You're saying if we find the alien, they might be able to track where the fragment is?"

I nodded, licking my lips. "But there's still the problem that Luriana said no one was ready to be the Primarch."

Jordan glanced around. "If they can hear us in here, they need to know that one of us has to touch the fragment to gain power over all the other elements. But Benedetti could gain it as well, and with how powerful he already is, they wouldn't be able to stop him from taking over the United States... or even the world."

I shook my head. "I know... we talked about this back in San Francisco, but even Luriana thinks Benedetti wants to change the world for the better. I mean, it's his skewed version of what better means, but still. They actually made it sound like we were wrong to hide the powers away."

Jordan raised his eyebrows. "Yeah, because exposing the fact that we have powers has landed us in such a great position here."

"I'm just repeating Luriana." I tried to avoid another fight by sounding as meek as possible.

"We need you to have another vision." Spencer stared at me.

I adjusted my head on my neck, looking around at everybody else. "Nobody else has had visions? Aliens that talk to them in their dreams? A dream you know is a dream?"

They all shook their heads. I sighed.

"I mean, how does it work?"

"I don't exactly choose when I have a vision. It just happens. And it doesn't happen every time I sleep, so I honestly don't know."

Spencer nodded. "Well, maybe if you try to fall asleep here, you'll have a vision? I mean, what else have we got to lose?"

Shrugging, I ran my hands through my hair. "I have no idea if I even *could* sleep."

"I could knock you out if you want," Will suggested as he sat on the end of a cot.

I rolled my eyes. "So sweet. No thanks."

"I don't mean like hitting you or something. More like making you pass out so you can fall asleep."

"I'd kind of like to try it naturally first. If I need your help, I'll holler."

He cracked his knuckles and laid on the cot. "Suit yourself."

I made my way over to a bed in the corner and laid down. Of course, all I was thinking was *fall asleep, have a vision, and hurry up about it,* so it took me a long time to actually find myself ready to rest.

Sure enough, I was suddenly standing in the middle of a blazing desert, the brightness and heat making my eyes water. When I looked around, shielding my face from the harsh glare of the sun, I saw the Praetorian.

I frowned. "I need answers."

"I cannot help you."

"Tell me where you are. How do I get to you?"

"You are close. So close. But I cannot tell you how to get to me. This is the last place I saw before I entered my stasis."

"Stasis? You're not awake?"

The Praetorian nodded. "I am aware enough of my surroundings to know I was taken to a desert location by humans. But from there, I do not know. Please, help me. You are so close to saving me."

"Saving you? I thought you were in hiding or something."

"I am in hiding. From my people and from yours. But once you find me and save me, they will both know."

"They'll know what?"

The Praetorian stared me in the face. "They will know what is coming."

"Jake."

I gasped and sat up to find Jordan standing over me. "What?"

He stared, wide-eyed. "I literally whispered your name to wake you up. Um, we have some visitors."

I looked up to find a woman in a lab coat and about two dozen Machine Gun Vaders walk in.

"Folks, I'm Dr. Bridget Stokes, and I've completed an examination of all your bloodwork. I'm going to divide you into three groups, and you will be taken in for some basic tests." She was the woman who had taken our blood on the plane.

"What kind of tests?" Ari asked.

"Coordination, eye movement, reflexes... that kind of thing." Dr Stokes flipped through her clipboard and then started calling out names. "I need the siblings over here. They're group alpha. Then Alexandria, William, and Ezekiel are group Beta. And over here, I need Jacob, David, and Aurora."

We all eyed each other, confused.

"Um, Dr. Stokes? No one here is related."

Her eyebrows shot up. She glanced at her chart, then at us again.

"Yes, there are. Last names... Bailey and Benedetti."

Chapter 14: Two Worlds Collide

Jordan and Spencer stared at each other, eyes and mouths wide. They weren't alone. My stomach was on fire, and an odd rushing sound filled my ears.

"... Jasper?" Jordan's eyes were glassy, but Spencer's were dry.

"Everyone, get into your groups, please." Dr. Stokes had an edge to her voice.

"Lady, calm your tits," Ari said. "Nobody knew they were related, including them."

"They can take a moment to adjust while they're standing over there." But she gestured to a nearby soldier, who nodded and discreetly left.

Spencer's jaw was clenched. "Doctor, are you sure? How are we related?"

"You're siblings."

"Full siblings? Or half-siblings?"

"You're full siblings."

Spencer frowned. "But... that means Benedetti is your father."

Jordan slowly shook his own head. "No... it means Benedetti *isn't* yours."

They both continued shaking their heads at each other.

It was all I could do to not run over to both of them. In a way, when I'd first met Spencer, I'd felt a connection of some kind. At the time, I thought it was because he was a Terra. Maybe it had been because he was Jordan's brother.

"Well, let's get to it." Dr. Stokes clearly wanted to move on. "Each group will be taken for tests at a different time. Group Alpha will be questioned first, then Group Beta, then Group Charlie. In the meantime, you will stay here. It will take however long it's going to take. And you will be provided any necessary medical care, as well as with nourishment." She walked towards the door but stopped and looked back at Jordan and Spencer. "I am sorry you were unaware, and sorry to drop that on you. It was not my intention. Come with me, please."

Jordan and Spencer, still pale and in shock, followed her out of the door, along with all the remaining soldiers.

"Well, what the fuck?" Will pointed after them. "Is Jordan right? Does that mean that Benedetti lied to Spencer, or... did Jordan's parents lie to him?"

I shrugged. "Benedetti lies a lot, so it would make sense that he lied about being Spencer's birth father. Or, maybe there was some deal where Benedetti handed his kids over to Jordan's parents and then... tried to get rid of them all?"

We fell silent at all the prospect of what could possibly have happened to these two in the past, and what could happen to them now as they were reunited.

Hours went by. There were no clocks, so I had no idea how many hours. We sat, making small talk on the cots, or sleeping, or—in Will's case—pacing incessantly.

"Hey." I patted the cot next to me after his millionth lap, and Will sat down. "You know, Zeke did seem okay. And he agreed to keep talking to his dad."

"I'm sure he felt pressured to do so to keep us alive." He sighed and slumped. "I know you and Jordan are new, but Zeke and I have been together for three years. And I... I'm so lucky to have him, Quakey Jakey. I'm worried about what his dad is saying to him... or what Zeke is sacrificing to keep us all safe."

I wrapped my arm around him, but he quickly shrugged it off and wiped his eyes. "Nope. Not gonna cry. Not again. God, I've done enough crying. I'm going to get some sleep."

Not too long after Will had laid down, Dr. Stokes returned with Jordan and Spencer. I took in their red faces and gritted teeth. Spencer was breathing heavily.

"We need Alexandria and William, please."

"What about Zeke?"

"He'll meet us there." Dr. Stokes gestured impatiently at Lex and Will. They walked out the door and it closed with a hissing sound.

"Hey." I followed Spencer as he and Jordan made their way to opposite sides of the room. "Can... can I do anything?"

"Yeah, make us not related," Spencer snapped.

"All I did was offer to tell him about our parents!"

"And I said there's no 'our!'"

"Spencer, just—"

"That piece of shit has been lying to me for the past twenty-five years," Spencer yelled, and we all jumped at his intense rage. "I want to find him and rip his fucking throat out!"

"Me, too." I stayed away from him. I didn't know what he was like when he was angry. "We're here for you."

"I don't *need* you," he roared, gesturing at me. "I don't need *anyone*! I didn't have anyone when I was born, or when I was growing up, so what makes that different from now?"

"We're here for you *now*," I whispered.

"I mean, to know that my father isn't my father... to know my entire beginning in this world was a lie... to make me *hate* my own b-brother..." He was breathing quickly, and I was afraid he was going to hyperventilate. "He knew... he *knew*! The-the whole time, and I never felt good enough... or strong enough... or l-loved..."

He sank to the floor, sobbing. Before I could step forward, Jordan was there, his arms wrapped firmly around his brother. Spencer hit his arm a few times, but accepted the hug.

"You're not alone," Jordan choked out, tears falling down his face. "He lied to me, too. I thought you were dead. This whole time... you're here. You're okay. You're here."

And they held each other. I cried as I watched the brothers find solace for the first time in a family they never had.

Hours later, we were all simply lounging on cots. I was staring at the ceiling when Lex and Will returned from their tests. David, Ari, and I left to go do our tests.

It was like getting a physical. They assessed our reflexes, our eye movement, breathing... It reminded me of when I was in the hospital at the end of August—over a month ago—after the explosion at Casa Pasta.

Then they asked us questions and had us stare at blobs and describe what we see. I sure hoped I passed, because the majority of the blobs looked like a cow's face to me.

It was like they were evaluating us to not only make sure we were sane, but that we knew all the things a normal human should.

Finally, we were escorted back to the room, where I found Spencer and Jordan sitting on a cot facing each other, talking quietly. I made myself scarce and went and laid down.

"Did you see Zeke?" Will asked me. I shook my head, and he let out a moan and slapped his thighs. "Well, they said we were in the same group, but he didn't do any of the tests with us. You didn't see him at all?"

"No. I'm sorry, Will."

"Well... fuck a duck." He stomped off to sit broodily on his own bed.

I guess I fell asleep, because I was stirred gently awake by Jordan crawling into the bed beside me and spooning me. He kissed the back of my neck several times, and I breathed a sigh of contentment.

"How is he?"

Jordan's breath tickled the hairs on my neck as he answered. "I told him everything I knew about our parents. I have a storage unit that has a lot of my—our parent's things in it, so... I dunno. When we get out this, things are going to be so different. I mean, he has a different name, a different social security number. A different birthday."

"Really? Benedetti couldn't even give him the same birthday?"

"No. My brother—Jasper—was born on April 28th. Benedetti had him celebrating his birthday on December 21st."

"Why?"

"Probably to be a cheap-ass piece of shit and combine it with Christmas. According to Spencer, anyway. Oh, and he said if we get out of all this and can resume life for ourselves, he wants to change his name legally and assume his identity as Jasper Bailey."

"That's amazing." I squeezed his arm with my hand. After a moment, I thought of a random question. "When's your birthday?"

"Me? July 2nd. What about you?"

"June 4th. I guess we have a ways to go before we celebrate birthdays."

"We can still celebrate Thanksgiving and Christmas together."

We fell silent and fell asleep. When I woke up again, Jordan was gone. I rolled over and found everyone standing, staring at the door, which had just opened. I quickly stood and saw General Breckenridge enter, followed by General McCormack. Then, Zeke.

Will let out a noise like a pterodactyl and rushed him, burning his face in Zeke's chest. Zeke's dad seemed to be trying to be okay with their embrace.

"Good afternoon, everyone." Breckenridge gave a curt nod.

"What's going on?" Ari asked nervously.

"First, I want to thank you all for your patience while we sort through all this new information," Breckenridge said. "I'm here now to take you to another area on the base. We've spoken to all the officials, and they've agreed on a course of action to get us some answers."

"And what have the 'officials' decided to do with us?" Jordan asked.

General McCormack cleared his throat. "I want you to know that your safety is our priority. We've made contact with Mark Buchanan—Sebastian Benedetti, as you call him—and we're bringing him in—"

We all objected at once. Zeke's dad held up his hands and we fell silent.

"Trust me, all of you, that we are more than equipped to deal with a man with the same kind of powers you have—"

"You can't bring him here." Spencer stepped forward. "This man raised me... he's murdered a substantial amount of people without any remorse. He's arranged for others to be murdered even more than that. Plus, you're not taking into account his big fucking army."

General Breckenridge looked at Spencer. "He has an army?"

He nodded. "And a lot of them have powers."

"I'm telling you, bringing him here is exactly what he wants," Jordan said. "Especially if you have something that was found in the cave in the Mariana Trench."

Breckenridge and McCormack stared at each other, then Breckenridge looked at me. "He can turn his body to diamond. Can a bullet still stop him when he's like that?"

"No."

Breckenridge and McCormack shared a glance.

"I'll take them, and you can get the base ready." Breckenridge nodded at McCormack's plan.

"You men, follow me. The rest of you, stay with McCormack and go with them to the object."

Breckenridge marched out of the room, a dozen soldiers following him. We were left with General McCormack and a guard for each of us.

"If Benedetti is as dangerous as you say, we better hurry. We don't have much time until he gets here. Come on."

He led the way out of the room, and a guard strode beside each of us as we followed him.

We half-walked, half-ran through more of the white halls, some gently sloping upward, until we made it to an elevator. There was no button, but a panel that General McCormack had to use a fingerprint, voice, and retinal verification on before the doors opened.

With a whirr, they opened to reveal a huge space that easily fit the eight of us, plus Zeke's dad, plus the eight soldiers.

"Good afternoon, General McCormack," the elevator said.

"Whoa, you have an Evie?" I blurted out.

Zeke's dad frowned. "How do you know about Evie?"

"They use it at Vostell headquarters in King!"

"What?" He glared at me. "Mark assured me it was only going to be used in military installations! What the hell is he doing, using government equipment in his building?"

"Don't be surprised if they have it in Russia, too," Spencer advised. "Vostell does a lot of contract work with them, too."

McCormack sighed. "Ground level, Evie." He turned to Will. "You worked for Vostell. Anything else I should know about?"

"I worked reception. The only thing I knew about was answering phones and looking good as I told people Mr. Buchanan was unavailable."

The general was unimpressed.

"Wait, why didn't we hear Evie when we first got here?" I asked him. "You know, when the bags were over our heads?"

"We used a different elevator that doesn't have Evie installed."

We rode in silence until the elevator dinged, and the doors opened.

"Have a pleasant day, General."

We all stepped out of the elevator into the middle of a short hallway. As we walked away from the elevator, I saw that it looked simply like a wall did. No seams where the elevator doors were or anything.

"You know, if Benedetti designed high-security features for this base, he knows how to get around them."

General McCormack shot me a 'you little know-it-all' glance but didn't say anything. We walked out through a door, and all of us had to shield our eyes as the bright afternoon sun beat down on us.

"I knew it." Spencer stared around triumphantly. "I knew that's where we were!"

"Where?"

"Area 51."

I took in the dusty landscape, taking in the buildings and the scenery before we all got into four Humvees and drove around the base for a few minutes. Finally, we pulled up to an unassuming warehouse.

At least, it was unassuming to everyone else. As we walked in, I realized I had dreamed about it—had a vision of it—before we'd even landed in San Francisco.

"Benedetti's going to make his move here." I shook my head, staring intently at Jordan. "I've seen this before. So has the Praetorian. This has to be where they're keeping the alien locked up."

"I knew there were aliens here, I *knew* it." Spencer was like a giddy kid getting candy.

We made our way to another elevator that needed more verification of the general's identity, and got in.

"Hello, General McCormack." Evie sounded as pleasant as ever. "Would you like to go to the vault?"

"Yes, please."

"Unknown presence in the elevator. Please verify security code."

"McCormack, Alpha Tango Beta Foxtrot Charlie o-eight three three one-niner."

"Identity confirmed."

And down we went. Music began to play, pop music from a girl whose songs I knew, but who I couldn't name.

"Uh, cancel music, Evie," McCormack said quickly. The music stopped.

"Would you prefer I play your other playlist?" Evie asked him.

"No music, Evie."

It was silent for a moment.

"What's your other playlist, Dad?"

"It… is… older music."

"Evie, play General McCormack's other playlist," Will said in a rush.

Classical opera began to play in the elevator.

Zeke frowned. "Is this Maria Callas?"

General McCormack turned to his son, impressed. "You remember?"

"Yeah, you played this all the time around the house. How could I not know who she is?"

The elevator stopped moving, the doors opened, and we were faced with a short hallway made of what looked like black metal. Only, as we began walking down the hallway, I realized the walls weren't metal—they were a two-way mirror.

At the end of the hallway, McCormack and a guard I recognized as Collins went through another verification of identity before the door opened. At this point, I was sure they were going to need a blood sample and a virgin sacrifice to get through the next door.

However, there *was* no next door. The door opened and we all wandered into an astonishing sight.

A green crystal about the size of a refrigerator was sitting in the center of a glass box. It had a bunch of wires coming from it, and video screens all around were displaying little wiggling lines. There were also video cameras filming every square inch.

It was all being recorded and watched by several scientists and soldiers in unusual uniforms around the room.

"What the hell is this?"

"We were hoping you could tell us," McCormack said. "We found it in that cave in the Mariana Trench back in 1973. A secret government exploration of the trench found this... thing sitting in the cave. We grabbed it and brought it back here. It's old."

"How old?"

Zeke's dad sighed. "It's been here for over two-thousand years."

I looked at Jordan. "It's like a giant Fragment of Terra. I mean... what if the fragments were originally a ton bigger?"

He shrugged. "I... I have no words."

"You and this object have similar qualities. We thought you might be able to do something with it."

"Like what?" Ari asked. "Take it on a date?"

"We're all in new territory here." General McCormack ignored Ari's comment. "We don't know what will happen, but, because time is pressing, we're willing to do an experiment. Now, who wants to get in the box with the big alien crystal?"

Jordan and I stared at each other. I imagined we were thinking the same thing—green meant it had something to do with the Fragment of Terra, and if that was the case, it had to be me or Spencer who touched it. And who knew what would happen then?

"I'll do it," Spencer volunteered. "That way, if something goes wrong and I get hurt or... well, there will still be people who could be the Primarch."

"Spencer, if we're related, that means we could both be the Primarch."

"If it's between the two of us—"

"I'll go." I stepped forward. "I'll go with Spencer. We're both Terras, so maybe things won't get too crazy with our powers in there together."

Jordan let out a breath, his jaw tightening.

"We'll be okay." I took his hand. "Trust me."

"Just... be careful."

Spencer and I shared a look, then slowly walked together toward the soldier standing by the glass door that led into the box.

"Ready?" I asked him nervously.

"A world of no," he said. "But, let's do it."

We nodded at the guard, who opened the door and gestured for us to step inside. We did, and the door closed behind us with a suction sound. Our footsteps echoed off the walls as we tiptoed toward it.

"What do we do?" he whispered.

"We probably should have thought about that before coming in here," I hissed back.

"Why are we whispering?"

"I don't know. Don't wake the baby?"

We laughed nervously. We were about a foot away from it. It seemed inert, not at all like the fragments had been in the bottom of the Mariana Trench.

"Well... here goes everything." Reaching out my right hand, I delicately placed it on the giant fragment. "Whoa."

It was warm, and much softer than I thought it would be. The fragments all felt solid, where this felt pliable. I pushed on it a little, and it shifted. It was almost like pushing on a car tire.

"What? Are you okay?"

"Yeah. Feel this."

He slowly brought his hand to touch it. "Is it... moving?"

"Jake, we're getting some readings from the object." General McCormack's voice sounded over the intercom. "Its size and temperature began increasing as soon as you touched it."

Spencer and I pulled away at the same time and stepped back. The general came back on through the intercom. "Size and temperature reducing."

I grinned at Spencer. "Well, what if we don't remove our hands?"

He shrugged. "I mean, we're already here."

Will's voice sounded out. "Hold, please."

Frowning, I tapped my foot impatiently while they all had a discussion on the other side of the glass.

"Okay, we took a vote, and we think you two should leave. It might not be safe for you in there."

"I'm going to touch it again."

"That's the exact opposite of what I said, *hon*," Jordan pointed out over the intercom, as annoyed as he was trying to be sweet.

"I know, but... I think I can wake them up."

"Wake *who* up?"

"The Praetorian." The answer formed in my mouth before I realized it was there. "I mean, it all makes sense, doesn't it? The visions, the sand... and if I'm right, I bet the Praetorian knows where to find the Omnia Fragment."

"Jake, please get out of there."

There was a scuffling sound and General McCormack's voice sounded. "Give me that. Ahem. Jake, you need to leave the box at once. That's an order."

I turned and gave a small smile. "Unfortunately, I don't take orders from you, general."

And I placed my hand on the fragment. Spencer smirked and did the same. The general started shouting, and the soldier opened the door behind us, but quickly closed it when he saw the fragment begin to change.

First, it started to grow, slowly and steadily. It was as big as a sofa. A bed. One of those smart cars. And the whole time it was tingling under my skin, but never hot.

"Jake, get out of there!"

Meanwhile, some scientist was calling out dimensions and temperatures over the intercom in increasingly panicked excitement, or excited panic.

When it had reached the size of a large SUV and Spencer and I were pressed against the glass, the fragment began to rupture. As each deep fissure appeared, a sound like a whip echoed through the room. The glass also started to buckle under the pressure of the fragment pushing on it.

"Let go of it, or you're going to be crushed and burned to death," McCormack shouted. "Get out of there, now!"

"It's not hot!" I yelled back as more cracking sounds filled the air. "Besides, I think it's almost done."

"Done *what*?"

"Done opening!"

As if on cue, the fragment burst, sending shards in every direction. The glass shattered and Spencer and I were thrown backward. It was like getting hit by a dodgeball thrown by an NFL player, except all over. And the dodgeball was a bowling ball. *Ow*.

We collapsed on the ground in a painful heap, hearing shouts of alarm throughout the room. But a loud voice sounded.

"Do not shoot. I am not armed." I heard the voice speak, but I didn't hear it with my ears. And it sounded all-too familiar.

"Identify yourself," General McCormack called out.

"Wait!" I groaned and rolled over, sitting up to take in the sight. "I know this alien!"

Blue alien. Four arms. Four eyes with hourglass pupils. Sideways mouth.

I inhaled shakily. "Hello... Praetorian." I glanced at their hands. "I believe you have the Omnia Fragment."

Chapter 15: A Totally Normal, Everyday Conversation

"Everybody calm your tits." Will held his hands out at Collins, the five guards, and general who all had their guns on the Praetorian. "If Jake knows this alien, it's probably from his visions he has when he sometimes falls asleep. It's a totally not-insane thing."

"You are right," the alien said. "I apologize for what must have been a rather alarming entrance." It looked around at the broken glass and shards of green crystal littering the smooth, black floor. "My... sincere apologies for any damage my awakening has caused."

It stared at me, and I blinked. *This is no big deal. It's just like meeting a new person. Well, a person that can read your thoughts. Oh, shit! Can they read my thoughts now? Um, elephants. Elephants on unicycles!*

The being laughed, their eyes strangely human somehow, even if there were four of them. "You are funny, Jake."

"Cool. Why did you take the Omnia Fragment?"

"To stop your government from getting it." The alien glanced at the general, still pointing his gun. "Representatives from the United States government came with fragments in the 1970s. I felt it better to hide than to resist, which is why I was moved here. I have been waiting for someone with the power to rescue me."

"Why didn't you communicate sooner? Or communicate with all of us?"

"Only the Primarch can communicate directly with those who have the power. I... worked adjacent to the Primarch and learned a few of their tricks. I was only able to find two with an open enough mind, and even then, could only communicate when their guards were down."

"When we were dreaming." The alien nodded, and I continued. "Um, Praetorian—"

"Cemparius."

"What?"

The alien smiled. "My name is Cemparius. My title is Praetorian."

"Okay, um, Cemparius... why didn't you contact anyone who had the power before us? Haven't you been here for, like, thousands of years?"

They nodded. "Originally, I was waiting for humans to come to discover the fragment. But when those without the power came and took me away, I began to reach out to those with powers. I managed to make contact a few times over the years, but they only ever thought I was a dream."

"But... why were you hiding the fragment? Why didn't you, like, take it back home or something?"

Cemparius opened their mouth to answer, but stopped, and looked at the general. "Yes?"

"Jake... Spencer... why don't you two step away and let me make first contact?" General McCormack stepped forward and slowly put his gun away. The soldiers lowered theirs, but stayed at the ready. "I have training for this."

"Well, I mean, I've actually already—"

"Shh." The general stepped forward, hands out like he was approaching a rabid raccoon. Then, he increased the volume of his voice. "My name is General Scott McCormack of the United States Air Force. I am an official representative of the United States government, the most powerful nation on planet Earth. Can you understand the words I'm saying?"

The Praetorian shot a quick look at me, then addressed the general. "General McCormack. You are currently thinking about how this first contact will get your name in the history books, no? But... you are also concerned how history will remember you as a father, especially to a criminal. And now you are thinking 'holy shit, it can read my mind.' I can read your thoughts as they occur. It would be like reading the same book—I can only see what page you are on."

General McCormack looked at Zeke, who tried not to look hurt. But, clearly, the general had more pressing concerns on his mind.

"So, you can read minds. To a point. And you can understand our language. What are your intentions on our planet?"

Cemparius blinked. "I intend no harm. In fact, I intend to help humanity."

"Help us how?"

"Help you stay alive in the war to come."

War? What war? World War III?

"No, Jake. The war between our peoples."

Nobody said anything for a good chunk of time. Finally, McCormack spoke again.

"So, you intend to betray your people?"

"No. My people have lost their way. I am standing by the values they originally intended, not as they are currently being executed."

"So, like, the spirit of the law, rather than what the law says?" Ari asked.

Cemparius nodded, meeting Ari's gaze. "Yes. From your thoughts, I am gathering you have people who created laws, and people who interpret them. We have a similar way on Oriach."

"Oriach?"

"My home world. I can show it to you on an interstellar map, if you have one."

"Hold on, I'd like to get back to the whole 'war between our worlds' thing." General McCormack swallowed. "When is this going to happen?"

"Never, if I can help it."

The general stared. "What?"

The Praetorian frowned. "Do you mind if we sit for this conversation? I am rather tired from being in stasis."

With that, the alien made a motion with their hands, and the floor around us warped and shifted into a black metal conference table with seventeen chairs.

Looking around, the alien smiled. "Ah. I see. Some of you do not wish to join us at the table. That is fine."

Nine of the chairs dissolved back into the floor, and the others moved closer together. The alien took a seat, and, after a few moments of hesitation, everyone began joining them at the table. Collins, the five other guards, and the three scientists stood back, eyes wide.

"Now, about this war—"

"Hold on." Zeke interrupted his dad, who looked shocked. "I say we hear what the Praetorian has to say before we begin making demands."

The being smiled at Zeke. "Thank you. That is quite kind." Their eyes wandered up to the ceiling. "However, we are running low on time, so the war is what we should discuss."

"How are we running low on time?"

"Benedetti is on his way."

"We know that. We're bringing him in."

Cemparius squinted at Breckenridge. "This is what he wants. He wants to be brought to the fragment. But he must not be allowed to touch it. No one can."

"You can." Spencer gestured to Cemparius's hands on the fragment.

"I do not have the potential to become the Primarch."

"Can you tell us more about these powers?" Zeke's dad asked.

"The eight of you—not including the general—as well as I have what is called Pethius. The power to control a single element. What this fragment unlocks is Ultimus—the power to control all the elements."

"Is it blood who decides who gets the power of Ultimus?"

"On our planet, it is not. But on earth, where Luriana tied the power to a bloodline, yes. It depends on blood." Cemparius stared at Jordan. "No, indeed, you did not find everyone who possibly has the power. However, the eight of you around this table could possess it under the right circumstances. As could Benedetti."

"Well, let's try it. Let's see what these circumstances are." Will stepped forward excitedly, but Cemparius tightened their grip on the Omnia Fragment.

"No. As I said, no one must touch it. It would set into motion a chain of events that could bring about the apocalypse."

I blinked. "I thought you said it could bring war."

"In the same way an ant has a war with a boot."

"Why do your people want to go to war with us?" General McCormack leaned forward, folding his hands on the table.

"Because you hold powers you should not."

"Pethius? Or the potential for Ultimus?" I asked.

"Both." Cemparius also leaned forward, two of their arms still holding the fragment in their lap, the other two mimicking McCormack's. "Luriana and The Dietat fled Oriach during a civil war. They make up a large portion of governmental power, so their absence caused more chaos. An opposing faction chased after them, reporting back that they had fled to this planet before The Dietat destroyed them. My people rebuilt, but they knew what would happen here on Earth."

"This has to do with the visions from the fragments, right?" Ari sat on the edge of their seat. "When you touch the fragments, you have a vision about what happened. The Dietat went to war with each other—"

"Yes, but when a Voranah dies, our body turns into these." They held up the Omnia Fragment. "These can transfer power. Our people had found peace, chosen a new form of government, and a new Primarch. When scouts first came to the planet, they found an Indigenous population of the first humans, none of whom had powers. So, it was assumed that the powers had been lost forever."

I gasped. "But then Luriana..."

Cemparius nodded. "Indeed. Luriana created a new Primarch in Mary, and the power passed down to her children. On our world, powers are given as a gift to only the Primarch, the Dietat, and the Cleimus, and only the Primarch is given the gift of Ultimus. So, you can see why it is a problem that there are so many here who could claim the gift of Ultimus."

"It's like the next step of evolution or something, right?" Will asked, but Cemparius shook their head.

"The powers are viewed as a gift that must be controlled, and only given to those who have proven themselves worthy. Here on earth, anyone who touches a fragment can gain its power—whatever their intentions or training. This is why the Primarch, the Dietat, and the Stratum all decided to... end the situation once it got too far."

It clicked, even though I didn't understand what a Stratum or a Cleimus was. "And if someone gains the power of Ultimus, that's too far. So, that's why we can't touch the fragment."

"Precisely."

"And what does it mean, to 'end the situation?'" General McCormack asked.

Cemparius met his gaze. "The Qualen."

"What's that?"

"It is the World-Ender."

Will shuddered and nudged David. "I don't like the sound of that."

"Definitely sus," David agreed.

"And the Primarch and... all the Voranah... have chosen to kill all the humans?"

Cemparius shook their head. "Not only humans. They have chosen to erase all life from this planet and leave it as it once was—a floating rock."

"But... they can't do that," Ari said, mouth slightly open. "We didn't choose to be alive. We didn't choose existence. They can't punish us for being born."

"We have already decimated more than a dozen other species. We have become exceedingly good at it."

General McCormack checked his cell phone. "Benedetti's here. I suggest we hide Cemparius here and the fragment in two separate locations."

Cemparius glanced up. "It is too late. We must evacuate all non-essential personnel."

"We have plenty of armed—"

"I can see his thoughts, general. He has broken free of the government's control. And he is close. He is close."

We all stood and stared at the door to the room. General McCormack pulled his gun. Lightning swirled around Zeke's hands, and Jordan's veins were aglow with fire.

"Why hasn't the intruder alarm—" General McCormack began, but he was interrupted by Cemparius.

"Look out!"

The ceiling above us began shaking violently, and large sections began to fall. Cemparius leaped and tackled Ari and Will out of the way, still holding on to the fragment. All three of them were buried under some cascading rubble.

Jordan jumped back and rolled, narrowly avoiding being crushed by a huge boulder. I raised my hands up to the ceiling to try and stop the cave-in, but it was no use.

Benedetti's men began repelling down ropes dropped in. General McCormack and the other guards opened fire, taking out three of the Disciples. But a fourth leapt from the dust, arm made entirely of sharp, pointed metal.

General McCormack was impaled through the stomach.

"*Dad*!"

Blood sprayed across Spencer and me, who were closest. Zeke ran to his father, but the rest of us began engaging in combat while, finally, an alarm sounded somewhere in the base.

David brought his hands together in a thunderous clap, and lightning shot out, getting almost everyone who was coming through the hole.

Lex began shooting ice shards out of her hands, dodging out of the way of a Disciple Ionis's lightning bolt.

Fire whips forming in his hands, Jordan began striking at those nearest, leaving them screaming as deep gashes formed across their bodies and limbs.

The five guards fell quickly against the Disciples, leaving only Collins to shield the scientists still trapped in the room.

But the man who had stabbed General McCormack went after Spencer, lassoing a vine around his neck and pulling him off his feet. The man pointed a gun at him and ordered everyone to stop fighting.

He removed his helmet, but I already knew who it was.

"Vic," I snarled.

"Long time, no see, Jake." His face was flushed with sweat, and the hole where his ear used to be was mostly healed, leaving an ugly scab.

"Let him go!" Fire swirled around Jordan's hands. "Take me, instead."

"Shut up," Vic tightened his grip on Spencer.

"What the hell are you doing?" Spencer grabbed at the tight vines around his throat.

"Well, at first I thought I was coming to help you tie up your loose ends," Vic hissed in his ear. "Then, after we paid off one of the sailors on *The Ashland*, we found out you had turned. Your dad was crushed."

"He's not my father! I found out from a blood test."

Vic blinked in surprise but tried not to get distracted as he backed toward the exit. "All we're here for is the Omnia Fragment."

"You can't have it." I carefully avoided glancing at the pile of rubble. "Seriously, we found out—"

"Enough!" Vic screamed. "I have had a long week, and I am sick of people telling me what I can and can't do. Give me the fragment, or I snap his neck."

"You're outmatched, Vic." I stepped forward slightly. "Besides, you think Benedetti would forgive you for killing his son?"

Vic rolled his eyes and blew a raspberry. He began pulling Spencer toward the door, and the four of his goons left standing followed. "Seriously? Jordan killed him. That's right, Jordan wanted revenge so badly that he killed Benedetti's only son for a chance to get back at Benedetti."

"He'd never buy it." Jordan was slowly inching his way forward. "He knows me too well."

"Back off." Vic pushed the barrel of the gun into Spencer's temple, then met my eyes. "Normally, he would believe that, but he saw Jake here push me off a bridge—his son, too—sort of trying to kill us. I'm a little upset by it, Jake."

"I didn't 'sort of' do anything. I threw you off that bridge knowing full well you could have died. But you keep coming back, like... like..."

"Herpes," David offered helpfully.

I shrugged. "You heard him."

His lip twitched into a snarl as he passed by Zeke holding his dad.

"Zeke, we can save your dad if you tell me where the fragments are." Vic glared at him, and Zeke looked back at me desperately.

"We don't know where they are!"

"I'm sure Daddy does."

We paused as the general tried to speak, but blood spurted out of his mouth.

"Dad, please tell us where they are. I can save you. I can save you!"

I glanced at Spencer, who jerked his head and eyes to the gun, and realized he had a plan. I had to keep Vic talking.

"Look, Vic, if Benedetti—if *anyone*—touches that fragment, there's going to be a war from the aliens who brought the powers here in the first place."

"Bullshit," he said. "You're just trying to scare us."

I looked over at the rubble, where Cemparius, Ari, and Will were still buried. I couldn't make out where the Omnia Fragment was. And as long as we knew where it was and Vic didn't, he and his men would die here, and we could still save Zeke's dad.

"Fine. You want Spencer, you can take him back to his father. But he knows the truth. And Benedetti will listen."

"He won't listen to a damn thing you have to say!"

"He might not listen to us, but he'd listen to Spencer. Especially after knowing you died trying to kill him."

"What makes you think you can kill me?" Vic asked, his eyes glinting. "I have the gun."

I tilted my head to the side. "Do you?"

And as he looked down, he saw that Spencer had used his powers to take the clip out of the gun and carefully remove the bullet in the chamber.

He jerked his head up, his eyes and mouth perfect o's.

Jordan and I acted as one. I shot off two stone fists that hit two of the Disciples in the face, and Jordan fire lassoed the other two.

Spencer whipped around and seized Vic by the throat, but Vic still had the vines around Spencer's neck. The two began choking each other. I ran forward, trying to pull them apart.

Meanwhile, David and Lex ran over to help get the rubble off Ari, Will, and Cemparius.

Spencer gurgled at me unintelligibly, but his face told me I was being stupid. Then, I realized I was.

Turning my finger into a sharp, metal point, I cut through the vines, accidentally cutting Spencer along the neck slightly in the process.

Spencer, now gasping for air, put both hands around Vic's neck, leaving Vic struggling weakly, his purple face contorted in rage.

We all simply watched as Spencer choked Vic slowly, but Jordan stepped forward and placed a hand on Spencer's shoulder.

"Who you *are*, not who he made you to be," Jordan whispered.

Spencer's sweaty, red face grew deepened in color. Then, he let out a strangled sob. He let Vic go and threw him at my feet.

"Here." He spat on Vic. "You decide."

Vic coughed horribly, gazing up at me. He was leaning heavily on the body of one of the Disciples we'd taken out.

"Well? What's it gonna be?"

I stood over him, and a terrible feeling entered my stomach, making it churn.

This man had arranged for me to be attacked and tortured. His actions set me on this path in the first place.

At the same time, he arranged for another attack on Jordan and me, he was arranging to have my family, including my baby nephew, killed.

I knew he would cause irreparable pain and damage if I spared his life. Now that we knew we could never touch the Omnia Fragment, he would continue to hunt us down, chasing us wherever we went. All on the orders of Benedetti.

All Vic wanted was to show he had power. For people to respect him for his power. There was nothing inherently wrong with that, but the way he'd gone about trying to gain more power? That had killed people. It had forced us all to make decisions on who lived and who died.

He had brought Bree and Kieran into the council chambers specifically for them to die.

I swallowed. If I didn't kill him, who else would suffer?

As soon as Spencer had told me to decide, I'd already made up my mind.

"Get up."

Vic slowly stumbled to his feet, and his eyes moved to the pile of rubble, where Cemparius was standing up.

"Is that... an alien?"

I nodded, turning my head to see Cemparius still holding the Omnia Fragment.

A shot rang out as I turned, and when I looked around to see who had fired a gun, I saw Vic holding a one and pointing it at my gut.

I clutched my stomach and pulled my hands away. They weren't bloody.

When I met Vic's eyes, however, I saw the shock of what had happened. He collapsed, and that was when I saw he'd been shot in the heart through his back.

As he fell, I found Zeke behind him, holding his father's gun in one hand, while still holding onto his father with the other.

Zeke dropped the gun and went back to his dad. Will rushed over, covered in scrapes and dust but otherwise okay.

General McCormack reached out with a shaking jerk and grabbed Will's hand.

"Take... care of... my boy..." Then, with a rattling sigh, he went limp.

"Dad..." Zeke leaned over his father's body.

Will placed his hands on Zeke's shoulders and held him as best as he could. But Zeke quickly sat up, his eyes dry.

"I'm... I'm not as sad as I thought I would be." He looked at Spencer with wide eyes. "I mean, we've grown so far apart. All the things he said—the things he did when he found out I was gay. And then, when he found us on the ship... all he wanted to do was talk. He'd changed." Zeke turned to Will, setting his father's head gently on the ground. "And in the end, he still couldn't tell me he loved me. Instead... he showed me by making sure the person I loved took care of me."

All we could do was stand there. Finally, Zeke closed his eyes and took a deep breath. Then, he stood. "We need to move. We need to get the fragment away from Benedetti before he comes here."

"He's probably searching where the other fragments are." I turned to Collins, who was on his radio, reporting everything that had happened. "We need to get to the room where they kept the smaller fragments. Now!"

As we all moved to head to the door and the elevator down the hall, Jordan stooped down to General McCormack's body and grabbed the things out of his pockets.

"Just in case," he told me, and we all ran, the three scientists and soldier with us.

We got in the elevator and Collins directed Evie to take us to the surface. Evie, of course, wouldn't shut up the whole way.

"Base in code red lockdown. Remember procedure and continue in an orderly fashion to your station. This is not a drill."

When we got to the surface, the doors opened to a terrible sight. Benedetti was there, along with a few dozen of his hired mercenaries. They were fighting General Breckenridge and a bunch of the Machine Gun Vaders, but it was obvious that Benedetti's troops, with their powers, had the advantage.

"Look!" Cemparius pointed with both right arms to Benedetti, who was holding the same bag I'd kept the fragments in on the submarine. And I was sure it held the fragments now.

"We have to stop him!" We rushed forward and each of us began to try to get to Benedetti.

Our influx seemed to revive the fight in the Area 51 soldiers, who began to push back against the Disciples.

Benedetti saw us, and his eyes widened as he saw Cemparius and the fragment they were holding. He let out a roar, and diamond spears began shooting out of his outstretched hands as he made his way to them.

"Cem, watch out!"

But my shout came too late. Cemparius was engaged in battle with two Disciples at once, and Benedetti impaled

Cemparius in the shoulder, causing them to cry out and drop the fragment.

Benedetti reached toward it, and I thought it was all over then. But he was wearing gloves.

"Dad, stop!" Spencer cried out, running toward him.

Benedetti turned, momentarily stunned. His expression turned from confusion, to pain, then rage. With a snarl and curl of his lip, he fired off a shard of diamond. Spencer conjured a shield, but the diamond pierced it and managed to catch him in the bicep.

Benedetti scooped the fragment into the bag, the ground breaking around his feet and, with a flourish, flew up and away from the battle, removing his gloves.

Jordan took advantage of the momentary distractions. He grabbed onto the edge of Bendetti's makeshift aerial platform and hauled himself up. Benedetti was caught by surprise, trying to hit him with the bag of fragments. This was exactly what Jordan wanted.

And as I watched, I knew in my heart he was the right choice to be the Primarch.

But it all went wrong. thirty feet above the ground, Benedetti kicked Jordan, who still had a hold of the bag of fragments. It split, and all six of the fragments came tumbling out and started to fall to the ground.

Benedetti released the bag, and Jordan fell.

Following Benedetti's example, I used the ground under me to propel myself up to catch Jordan. But as I flew up, I realized Benedetti was going to grab the Omnia Fragment. Jordan couldn't reach it.

I jumped off the platform and kept it moving to catch Jordan.

The fragment was right there.

Benedetti and I both reached for it, and—

Chapter 16: Wormhole? Blackhole? Hellhole.

There was no flash of light, no big bang or explosion. Benedetti, Jordan, and I had all been falling through the air one moment, and the next, I was in a white void, floating.

But I wasn't alone.

"Where... where is this?" I looked to my right and saw Benedetti floating. "Jake?"

"What happened?"

"What happened is you tried to take my hard-earned power." He glared at me.

"You didn't hear what I did." I shook my head. "The alien who's been contacting us said the Voranah were waiting for someone to activate the Omnia Fragment in order to start a war with Earth."

I knew he could sense the truth in what I told him, but he didn't want to believe it.

"No... no. There's always an option. There's always an out."

"This is why you were not chosen, Sebastian."

A figure began to form in front of us, but I was surprised to see it wasn't a Voranah. It was a human. A man, brown skin, black hair, and black beard appeared before us. I didn't recognize him. Benedetti frowned.

"Who are you?"

He smiled, looking at both of us. "Who I am is not important. What I have to tell you is."

"I demand to know who you are, right now."

Holy shit. Holy... holy shit! Wait, if it's actually him, *maybe watch your mouth, Jake.*

"Benedetti, I think this is... Jesus."

The man smiled and nodded. Benedetti's jaw dropped.

"So, it's true. You were the Primarch?"

Jesus nodded. "And I am here from the afterlife to warn you. We do not have much time."

"Why... why are you here? Why is Jesus here?" Benedetti seemed perplexed.

"When Christ died, his body became the Omnia Fragment," I said. "His disciples hid it in the Mariana Trench, in a cave that you could only get to if you had all the fragments."

Benedetti shook his head. "We knew you were off searching for it, but I never thought it was actually there."

"It was, until 1973. The government brought it back to Area 51, along with Cemparius."

He sighed, seeming to deflate. "So, what, now you tell us which of us has been chosen?"

Jesus stared calmly. "Jake has been chosen."

My eyes immediately began to water. Benedetti's mouth formed into a tight line.

"Why?" I asked. "Luriana told me—"

"They told you what you needed to hear," Christ said. But he still frowned. "We both know, deep down, that you wanted it to be you. You were scared of what it would mean, but you desired the power."

"Then give it to me, not him!" Benedetti gestured at me wildly. "I know what to do with it."

"He's right," I admitted. "I only tried to grab the fragment because I thought others would be in danger if he got the power."

"Which is why I chose you," Jesus said. "However, who the Primarch turned out to be is not as important as what they need to know."

"This is bullshit," Benedetti spat. "I am the one with the resources to make a difference on the planet. I'm the one who has the power to influence change. I was going to feed the hungry, and keep away famine, and—"

"Only after helping yourself." Jesus's voice was surprisingly hard. "Even in my time, the rich were worshipped and glorified, yet those who refused to share their abundances sinned in the eyes of God. You have lost your way."

"Oh, don't give me that God crap. We know humans came from the aliens."

"And where did they come from?" Jesus stared intently at Benedetti. "Who has given me the power to appear before you now, and warn you of what is to come?"

"What? What is it?" I interrupted Benedetti.

"Jake, you have touched a piece of a power which you do not fully understand." Jesus grabbed my hands in his, my stomach flipping at the touch. "Even I did not truly understand it. But you must to face the war that is to come."

"Cemparius said war was coming. Isn't there any way it can be avoided?"

"You may try." He sounded like a parent who says okay, knowing their child is going to fail. "But remember this—every beginning must have an end."

My eyes widened. "What? What does that mean?"

But Jesus seemed to be dissolving, and as he did, a Voranah appeared in his place. Their eyes were closed, and hands were raised, palms up, as if feeling and sensing what was around them.

This Voranah was not one I'd seen before. It was dressed in elegant and complexly draped fabrics of silver, blue, green, red, and purple. The tendrils along their head fell to the floor, were painted in the same colors as their clothes, and decorated with many jewels, symbols, and odd-looking trinkets.

The figure turned in a slow circle, continuing to exude an air of mysterious observation, taking in everything. When they were facing me, they opened their eyes. Their shimmery silver eyes had no hourglass iris like Cemparius and Luriana.

And as I stared in their eyes, I realized I had rotated in a circle with them. We were no longer standing in the white void, but an alien desert. Literally. The sand was purple. Crystals the size of small boulders dotted the landscape and, in the distance, islands and mountains were floating in the air, though they seemed to be upside-down.

The mountains were covered in an overwhelming variety of plants. Flowers the size of beach balls, trees with bright blue leaves and trunks that were made of a swirling liquid. Some of the plants had purple fruit with thick spikes that ended in a yellow point. The fruit hung from branches that were covered in short, black fibers.

I've seen all this before. I saw it in my vision of the first beings on Earth. So, they tried modeling our planet after theirs at first.

As I took it all in, I noticed there was a crowd of thousands, maybe tens of thousands. But they were humans. They were all blurry around the edges, and when I looked at my hands, I noticed I was as well.

I only recognized my friends, but the rest of the humans were unknown to me. They all were as alarmed as I was to suddenly be in such an intense vision.

"This is not a vision," the Voranah in front of us said. "I, The Augury, bring you before the leaders of the Voranah.

They gestured, and Benedetti and I turned around.

A Voranah was sitting on what had to be a throne. And if it was sitting on such an important piece of furniture, I had an idea of who it was.

"You must be the Primarch."

They were dressed in robes of white and gold, but the robes seemed to emit a light of their own. Their tendrils were also long but formed around their head to support a crown that had five jewels, one each for the colors of the fragments.

But they weren't alone.

On one side of the throne, on a platform shaped sort of like a small jury box, were five more Voranah. Each wore a solid color, likely representing the fragment power they had. The Augury joined them in the box.

On the Primarch's other side was another box, this one with three Voranah. I had no idea who they were representing.

And, standing off to the side of the box was a warrior. I could tell because they were wearing red crystal armor, not robes like the others.

And they were staring at me like I was their next meal.

"Where are we?" Benedetti asked.

The armored being stepped forward, eyes flashing. "Know your place! Only the imposter may speak."

I'd never seen Benedetti truly afraid, but he knew he was in over his head. We all were.

The Primarch leaned forward. "Imitor. The Pretender." The words echoed across the landscape. I felt like they were speaking to an unpleasant bug—me. "I am indeed the Primarch, leader of the Voranah. You were brought here to face judgment."

How do they know English? If I were Chinese or French or something, would they be speaking that language? Maybe that isn't an important question to ask right now, Jake.

"Indeed," the Primarch said. "I believe introductions are in order." They gestured to the five sitting next to them. "You have met The Augury, my seer that has brought your consciousness here from Earth."

"Whose consciousness? What about our bodies?"

The Primarch blinked a few times, and I realized I had interrupted them. *Oops.*

"The bodies of every person with Pethius will simply appear to be unconscious until we are finished here." They cleared their throat. "Continuing on. Here is the Dietat, my five Prefects that oversee the Cleimus." They waved their hand to their right. "And these are the three leaders of Stratum: the Cardinal, the Ascendant, and the Anointed."

Yeah, I have no idea what anyone does or what their names mean.

"You do not need to know." The Primarch responded to my thought. "Finally, this is the Invictor, leader of our armies."

Then, they looked over to the crowd of people, where a figure was making its way through.

"I believe the humans *do* have the right to know about our government. They are, after all, a part of us."

Cemparius stepped forward to gasps from the Voranah.

"Praetorian?" The armored Voranah stepped forward, furious. "You have been gone for many cycles. We thought you dead. The Augury could not find you."

"I was in stasis until today." Cemparius gestured at my friends in the front, then gestured to Benedetti. "These humans awoke me, but this human did not know about the vote cast over two-thousand years ago."

Benedetti's eyes darted around as if expecting to be attacked.

"If that human was not aware of the decision, why is *this* human The Imitor?" The Primarch pointed at me with two hands.

"I was trying to stop Benedetti from getting the fragment."

The Primarch leaned forward. "And now that you have the power?"

I bit my upper lip, looking around at the humans gathered. "I guess I'm going to have to use this power to protect all of them."

While the Primarch only narrowed their eyes, this gesture made them seem ten times more intimidating.

"Protect them from what?"

"You, apparently."

The armored being made a noise of disgust and gestured angrily at Cemparius. "What have you been telling them, Praetorian?"

"The truth—that the people from which they originated have decided they do not deserve to live."

"Their existence was never supposed to be in the first place," the Invictor said loudly. "You were always a sympathizer of the traitor, Luriana!"

"I sympathize with anyone fleeing a war to find peace."

"Enough," the Primarch ordered. "You have made your allegiance clear."

"You have forced there to be two sides," Cemparius said. "Humans have developed a saying—two sides of the same coin. If you look between the Voranah and humans, they are quite similar. They may look different from each other, but they are one family. One people."

"They are an unfortunate side-effect." The Primarch dismissed Cemparius's words with a flip of one of their hands. "Remember your place, Praetorian."

"My place has been decided for me, it seems." Cemparius straightened. "I stand with the humans."

The Dietat and the three other Voranah looked scandalized.

"Truly?" The Invictor acted like they'd been slapped.

Cemparius nodded. "I will defend those who have done no wrong."

"That claim is false. But as you have chosen to side with the Imitor, your name and rank will be removed from our records. You are hereby banished to Earth."

Cemparius didn't seem surprised, but it must have been a blow, nonetheless.

"We will now move to the judgment of humanity."

"Wait, wait." I held up my hands. "Don't we get any kind of defense or... like, to plead our case for ourselves?"

"The decision has already been made." The Primarch sounded annoyed.

"Yeah, it was made two-thousand years ago. So much has changed on our planet since then."

"Has it truly? Or has your technology advanced to where you can kill and enslave each other more effectively?"

I came up short. Was I actually having to defend all of human history right now? "I... I mean, yes, those things still happen. Based on how long life has been on our planet, and how long humans have been the dominant species, we're still in our infancy. We have people who are power-hungry..." I glanced at Benedetti, but he refused to look at me. "And we have people who just want to live in peace."

"Your species is failing. It is failing your planet, and it is failing itself."

"I know. We know that. We can change. We *have* been changing. We're constantly evolving and learning and growing. I mean, we barely developed space flight. We're starting to plan missions to a nearby planet. We already have robots on that planet. We're a young species. Please, give us time to learn, to grow up."

The Primarch considered me carefully. "You do not know of Voranah history, do you?"

"I only know Luriana fled a war on your planet."

"Ah, but it was a war Luriana started." The Primarch stood and gestured to their right. A bunch of crystals floated up into the air to form a sort of screen. There, a vicious battle began to play out, and the Primarch described what was happening.

"Luriana turned their back on our people, declining to follow their will. At this time, The Stratum did not exist, but rather the people worshipped the Primarch as their singular leader. An equivalent to your Kings and Queens. Some of the people turned on the Primarch, saying their power was too great. Others said the Primarch's will alone was to be heard."

The scene turned into graphic violence. I wanted to look away, but I knew it was important for me to see. The Primarch continued.

"The people turned on each other, and Luriana could not diffuse the fighting. Eventually, those who were angry at the Dietat and the Primarch came for them, but they fled with others to start anew. The others did not survive as they were pursued, and they left the planet in chaos, with thousands crying out to be the next Primarch. It took thousands of years to come to the form of government we have now."

It showed the people coming together, shaking their hands, seeming to bond.

"By the time our world was back in order and our outposts were notified of the decision to bring Luriana in to answer for their crimes, the second moon in orbit had already been smashed into your planet in their own war. We assumed all had died, and their remains had been destroyed in the impact."

Then the screen showed an image of a young girl, brown skin and black hair, being greeted by Luriana as they floated through the air.

"Then, when Luriana mated with the human Mary, we discovered the truth—Luriana had been in hiding, waiting, biding their time to impart the powers to a human bloodline. *Your* bloodline."

The screen disassembled and the pieces returned to the ground. I frowned, considering. Finally, I spoke.

"I understand that Luriana was a traitor to your people, and that you would view their creations as part of that betrayal. But only the people who have, um, Pethius know about this. The rest of humanity believes in an evolution without alien contact. It's not right to hold them accountable for something they don't know anything about. They don't even know people with Pethius exist."

"And why is that?" The Primarch sat back down on their throne.

I licked my lips nervously. "Well, because we're still so young, there are those of us who are afraid that people who don't have powers would try to hurt us, or make us use our powers to their will."

"Now, even you admit that humanity is not ready for Pethius. Do you truly think you are ready for Ultimus?"

I sighed. "No," I admitted. "But we also aren't being given any choice of time. You've had... however long to mature and learn and grow. Voranah have been around a lot longer than humans. We could absolutely get to an enlightened stage like yours, given time."

"You have had time. You have not used Pethius in the way it was intended, therefore we can reason you will not use Ultimus properly," the Primarch said.

"Well, what are the powers supposed to be used for? Help us learn, don't condemn us for not knowing what we've never been taught."

The Primarch tilted their head to the side. "Pethius and Ultimus have been used for many purposes. Peace, and war; creation, and destruction. Once we developed our ability for interstellar travel and expanded to live on other planets, Pethius and Ultimus became a model, a symbol, for what knowledge and peace can attain. You have used your powers to destroy, and to harm each other. You perpetuate the cycle of violence inherent in your species' genes."

I nodded and looked at Benedetti. "You were right, in a way. We should never have been keeping our powers a secret. We should have been helping to better the world."

Benedetti's eyes, for the first time, softened as they met mine. "And you were right. I think humanity needs to be introduced to the idea of powers slowly, or they will be used for more destruction."

His words shocked me. He'd been an enemy, so I'd never truly stopped to consider what we had in common. He was still responsible for too much death and destruction for my taste, but... he could reason. He could change.

Maybe we all could.

"As I have said, it is too late for change." The Primarch sat up straight.

"No!" Cemparius stepped forward, but The Augury stood, eyes fixed on them. Cemparius could no longer move but could still speak. "Think about this. Human beings are formed from our powers. They are formed *from* us. You are condemning your own people to a life without Pethius and Ultimus."

I frowned. "Well, that doesn't sound so bad." I looked around at the others. "I mean... we wouldn't have powers, so we wouldn't need to keep secrets. And we could still work together to make humanity better."

"That is simply not going work," the Primarch explained. "As The Praetorian has said, you are all formed from us. You would not exist if it were not for Pethius and Ultimus. Therefore, we have decided to remove them from your world."

"How?"

The three beings that had been silent this whole time finally stood. The being on the right spoke. "It is the proposal of the people of Oriach that The Qualen be enacted on the planet Earth. The Stratum has voted."

The being on the left, The Cardinal, spoke. "Prolus, The Hand, votes to enact The Qualen."

The being in the middle, The Anointed, spoke next. "Synodos, The Heart, votes not to enact The Qualen."

My heart leapt. They voted no. What did that mean?

Finally, The Ascendant opened their mouth. "Asisus, The Head... votes to enact The Qualen."

"This is... this isn't fair!" I was desperate to try and stop the war. *Come on, Jake, think of something.* "Please, give us time to change our ways. You can't just kill us!"

The Primarch shook their head.

"You cannot kill something that will never exist."

Chapter 17: I Make a Choice

I don't know how long I stood there, looking at the beings around me, both alien and human. Every human was stunned, shaken to their core. Each alien seemed to be waiting for a reaction.

I wondered if the Primarch could keep track of all the reactions in my head. Could the other Voranah also read minds? Finally, I decided to say the general focus of all the thoughts going through my head.

"You can't do this."

"It has already been decided." While it didn't seem like the Primarch was cold, they certainly didn't seem to care.

"Let me get this right." I frowned and shifted my weight. "Voranah warred millions of years ago. Some escaped to Earth and created life. We are a result of that life, and that power. But because humans can be violent—like you were in the past—you're going to wipe us from existence?"

"That is correct." The Primarch stood. "Voranah have a responsibility to control who has Pethius and Ultimus. On your planet, every single living thing could gain that power. It is chaos. It would result in your self-destruction anyway. We are taking responsibility for a mistake of the past."

"But... we're not a mistake! We're alive... living beings, with souls and love and families. You aren't even giving us the chance to change." My heart was thundering in my chest.

"We've given humanity their entire existence to change. The situations of violence have only gotten worse. We cannot let a race of violent beings tarnish the reputation of Voranah across the galaxy. If it were found out that Voranah helped speed along the evolution of a planet's life, other worlds would beg us to do the same for them. Evolution is a natural part of a species learning and growing. It is a test to ensure only the strongest and wisest survive."

"But... we're not done with evolution yet. It took you probably millions, or billions of years to get to where you are now. You haven't given us that time."

"You must not be allowed to evolve further," the Primarch said. "If your violence spreads into the galaxy, you will undo the eons of work we have put into preserving the peace we have found."

"You can't see the error in your logic? Like you said, it took you eons. Modern civilization has only been around for, like, thousands of years. This is injustice. This is... this is about you and your reputation. It's about control."

The Primarch began stepping off their platform toward me. They were terrifying in their grace.

"Humanity does not know about its true history, and therefore can never fully realize its purpose."

"We *have* purpose. We may not know where we truly come from, but people are still finding purpose in their everyday lives. They have jobs, they make families, they love, they cry, they learn. They... they *live*. You can't decide for us that we have no purpose because not all of us truly know where we came from. Humans find meaning beyond the past."

"A career and choices in a life are not a purpose." The Primarch was standing a few feet from me, about seven feet tall. "Your people are individualized. There is no unity. That means there is no true purpose for your people."

"We may not all have the same desires and goals, but that doesn't equate to purpose," I argued. "Some humans devote themselves to education—making generations of people smarter and leaving the world in better hands. Some people want to travel into space, and work to move humanity forward to space travel. Some want to make the planet more beautiful and create music, or paintings, or whatever. The one thing they all have in common is that they live. Maybe that's their purpose, is to live. You're not there, so you can't know."

"But we are there," the Primarch replied, taking a small step forward and reaching out their hand to my chest. "We are there, in your heart, and there, in your mind. I know you changed college majors, but you still don't feel like you belong anywhere. You don't know where you fit in your own existence. The others around you all feel the same way, and some continue to do so. Humanity's behavior indicates that the only thing that unifies you is selfishness. The accrual of wealth, war, genocide, famine... even wars of religion are all based in selfish desires. What purpose is that?"

"Greed and violence condemn us? Our teachers, our advocates, our historical leaders who spent their lives leaving positive messages and results... who pioneered for progress—they count for nothing?"

"As you've gotten older, have they made a difference? Is there not more war, more death, more violence, more ignorance?"

"There's also more acceptance, more love, more growth, and more tolerance," I argued. "Just because elected officials enact laws restricting the rights of some doesn't mean people agree with those laws."

"Then why are they your elected officials?"

I shrugged. "Because they have the most money. Look, I know our system of government in the United States is broken. But there are people who want to change it for the better, to make it more representative. What if—"

"No."

"But—"

"No." The Primarch wasn't even letting me voice my idea out loud.

"You could help us. We're your people. Humanity doesn't know about life on other planets. Be the first! Give us an example—help us be the best we can be. Please, I'm begging you to reconsider. Please... that decision was made thousands of years ago. So much has changed. So much *can* change."

The Primarch turned away from me, seeming to reconsider. At least, I thought they were.

"No. I will not be like Luriana and defy the will of the people. The Stratum *is* the people, and they have voted." They swiftly glided back to their throne.

"But one of them voted no!"

"We cannot please everybody."

Suddenly, a light clicked on in my head. "You'd already made the decision. Why did you bring our consciousnesses here?"

"It was the moral choice. The only stipulation given in this decision was that those with Pethius and Ultimus on Earth be given notice. Be given time to prepare the people of Earth. We are giving you time to say your goodbyes to each other before The Qualen."

"That's it? There's no other option?"

"No."

I looked around at my friends. Jordan almost appeared peaceful, but his jaw was set, and his eyes were shining with passion. He gave me a sad smile. I understood.

Lex, Ari, Spencer, David, Will, and Zeke all had similar expressions.

I frowned at Benedetti, who glared at me, then turned the glare defiantly up at the Primarch.

Then, as I scanned the crowd once more, I saw one more familiar face.

My father. His eyes were shining with pride, and he nodded.

Everyone was saying the same thing.

Resist.

They'd made their decision. They weren't going to give us any other options. I could beg, cry, threaten... and nothing would change. There was only one thing I could do. One thing I could say. I had to make a choice for all of humanity.

No big deal.

"You've told us all here that humanity is going to be coming to an end. You've declared war on a species simply because we exist. You claim you are peaceful, but you're planning a genocide. Pretty it up however you like. The murder of billions of innocent people will be on your hands. But I believe I speak for all of humanity when I say this: fuck around and find out."

"We did not bring you here to fight," the Primarch said. "We—"

"You brought us here under an illusion of choice and mercy." I stood as straight as I could, turning to The Invictor, leader of their armies. "You want us to submit to you, to go peacefully. We will not. You will face an army made up of the entire world. You wanted to see us united? Watch. We will fight."

"You will *die*," The Invictor hissed.

"Then we'll die fighting." I turned back to the Primarch. "You tell your citizens everything that was said here. And you ask them if they're willing to sacrifice the lives of their loved ones in a needless war."

"You will not listen to reason? You are being given the chance to find peace for a short time before we come. Will you not seek peace?"

"Won't you?" I challenged. "You said you had a responsibility to humanity. And you're choosing to simply eliminate that responsibility through murder. You said the decision's already been made, so I won't waste breath. We'll fight you to the end."

"You will only prolong your suffering." The Primarch actually sounded sad. "All of humanity will suffer seeing their world end. Under our plan, it could have been as peaceful as going to sleep. Now, your people will suffer a violent and painful death as they struggle to escape the war you have chosen. We... regret your decision."

They waved at The Augury, who nodded and raised their hands, beginning to move them in various patterns, their eyes pools of silver once again. The people around me began to disintegrate.

"You're going to regret *your* decision." I was able to get in the last word before the alien landscape around me blurred into darkness.

I opened my eyes with a gasp. I was staring at the ceiling of the warehouse.

"They're awake," I heard a voice call out. "Nobody moves or we will shoot!"

"Breckenridge?" I sat up and met the barrel of a gun.

"Jake, what the hell happened?" He walked over and I stood, along with everybody else who was still alive.

Apparently, in the time we were out, Breckenridge and his soldiers had won the fight in the warehouse over Benedetti's hired mercenaries. Benedetti's hired people were nowhere to be seen. Only the people with powers remained.

I looked around. No one was fighting. Everyone was in shock. And everyone was staring at me.

"Jake—what the hell happened?" Breckenridge asked again. And that was when I saw Benedetti. He walked over to me, his brown eyes a dull blue, and his formerly lush brown hair seemed flat, and was flecked with gray. He was older, paler, and much weaker.

I stared in disbelief. "You... you lost your powers."

He nodded. "They must have been taken by... by *him*."

I knew he meant Jesus.

I felt a rough hand on my shoulder, and Breckenridge made me face him. He had a gash above his eyebrow that made him look even more terrifying.

"Dammit, what happened? We were all fighting and then most of you collapsed. You've been out for twenty minutes."

"It was... the Voranah. The aliens. They... um, they called us."

"And?"

"They're coming."

Breckenridge's face hardened. "They're not coming to talk, are they?"

I shook my head.

"How long?"

"I... I don't know."

"General?" Cemparius stepped forward, and Breckenridge took a few steps back. "I apologize if my appearance has alarmed you, but I have an answer to your question. It will take the Voranah some time to gather their forces, but once they do, travel to Earth only takes six months."

He looked stricken. "Six months? And, what the hell are you?"

"I am Cemparius," they said. "I was... I am..."

"They were in the big green crystal downstairs," I explained.

Breckenridge sighed. "Well, as far as first contact goes, how am I doing?"

"Fine," Cemparius said. "It is I who must apologize for my people. They are initiating an invasion after making a decision based on outdated information."

"So, they've been planning this for a while, now. Why send you?"

Cemparius hung their head. "I was sent when they found out the power of Ultimus had been transferred to a human. It was... they based their decision off my report over two thousand years ago."

Breckenridge raised an eyebrow. "So, you want to fix what you broke, huh?"

"Yes. I made harsh judgments about humanity and have learned much while in hiding these last two-thousand years."

"How old are you?" I asked. "Sorry. Maybe that's a rude question."

"I am three-thousand, one-hundred fifty years old. Voranah live to be ten-thousand years old on our planet."

Breckenridge suddenly realized we were being watched by all the soldiers, as well as Benedetti's people and my friends.

"Here's what we're gonna do. Take Benedetti and his men into custody. The others you're going to transfer onto my plane, and we're going to take a little trip. You." He looked at Cemparius. "Can you disguise yourself?"

Cemparius nodded and, suddenly, I was looking at two Breckenridges. He stared, eyes wide.

"How can you do that?"

"It is simply holographic emitters I have installed throughout my body." Their voice was still the same. "They were implanted for my trip to Earth. I hid as a human for many years before I discovered the Omnia Fragment was in danger of being found.

"Right. Well, you can't be me. Choose one of your friends or something."

Cemparius turned around and began examining everyone in detail. Finally, they smiled at Ari, whose eyes went wide.

"No. No way. Do *not* mirror me, please."

Cemparius nodded. "I like your look, but I have examined all of you and determined a compromise." Their body flickered in and out, mixed in with all my friends, until there was a completely new person standing before me, a mix of all of us.

"That's... wow. Um, what do we call you?"

Their head tilted to the side. "My name is Cemparius."

"We should try to give you a more... human name so you can blend in."

Cemparius blinked. "My... my former friends used to call me Cem."

"That sounds like Sam," I said.

"Sam it is. I'm going to have some men escort you all to a holding location." He turned to his soldiers. "Arrest Benedetti and his mercs."

The Machine Gun Vaders all came in and grabbed the remaining seven, plus Benedetti himself, who didn't put up a fight until he noticed Spencer wasn't being handcuffed.

"Wait. Spencer's with me."

Spencer simply crossed his arms over his chest. "Don't you mean 'Jasper?'"

"No. You are my s—"

"*Don't*!" Spencer screamed. "I am *not* your son!"

"I raised you!"

"You didn't raise me. Nannies raised me. You used me for your own power. You trained me to be a tool. You manipulated me and you lied to me! You wanted me to kill my own brother and you were never going to tell me!"

Spencer lunged at Benedetti, knocking the soldier holding him off their feet. Benedetti landed painfully on his handcuffed arms while Spencer choked him.

"Spencer, stop!" Jordan pulled him off of Benedetti, but Spencer tried to shove him away. David stepped in, and the two of them were able to get Spencer under control.

"Get him out of here," Breckenridge told the soldier, who hauled Benedetti to his feet and began walking him away.

"You're my son," Benedetti cried out. "You're my son!"

But Spencer could only glare as his 'father' was escorted away.

"Get them on a plane," Breckenridge said. "I'll be there shortly."

"Wait." I gently grabbed Breckenridge's arm. "We need the fragments."

"They're safely inside the base."

I cleared my throat. "General, I promise you: we need the fragments with us."

He took a deep breath, considering. "Fine. I'll grab them. But you don't get to be near them. I don't know what they mean to you now, anyway."

"Healing," I said, gesturing around at us all. "We're a little banged up."

"Oh. Then, sure."

The remaining soldiers walked us out of the warehouse and toward a nicer-looking plane. *No more cargo planes. Yay.*

Nobody spoke until we were walked onto the plane and shown our seats. Finally, Will spoke.

"This is pretty luxurious for a government plane, isn't it? I mean, my taxes went to pay for this?"

"I was thinking the same thing in the base." I was glad to have something to talk about besides the end of the world. "All those fancy hallways and rooms? We need to write a strongly-worded letter."

"I can't believe you're joking right now." Lex's voice was shaking. "We just found out the world is going to end."

"In six months," Zeke added.

"It's a coping mechanism," I said. "I mean, freaking out isn't going to do any good."

"You're not freaking out even a little bit?"

"Oh, I am on the inside for sure."

"But you have all the powers now," Jordan said, and I looked at him for the first time since we'd come back to consciousness. His face was blank, but I was concerned about how hurt he was under all of that.

"I don't feel like I've changed," I said. "I mean... I don't feel weird at all."

"You look a little different," he said. "But not really. Maybe it's me."

I held his gaze. "Are you okay?"

He smiled, but it didn't reach his eyes. "I will be."

"So, Sam, huh?" Will winked across the aisle at Cemparius in their new form. "I like it. I dig it. It must be cool to walk around being all naked but looking like you're wearing clothes."

"Don't get any ideas, please." Zeke normally had a small smile on his face when teasing Will, but this time he didn't.

Right then, Breckenridge got on the plane and walked to the front, bag of fragments in his hand. The engines started and we began to taxi.

"Everyone buckle up. We've got a bit of a flight ahead of us."

"Where are we going?" Ari asked, but Breckenridge ignored them.

"I need to see Jake and Sam at the back of the plane."

I stood and followed the general and Sam to a small little table in the back. We sat down and buckled in as the plane began speeding up for takeoff.

"Oh, I hate this, I hate this, I hate this." I gripped the seat tightly.

Breckenridge frowned at me. "You must not fly often."

"Nope. I was a Terra for a reason. Very much like the ground."

"But you can fly with your new powers." I looked at Sam, shocked at what they were saying. "Yes. The power of Fortis allows you to fly."

"Well, I guess I knew that, but I didn't really think about it. Man, this is crazy."

"Tell me exactly what happened," Breckenridge said. "I want to know what happened in the last hour that started an attack on the base, killed a general, gave you all even more powers, and brought a goddamn alien awake."

Sam raised their eyebrows. "Would you like to see what happened?"

Breckenridge raised an eyebrow. "I saw what happened."

"No. Would you like to see what happened through my eyes?" Sam asked. "We can use our telepathy to communicate via physical contact. If you'd allow me, I can show you what transpired in the base and on Oriach."

The general looked between us. I couldn't imagine how he was feeling.

"Fine. I guess there's not much I can do but trust you people."

Sam extended their hand out to the general, and the general took it, making an interesting face as he touched Sam's skin underneath the hologram.

"This is called The Nexus. It is a transference of experience. You will hear what I heard, see what I saw... feel what I felt."

Breckenridge nodded in consent. I watched in fascination as Sam's eyes through their hologram shimmered into silver, just like The Augury's did. And they were that way for about five seconds until Sam let go.

Breckenridge gasped and sat back, clutching at his heart. He undid his seatbelt and stood, beginning to pace. I leaned forward, extending my hand, but Sam put out their arm to stop me.

"Give him a moment. He lived the last hour in a few seconds."

He continued breathing hard, eyes watering. After a few moments, he shakily sat back down in the chair, running his hand through his hair.

"Okay. I believe you. They're coming and they're not happy."

"General—"

"Jake... thank you." His words surprised me, and I stopped talking. "You represented humanity well, I think. I would have chosen my words, ah, a little differently, but the message was the same, I think."

"Oh." I had about apologized for dooming us to a war. "Um, thanks."

"Now, what kind of force are we looking at here?" the general asked.

Sam rubbed their fingers together. "When I left two-thousand years ago, their army was one billion strong. But that is not the issue. The issue is The Qualen."

"What's the difference?"

"They're not sending an army to kill us. They're sending a beast to erase you from time."

I frowned. "A beast? They never said anything about that."

"It is how they conduct The Qualen. The beast is called Lusus, and it is... gargantuan. It is vast in size and weight, and it has never been defeated."

"They've done this before?"

"To fourteen other species across the galaxy."

I tsked. "So much for 'we like peace' and shit."

"The Voranah did not initiate those conflicts." Sam gave me disapproving look. "But they know how to end them. Devastatingly so."

"Well, then we nuke it," Breckenridge said.

"It will not work."

"Why not?"

Sam sighed. "Lusus is not made up of one being, but trillions of beings that all work as one to simply undo life. Anything fired at Lusus has always gone through it to the other side."

"The resulting explosion wouldn't even get it?" I asked. "I mean, nuclear weapons are huge. What if we fired it in space before they arrived or something?"

Breckenridge shook his head at Sam. "This is more than the U.S. can take on. We're going to need allies. All of them."

"It will be difficult, given the divisions between nations. They were bad when I went into the ocean in the 1950s. I can only imagine how they are now."

"Much worse," I said simply, looking at Breckenridge, who nodded.

"Then we had better get started soon," Sam said. "Where are we going now?"

"Washington D.C."

My heart stopped. "We're not... you're not taking us to meet..."

"Oh, yes." Breckenridge nodded impressively. "The President of the United States is about to make first contact with an alien."

Chapter 18: Fragments of Truth

Halfway through the flight, Jordan found me sitting in the back. Breckenridge and Sam had moved to other seats, but I stayed, not wanting to move during the flight.

"Hey."

"Hi." I patted the seat next to me.

"How are you?"

"I'm... all the feelings." I shrugged and smiled. "I'm scared about what's to come, I'm scared and excited and overwhelmed about what happened with me, I'm happy we defeated Benedetti, I'm nervous about meeting the president, and I'm... I'm scared what this means for us."

He took a big breath. "I know we said it doesn't have to mean anything, but I feel like things have changed."

"Are you... mad? I know you were trying to get to the fragment."

His eyebrows creased, but the look vanished so quickly I might have imagined it. "No. I'm just worried about you. And I'm worried about... well, about what you said to the Primarch."

"I... I didn't know what else I could say," I admitted. "I mean, they told us what they were going to do, and I thought... no. No, you're not. I checked in with you, too. Is that not something you were thinking?"

"No. I would have tried to negotiate more. But you have the power now, so I guess we need to defer to your judgment."

"No, we don't. If it were up to me, you'd have the power and you'd still be in charge."

"Yet you didn't help me get to the fragment."

I blinked. "What?"

He swallowed, and I felt his words as if he were stabbing me.

"You made a choice. To get the fragment for yourself. You could have hit Benedetti, or controlled the ground he was on, or helped me with vines or something. But you wanted it. You wanted the power for yourself."

I let out a noise of indignation. "That's... not really true. I mean, at first, I did, but when Luriana told me I couldn't have it, I let it go. I honestly thought I could keep it away from him and give it to you—"

He stood. "I can't do this."

I stood as well, and he took a step away. I could see Breckenridge watching closely. "Do what? What's going on?"

"You made me the leader," he snapped. "Yet, you've never once deferred to any of my decisions. You decided to open the shell with Cemparius inside. You've never respected me or my decisions, and that's why you chose the power for yourself."

"Jordan, that's not true!"

"Yes, it is." His face was ugly, filled with pain and anger, and it completely blindsided me. "If you had listened to me, we could have secured everything first, dealt with Benedetti, and then handled the fragment situation. You're reckless, and you don't think before you act."

My mouth fell open. "I do *too* think before I act. I hesitated and watched as you went after Benedetti, Jordan. I wanted it to be you."

He clenched his jaw. "I think you're lying."

Hands shaking, I wet my lips and decided then and there. "If anybody lied here, it's you."

"Oh, this again."

"No, Jordan. When I spoke to Luriana in the cave, she told me why you wanted the fragment. Why you *really* wanted it." His face fell and I continued. "You have your brother back. But this power can't bring anyone back from the dead."

"You don't *know* what it can do."

I folded my arms across my chest. "I have the power, Jordan. Whether that's how it's supposed to be or not, that's how it is."

He shook his head, his lip curling in disgust. "So I guess you're in charge, now."

"No. I'm still new at this, Jordan. I still need guidance, and support."

"Well, you'll have to get it from someone else." He took a deep breath and rubbed his eyes. It seemed to help him clear his mind as his eyes were filled with pain when he pulled his hands away. "I feel so betrayed, Jake. I never wanted this for you in the first place, and now... now you're the Primarch."

I scoffed. "According to the big alien, I'm the imitator."

He bit his lip. "Well, we'll see how you stack up to them. You have six months."

I blinked back tears. "I... I didn't think you of all people would be so bitter if it was me."

"You're damn right I'm bitter!" The plane fell silent at his shout. "I sacrificed *everything* for the fragment—my family, my friends, my home! And you came in and decided it was yours. It should have been me. It should have been *me*."

I shook my head as if seeing him for the first time. "Wow. I had no idea you were so alike."

"What? Who?"

"You and Benedetti."

Jordan slapped me across the face. Spencer jumped up, and immediately stepped between us.

"Jordan, take a break. It's alright."

"Fuck you, Jake. *Fuck. You.*"

He stalked to the front of the plane and took a seat while Spencer put his hands on my shoulders, staring as I clutched my face.

"Are you okay?"

I shook my head. "I would have thought you'd be more like Benedetti than him. But you're not."

He smiled softly. "I'll talk with him. You'll be okay."

My lip began to tremble and, before I knew it, Spencer was holding me while I cried. After a few minutes, he let me go and I found Breckenridge standing nearby. I quickly rubbed my eyes and stood as straight as I could.

"I'm going to need a minute with you, Jake."

I nodded at Spencer, who went back to the front and slowly approached Jordan, whose head was in his hands. I wondered if he wasn't crying as well.

Breckenridge and I sat down at the table, and I waited for him to speak. Finally, his voice low, he leaned forward and asked me if I was okay.

I let out a snort of laughter. "Obviously not, but that doesn't really matter."

"You're right. We've got war coming, and I want to get an idea of how you and your people are going to handle that."

I frowned. "I mean, they're not really *my* people. Jordan's in charge."

"No." I stared, and he continued. "I saw that quite clearly. When the chips are down, Jordan can't handle working as a team."

"I mean, he's been a great leader so far—"

"Has he really?"

"Of course." I said it defiantly, not thinking about whether it was true.

Breckenridge shook his head. "You're young, Jake. But I'm going to need you to shape up real fast. You've been in fights, but you've never seen war. You and your friends are soft. I'm going to need to toughen you up to face what's to come. And that includes making decisions that affect whether they live or die."

He gestured to my friends, who were gathered around Sam, asking questions. I felt something cold enter my chest, a barrier. It settled there, and I knew it wasn't going anywhere any time soon.

I looked back at him and sighed. "General, I don't think you have to worry about me making hard decisions. Yes, I care about these people, but I care about my family more. If it means sacrificing them to save my family... I'd do it in a heartbeat."

His eyes bore into mine. "And if it meant sacrificing your family?"

That I honestly couldn't answer. It was a complicated situation there, after all. All I could think about was my little nephew, who I basically hadn't seen in two months. I blinked back tears.

"Okay," he said, patting me on the arm. "I get it. You're new. But you're going to have to learn, and fast. Because when the world is literally on your shoulders, you don't have the luxury of having anyone you care about be a priority. If they have to die so others can live... that's a decision you *have* to make."

I nodded. "I'll... I'll do my best."

"That's all I can ask. Now, while I want you in the meeting with the president, it's basically to show her that powers exist. You think you can do that for me?"

I gulped. "I mean, as long as I don't get shot or something for snapping my fingers and lighting a fire, sure."

"You won't be shot, I assure you."

"Does the president know why we're on our way?"

"I've kept the details to a minimum for everyone's safety."

I grinned. "I can't imagine you describing Sam over the phone, anyway."

He gave a short laugh. "Now, when we get to D.C., I have us set up in a hotel with a boutique. You need to look presentable for the president. Just drop my name and you'll be able to buy whatever is necessary."

"Whatever I want?"

"Whatever is *necessary*."

I nodded. "Sounds like a plan. So, I've been dying to know... the crash in Roswell in the 1940s... was that another alien or—"

"And we're done."

My mouth fell open in protest. But as the general stood to walk away, he winked.

Wanting to distract myself, I stepped over to stand by Sam.

"So, you were the second-in-command of the Voranah army?" Ari asked.

Sam nodded. "Yes. However, I... I come from a line of Voranah that have always held a position of power. My parents set the goal for me to become the Primarch, and I was on my way to doing so with this trip to Earth."

"What sorts of things did you do on Earth while you were hiding?" Will asked. "Were you ever anybody famous?"

Sam smiled. "That is a much longer story than we have time for. I tried my best to live in the background as much as possible, but sometimes I couldn't help gaining a little attention. Often, I traveled. I... I was present at the crucifixion of Jesus Christ. I was among the first to travel to the new world and see the genocide committed against the native people here. I... I wish I had interfered more, and helped the people become kinder and gentler."

"Well, with the decision already made against us, you could have also tried to build us up into a world of warriors," David offered.

"I do not know how helpful that would have been." Sam yawned, something I didn't know they did. "Apologies. Though I have been in stasis for decades, I still find myself tired."

"Do you sleep like humans sleep?"

"I sleep in the evening hours like most humans, but not nearly as often. I sleep every four days. However, on our planet, services are open all the time. There are four shifts to choose from throughout a full day, but Oriach counts days as 16 hours."

"I know we kind of saw it, but what's Oriach like?" Ari leaned forward, eagerly hanging on their every word.

As Sam began to describe the three moons orbiting their planet, their gargantuan blue sun, and the five other planets in their solar system, I glanced over at Jordan, who I saw staring at me.

His eyes were shining and his eyebrows met each other in an upward curve. Gently touching his face and pointing to me, he mouthed the words, *are you okay*?

I nodded.

He stared for a moment more before mouthing, *I'm sorry*.

Me, too, I mouthed back.

A few hours later, Breckenridge had told us all who was doing what to meet the president, and to be prepared to move quickly once plans were formed in the Oval Office.

The loudspeaker came on, telling everyone to fasten their seatbelts. I got into a seat next to Jordan and tried to take deep, calming breaths as we landed at the airport in Virgina.

When we got off the plane, we were loaded into three black SUVs with tinted windows. I felt so cool. Then, we were on our way to the hotel.

Sam debated between wearing a dress or wearing a suit while in the car, saying, "Neither feels right."

"Exactly," Ari said from the back seat. "But wear the suit. It will look cute with your short hair. I mean, good. It will look fine. Whatever."

They sat back, their face as red as a tomato.

I glanced over at Jordan, who was watching the scenery go by.

"You still doing okay?"

He sighed. "I feel awful. I lost control."

"I know. I... I didn't mean what I said."

"Thank you."

Something was still off between us.

Is it ever going to be the same? No, Jake, because you're at war now. You have to make choices. Make sacrifices. Focus on the war, not on your love life.

When we got to the hotel, I went to the boutique and picked out a grey suit, light blue shirt, yellow tie, and black shoes and belt. Then, I picked up a pair of black sunglasses. I know, unnecessary, but so cool.

After I had gone to the room I was going to be sharing with Jordan, Spencer, and Sam, I hopped in the shower, still missing the tattoo on my arm. I had paid a lot of money for that phoenix tattoo, and I didn't know how I was going to tell Kate that it was gone. She'd gotten one as well, of course, but with purple fire, because purple was her favorite color.

We'd gotten them after Zane had been sent to prison. She felt guilty she had never told anyone about what he'd done to her, as it may have stopped him from raping the victim, as well as his ex-girlfriends who later came forward to discuss their rapes.

Now... I had nothing to remind me of rising out of the ashes of the past.

I got out of the shower, put on the suit, and made my way into the room.

"You look fantastic," Spencer said, quickly looking away.

Jordan's eyes lingered, however. "You do. You really do."

I sighed. "I'm not ready for this. But I was also wondering if you could start the process of trying to track down my family? I haven't been in touch with them this whole time, and I'm sure they're worried."

He nodded. "I'm sure our confiscated phones are still back at Area 51, but someone can at least give me the number off your phone that your parents texted you."

"Thank you." I looked over at Sam, who was studying their reflection in the mirror. "You ready?"

Soon, I was sitting in the SUV again, but only with Sam and Breckenridge. Everyone else was staying at the hotel to recuperate.

"Here's the plan," Breckenridge said, turning to face us in the backseat. "I explain that you're here to talk about a serious situation I'm already aware of. You show your powers... maybe wind, a little fire, then end with the lightning. We don't want to scare the president. Then, we show Sam as... not Sam. From there, I'm betting President Walsh will agree to the same thing I did."

“The Nexus,” Sam said.

“Yes. From there, we can all sit down and hash out a plan.”

I drew a short breath. “Boy. I don’t think anything could possibly go wrong.”

“It actually sounds like many things could go wrong,” Sam pointed out. “We do not know how the president will react, so everything hinges on this moment.”

“Thanks, Sam.”

“You are welcome.”

In a whirl of guards, gates, and turns through the lavishly decorated and historic halls of the *freaking* White House, I found myself sitting on a couch in the *freaking* Oval Office, my leg twitching nervously while I bit my lip, waiting to meet the *freaking* president.

“I’ve never known a human to bite their lip so intensely.”

I looked at them, perturbed. “I’m nervous.”

“Oh. When we get nervous, we sit still and work to control our thoughts.”

“Do you?” I was about to ask Breckenridge where everyone was when the door opened. We all jumped up as a group of people entered, led by—

“President Gwen Walsh.” She stepped forward and held out her hand for me to shake. “This is my Chief of Staff, Stephen James. My assistant, Madeline Thomas, and my advisors, Brandon Benson and Gene Fowler.”

I shook everybody’s hands, nervous mine was wet with sweat. “It’s nice to meet you all. I’m sure you know General Breckenridge, and this is Sam... Sam.”

As she stepped around to unload some of the papers she was holding onto her desk, I couldn't help but take in the air around her. Her eyes were downturned, which made her look kind. She kept her wavy hair about shoulder-length, and had it pulled back in a low ponytail. Her mahogany pantsuit was paired with a bright blue button-up shirt. She was equally professional and intimidating.

She had always been a woman of incredible charisma and persuasion. Her speeches and policies were direct and no-nonsense. She had gained the respect of many world leaders through not only her logic, but her passion for preserving peace and the future. The way she'd turned things around after the previous three presidents had nearly sunk the country into war was hard-fought.

In addition, she had done more for human rights in the U.S. than any of the other presidencies combined. The nation was in a much better place after she added justices to the Supreme Court, got some non-crazy people in there, and they began progressing things forward for the people of the nation.

President Walsh had gone on record saying the proudest moment of her career so far had been signing the bill that had legalized marijuana for medicinal and limited recreational use nationwide, with the new funding going toward education reform.

Granted, she still had plenty of people who criticized what she did and didn't do, thought and didn't think, and whether she was neglecting the presidency for her family, or her family for the presidency.

You know—basic woman stuff.

I had an immense amount of respect for her and was *not* happy that I was meeting her for the first time only to tell her about the apocalypse.

She directed us to sit on the couches, then sat on the couch across from Sam.

"Well, General Breckenridge, I was pulled out of my weekly security briefing for this meeting, so it had better be important."

"I assure you, it is important... and that you will want to hear this news alone."

She nodded at her staff. The three other people left the room, leaving the four of us.

"Well, what's so pressing?"

"Madame President, you know I don't like to beat around the bush. And I'm here to tell you some things that are going to sound very hard to believe."

"Okay. I'll do my best to keep an open mind," she said slowly, carefully watching Sam and me out of the corner of her eye. "I'm also not a fan of suspense."

"Right. Well, as you know, we found a crystal in the Mariana Trench in 1973. The circumstances were curious, and we've been keeping an eye on it at Area 51 ever since. A few days ago, we received word of a stolen submarine diving in the Mariana Trench right where we found the crystal. That was when we found five smaller versions of the crystal we had, only they were different."

President Walsh was following the story carefully. "How were they different?"

"They changed the humans they came into contact with."

"Changed how?"

General Breckenridge gestured to me. I cleared my throat.

"Okay, um, Madame President... so I started out only having control over one of the elements. Now I have control over them all."

Her eyebrows raised, and she smiled slightly. "And now I'm lost. The elements?"

"Earth, water, fire, that kind of thing. I can show you, if you're up for it."

She squinted at me, eyes darting to General Breckenridge. He nodded encouragingly.

"Okay, so I'm going to show you wind." I focused my hands out in front of me, and a gentle breeze began to blow through the room. It picked up some speed, ruffling everyone's hair.

"I've seen enough," she said, patting her head, eyes wide. "How many like you are there?"

"Well, I'm the only one who has power over all the elements, now. But we're all scattered, now. The sinkhole in King? That was caused by the collapse of our home there."

"How did it happen?"

"Sebastian Benedetti. He was the CEO of Vostell, and he has—had—the power over earth. He... *we*... caused the collapse."

She stared at Breckenridge. "Do we have him?" He nodded, and she turned back to me. "How many were there before the collapse?"

"There were about four-hundred people, all with powers. They're called The Keepers."

She let out a breath. "Okay. Do we need to go public with these people and their powers?"

Breckenridge cleared his throat. "Madame President, the powers he has aren't the issue. It's where they come from."

She blinked. "Not the ocean?"

"No."

She clenched her teeth. "Space?"

"Yes. And we know exactly where."

"How?"

Breckenridge swallowed. "Today, General Scott McCormack was killed right after he made first contact."

Her eyes seemed to bulge out of her head. But she kept her chill.

"How did he die?"

"Benedetti, Madame President. He sent a small army to the base to attack and steal the crystals."

She let out a whistle. "Does his family know?"

"His son was with him at the time."

She nodded, refocusing herself. "This first contact... how did it happen?"

"In person."

Her jaw dropped. "They're *here*?"

"Not all of them," Breckenridge said. "Just one."

It seemed to click for her, and she turned her full attention to Sam.

"Who are you?"

Breckenridge sighed. "Now, this is a friendly, Madame President. You're not in any danger. I would never do that to you. But they can show you what they actually look like."

President Walsh swallowed hard and nodded.

"Sam, go ahead."

Sam stood, and the air around them shimmered for a few seconds. Where a human had been standing, there was now the four-armed, four-eyed alien that, not even eight hours ago, was in Area 51.

President Walsh took a deep breath and stood, her eyes wide. Sam focused on me for a moment, then said, "Madame President Gwen Walsh, my name is Cemparius. I am a Voranah from the planet Oriach. One of the humans I met earlier told me saying this would help: I come in peace, earthling."

I stifled a laugh. Will. I needed to tell Sam to *never* take Will's advice.

Sam held out their hand. The president hesitated for a moment, but then reached out. I felt my eyes well up as I witnessed one of the most powerful leaders on Earth greet a being from another world.

I was seeing the beginning of a new chapter of humanity.

Just in time for it to end.

"Well," President Walsh said, "Since we're getting everything out in the open, I also have some news, and I think it might have to do with what the three of you have been up to today."

She walked over to the desk, then turned back around. "Sam, if you wouldn't mind... looking human again? There's someone I think you all should meet."

Sam nodded and instantly assumed their human form. The president hit the intercom on her phone. "Madeline? Could you show our guest in?"

There was a soft knock on the door and the woman from earlier entered, followed by a Middle Eastern woman in a crisp, white pantsuit.

She had long, flowing black hair that was half-up, falling to her lower back. Her eyes were extraordinary. They were almost black, with flecks of blue around the outer edges. No, not blue. Purple.

Madeline left, and the woman stepped forward to shake the president's hand.

"Madame President, it's nice to see you again." Then she reached out to shake my hand, and I felt a tingle as I took it. "Jake. My name is Mirum Hijazi. I was in New York when I was pulled into... the connection we experienced earlier today."

"You're a Keeper."

She smiled. "In a way. I'm the leader of a group we call Hadaya Alkhaliq."

"What does that mean?"

"Creator's Gifts," she said. "We are devoted to the preservation of the Fragments and maintaining the secret of their existence. We're based out of Yemen."

"Yemen?" I was stunned. "That's... how?"

President Walsh stepped forward. "In full honesty, we've known there are people who can control the elements for some time, thanks to Mirum's group. They fought against terrorism in the Middle East for decades before the U.S. became involved. They went underground at that point."

"You know about people with powers?" I asked the president, shocked.

"I knew of this particular group as an underground railroad of sorts for Muslim women all over the Middle East." President Walsh gestured at Mirum. "We met for the first time today."

"But... how do you know about the Fragments? How do you have your own group?"

"We've kept our existence secret from your group here in the United States," Mirum said. "It was determined to not be settled enough to trust. But now that's all over. I'm the leader of a group of about two hundred. Each of them has powers from the fragments. Of the Voranah."

"How have you kept this a secret?" I asked, sharing an astounded look with Breckenridge. "The Keepers have had most of the Fragments for a long time. Like, decades."

She shook her head and smiled. "This is precisely why we kept ourselves a secret from you. You Americans seem to think you have all the power."

"But... we have all the fragments."

"You truly think yours are the *only* fragments?"

TO BE CONTINUED IN ***Fragments: The Defiance***

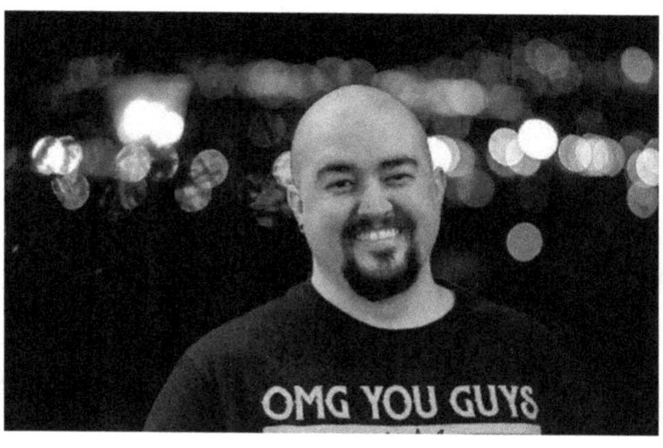

About the Author

Cole Stephens began writing when he was 13 years old. He enjoys a variety of genres, including fantasy, romance, and mystery, all with queer themes. He also has written several screenplays that he's revising and shopping.

Cole just finished obtaining his master's degree in counseling, where he hopes to work with youth.

He lives in Idaho with his husband and their adorably stubborn dog.

Read more at https://www.chriscolebooks.com.